Suddenly, I sensed, more than saw, another movement. Adjusting the side rear mirror from the inside, I pretended not to notice a child crouched by my left rear wheel. Another girl, hunched down and hiding from the fat guy.

A family quarrel. I'd better stay out of it.

By now, the woman in the Buick's front seat had slid over to the driver's open door. "Hurry up, Frank. The ferry's comin'," she shouted. "Can't you find her?"

Fat Man had walked up the dock to the water. And though I kept an eye on him, ready for any more violent moves, I mostly watched the kid. Her short, dark hair framed a round face - twisted now with fear, the olive skin bloodless and drawn.

The exchange between them looked bad enough - I never have bought the idea that teenagers would run away from home, risking their lives on our inner-city streets strictly as a means of escaping some dirty dishes. Not to mention that slap - a severe if not criminal punishment for a little boy.

My gut feeling was even more unnerving. I barely resisted the urge to put the girl in my back seat and head for the nearest police station.

Too bad, gut feelings don't hold up in court.

Other books by
Ruth Raby Moen
Hayseeds In My Hair; A Memoir

A "true, rough and tumble story" set in the 1940s, of the authors child-hood in the Cascade Mountains and on the Olympic Peninsula of Washington State. To order, send $13.70 (includes tax) to Flying Swan Publications, P.O. Box 46, Sedro-Woolley, WA 98284.

All Flying Swan Publications are available at special discounts for bulk purchases or to wholesalers/distributors. For details, write to above address.

Deadly Deceptions
Copyright 1993   By Ruth Raby Moen
ISBN 0-9635653-1-1 $7.95
Cover art by Arnold Moen

This novel is a work of fiction. Any similarity to actual persons or events is purely coincidental. I would like to thank the City of Poulsbo, North Kitsap County, North Kitsap County Sheriff's Office, and the Duwamish/ Suquamish Native-American Tribe and members of their Reservation for their indulgence. Any remarks or references in this text is by the fiction characters only and not meant to inflect upon the above institutions or and any institution or organization which may be connected to them.

To Teri.
This one's for you, kiddo. You've earned it.

DEADLY DECEPTIONS

A Mystery Novel

By Ruth Raby Moen

The President in Washington sends word that he wishes to buy our land. But how can you buy or sell the sky? The land? The idea is strange to us. If we do not own the freshness of the air and the sparkle the water, how can you buy them?

Every part of this earth is sacred to my people. Every shining pine needle, every sandy shore, every mist in the darkwoods, every meadow, every humming insect. All are holy in the memory and experience of my people.

We are part of the earth and it is a part of us. The perfumed flowers are our sisters. The bear, the deer, the great eagle, these are our brothers. The wind...gives our children the spirit of life.

So if we sell you our land, you must keep it apart and sacred......

Chief Seattle, 1852

CHAPTER ONE

It never fails. Feast or famine. I can wait for weeks for Gunner, the managing editor at the Seattle Gazette, to assign me something - anything - more exciting to write about than the Ladies Garden Club luncheon or some brat's wedding extravaganza. When those were done, he'd hand me the obituaries.

I was hungry for my own front-page byline. I wanted it - bad. The rules were, that any reporter who dug up a new story had the right to pursue that story and write the article - supposedly. But since I was still new and untested, my chances to propel my career into the status of investigative reporter were slim to none. The problem was, my editor still deemed me a rookie - a questionable status, held in the same high esteem as a dingbat with an IQ in the same range of a gnat.

Unless I could find an exclusive scoop.

I'd just gotten a great lead from a local politician's wife in Tacoma. This story could be my finest hour. It seemed the Mayor had been seen with his hand in someone else's pie at a party. He'd been found, so his wife said, crouched in a corner behind a case of Jack Daniels with Ruby Walden - the very buxom wife of Randy Walden, a City Councilman. Ruby was naked to the waist, her huge breasts pillowing the Mayor's bald dome, her hand jabbing a needleful of Columbian coke into His Honor's arm.

My informant wanted the creep impeached and forced to take an AIDS test. I doubted her motives. But then, in an election year, I doubted everyone's motives.

A few minutes later, I took another call. One that would forever change my view of the world in which I lived and I had more damn news than I could handle.

I was on my way to Gunner's office, ready to argue my rights and abilities to cover a real event, when the phone rang. Tom Goss, one of the more lecherous reporters in the office, picked it up. "Just a minute," he mumbled and handed it to me.

"Miss O'Shaunessey?" a girl asked. She sounded quite young, and close to hysterics. "Is that you?"

"Yes. Kathleen O'Shaunessey. Can I help you?"

"Oh, please. You gotta help me. I don't know who else to call."

"And your name is...?"

"Camille. Oh, I can explain it all later. You gotta hurry. They could be here, any minute."

With one jabbing finger, I motioned to Tom to switch on the recorder. We used it occasionally to check for accuracy, and as a back up. Too many times, the paper has used a source who later claimed we distorted a quote or a disclosure. Turning up the volume so he could also hear, Tom's eyes twinkled with the prospect of a breaking-news headline. Into the phone I said, "You'll have to calm down and tell me why you called."

She took a deep breath, speaking carefully in a hoarse whisper. "It's kinda hard to explain. My dad's gone. And I'm really worried."

I leaned on one foot, my hip resting on Tom's desk and said, "A missing person's report should be filed at your local police station, Ma'am."

"Oh no. I mean uh, they can't do nothin'. You see, its Indian business. Here on the reservation. We uh, some guys came here and took him away."

I almost hung up. We'd done it lots of times - say something polite about going to the proper authorities, wish them a good day, and drop that sucker like a hot potato.

But...this time I didn't.

The plaintive quiver in her voice and my own inclination to snoop, stopped me. Already softening, I said, "Do you mean he was abducted, coerced, or just called away?"

"He was taken. I guess you'd call it, abducted. It's the uh, first warning." Then she began to cry. "Please, Miss Shawnee, or whatever your name is, don't let them hurt Daddy. They're making it all up. And I'm gonna be next. I'll have to go with them, too."

"Hey," I said, ignoring the warning little voice in the back of my head. "You don't have to go anywhere with anyone you don't want to."

"But they've got everybody convinced that I lied. And I'm not. I'm not lying!" She started crying again.

"But, why me? Why did you call me?

"I was told to. That man you wrote about. The one who died. He was one of Chief Seattle's descendants. He came to the Tribal Council and told me you'd help."

"I thought you said he died."

"He did."

"What was his name?"

"His real name was in our native tongue. You wouldn't recognize it."

"Did he have another name he went by? A last name?"

"Some people called him 'George.' It wasn't mentioned in the paper, though."

Who could it be? Searching my memory I tried to remember who I'd covered that might have died recently - other than the obits. Couldn't be too long ago. I'd only worked here a few months. The only one I could think of was the guy from Pier 57.

While job hunting last February I'd done a write-up, as part of my resume, on a dead wino the police had found the night before. The St. Jude Mercy Mission had been full to the gills with families and they'd had to turn him out for being drunk. That night, a storm blew in. The next morning, they pried his body - frozen stiff - off a wooden bench down on the docks.

The story of his death got me the job and prompted my editor to assign me one measly little article, featuring the lack of a sufficient number of shelters for Seattle's homeless - an issue which I thought deserved at least a full page. But, this was the middle of May. That poor soul was dead long before this gal on the phone was in trouble.

Since then, I'd been confined to the society page. Some potted ladies with their potted plants, a style show at the mall - all women. "Where did you see it?" I asked. "What edition?"

"I think it was a couple weeks ago. Can you come? Oh. Somebody's here. I gotta go...are you coming?"

"How can I find you?"

Talking fast, she whispered hoarsely, "The Suquamish Indian reservation - just outside of Poulsbo. I'll meet you in the parking lot."

"How will I...?"

I tried asking better directions but she'd already hung up. I heaved a sigh, puzzled. She sounded sincere enough, but her story didn't make sense. Still leaning on the desk, I felt a tickle on the part of me that was sitting down. I looked behind me and slapped Tom's hand away from my fanny.

Giving me an obnoxious grin, he said, "So close and yet so far away."

"Does your mother know where you are?" I walked over to the senior editor's office and jiggled the door knob. It was locked. I then tried another door, the next down in the line of editorial hierarchy. "Where's Gunner?" I asked, knowing Tom's eyes were still glued to my backside.

I ought to sue the old lech for harassment.

"Gone on a three day weekend," Tom said. "They're all gone. Won't be back 'till Monday." Then, in a theatrical whisper, "It's just you and me, Doll. Yer place 'er mine?"

"In your dreams."

Tom had been flirting with me since the day I first walked in, looking for a job. He was harmless enough - divorced long ago, a good twelve years older than me and prematurely bald. But because he had at least one food stain on every tie he owned and shirts that strained the duty of most decent buttonholes, he was a known risk at any reputable restaurant. "Come on, Kath," he whined. "I got a couple a tickets to the Mariners' game...a nice dinner...who knows? You may like it."

My heels clicked in the old tiled hallway as I headed for the ladies room. "Tom," I said over my shoulder, "if you were the last man on earth, I'd demand a recount."

I washed my hands and checked my make-up in the mirror. Not too bad. I reapplied some lipstick and removed some smudged mascara. *Damn, this is frustrating. Just when I get a lead, my boss takes off.*

As I hurriedly brushed my long, blonde mane, I thought once more about a shorter, shoulder-length style. *Naw.* There was something about the feel of it as it swept the middle of my back and the way the little corkscrew curls always bounced up - no matter how many times they were straightened, flattened, brushed, or just plain ignored, they still retained their original character.

In the full length mirror, I sucked in my tummy and smoothed out a few wrinkles in the grey, wool slacks I was wearing with the matching herringbone-tweed jacket. They'd have to do. There wasn't time to go home.

Poking my head in the door, I hollered to Tom, "I'm going to Suquamish. I'll check out that kid and see if there's a story." The phone receiver cradled between his ear and shoulder, he was jotting some notes on a pad. "Tom?" Mumbling something into the mouthpiece, he covered it and glanced up at me. Talking fast, I said, "If Gunner calls in, tell him I left for the Suquamish reservation. Just tell him, 'Native Americans.' Missing person or human interest. I'll bring one or the other in on Monday." He nodded absentmindedly and waved a left-handed goodbye while still writing.

On the way out, I said in a raised voice, "And I'll start on that Mayors' wife story when I get back. Don't forget to tell Gunner - I got the original phone calls and I've already started the follow-up."

The elevator ride deposited me on the garage floor where I unlocked my '75 Porsche. It started on the third try, the old engine sputtering and spewing blue smoke out the back. Finally, it thrummed a little more evenly and I eased it up to the edge of the sidewalk. Waiting for a break in the traffic, I gunned it a few times and chuckled at some teenage boys hanging out at the entrance to the parking garage and toting a portable radio the size of a suitcase. I could hear them brag and debate the horsepower of the roaring engine under my hood as I pulled in front of an old, white van.

Cruising at 75 in the express lane, I recalled my last Washington State history class in high school and the two weeks we'd studied the Pacific Northwest Indians. I seemed to remember that the Duwamish and part of the Suquamish tribe, led by Chief Sealth, or Seattle, as we know him today, were happy, peace-loving Indians, making their homes on the shores of the Puget Sound. At one time they were a large tribe, with offshoot tribes stretching into what is now Canada. Then the white man came and within only a few years they bought this land for next to nothing. By then, these once proud and prolific Indians were sickened almost to extinction by disease. Diseases previously unknown in their society and to which they had no immunity - small pox, measles, diphtheria, and alcoholism.

They've never, totally, recovered. *The hell with it. I'll write this girl's story as a freelance, and if the Gazette won't run it, I'll sell it somewhere else.*

Ten minutes later, I exited at Edmonds and wound down past the park. Faking out a Ford camper, I maneuvered the Porsche into the ferry lane, bought a ticket and parked on the dock.

In the next lane, an old Buick rattled up alongside and shuddered to a stop. I glanced over, casually, getting an impression of a large family with clothes and blankets crammed into the back window.

About then, a grey plop of bird dung splattered my car window. I looked up to see a flock of seagulls squawking and circling over the heads of three fishermen. Two grown men and a boy were hunkered on the edge of the dock, cleaning fish. The older man dug out a handful of fish guts and tossed them in the bay. In one frenzied swoop, the gulls descended on the entrails, gobbling and cawing and beating one another with their wings.

Vaguely, from some corner of my mind, I heard the rusty squeak of a car door. A deep guttural voice grunted, "Hey. Get your ass back in here." A movement, no more than a flash of color, streaked across my rear view mirror from right to left. Pure instinct made me jerk my head toward the Buick as the driver slammed open his car door into the side of the red Chevy wagon just ahead of me.

With a clear view into their front seat, I could see a woman on the far side. She'd grabbed a struggling young boy, talking sternly to him as she pulled him onto her lap, pinning his arms to his side with her own.

The boy hollered. The driver reacted. "Goddamn kids, always running off," he snarled, and reached across the seat to slap him.

The woman immediately raised a fat arm to protect the boy and moved him to a spot between her back and the other side door. "I told you, to leave this boy alone," she snapped. "He's mine."

The driver, a disgustingly fat and shabby man, then got out of the car and stepped up onto my bumper, looking for whoever had jumped out. As the long snout of my Porsche bowed almost to the ground, springs squealing, I rolled the window down and made ready to order him off.

Suddenly, I sensed, more than saw, another movement. Adjusting the side rear mirror from the inside, I pretended not to notice a child crouched by my left rear wheel. *This must be my day for kids*, I thought. *First the girl on the phone and now this.* Another girl, in her teens, hunched down and hiding from the fat guy.

A family quarrel. I'd better stay out of it.

By now, the woman in the Buick's front seat had slid over to the driver's open door. "Hurry up, Frank. The ferry's comin'." she shouted. "Can't you find her?"

Fat Man had walked up the dock to the water. And though I kept an eye on him, ready for any more violent moves, I mostly watched the kid. Her short, dark hair framed a round face - twisted now with fear, the olive skin bloodless and drawn.

The exchange between them looked bad enough - I never have bought the idea that teenagers would run away from home, risking their lives on our inner-city streets strictly as a means of escaping some dirty dishes. Not to mention that slap - a severe if not criminal punishment for a little boy.

My gut feeling was even more unnerving. I barely resisted the urge to put the girl in my back seat and head for the nearest police station.

Too bad, gut feelings won't hold up in court.

The woman in the Buick, probably in her late forties, showed no resemblance to either the teenage girl or the little boy. Slick, grey-streaked hair had been fastened back with bobby pins, the dusky tan of her doe-skin cheeks replaced long ago with fatigue and middle-aged, liver-spotted bloat.

I knew I shouldn't - but the driver was coming back this way and would soon see the girl hiding behind my car. I hollered at him. "Do you know, that its a criminal action to be beating up on kids?"

"Stay out of it, lady," he shouted back. "If ya know what's good for ya," and stalked in my direction.

My first instinct was to react. Get out and battle with him. Instead, I locked my door, my hand resting on the handle, trembling with anger.

God, I hate men like that.

Just then the ferry whistle blew.

The kid must have panicked. She bolted over to the rail on the other side - running back down the dock and towards town for all she was worth. He spotted her and made a flying leap over the trunk of my car. She never had a chance.

He caught up with her in ten or twelve short strides. Grabbing her arm, he cuffed her about the ears when she cried and wrestled her across the two lanes of cars and back to the Buick. Still in my car and quivering from the brief exchange, I forced myself to think logically. There were several things I could do. One involved bashing the Buick's windows in and dragging the kid out. It would mean a confrontation with the driver. *That might be all right, too.* He didn't look to be so tough.

Just pure damn mean.

The other move, although less satisfying, was more rational. I could always mind my own business.

My lane of cars began to inch forward. I started the engine. On the right, the kids had flopped on the blankets and the fighting had stopped.

Should I get out? Start a screaming brawl with the fat guy and give the kids a chance to run? Surely the ferry crew would come to my aid. And should I get socked in the jaw for my trouble, they could always drag my lifeless body from the cold bay and give statements to the paper about what a gutsy broad I must have been.

Maybe she is his daughter. Might just be acting up. Mad about having to turn down the volume on the car radio. And maybe the sick dread churning in my belly is not a premonition at all but an over-reaction to the cold piece of pizza and handful of peanuts I had for breakfast.

Five minutes later the ferry disgorged its load of cars from the other side. The attendants waved me aboard. Since my whole lane loaded before the Buick's, they were a good ten or twelve cars behind me. And since I didn't see them get out and go upstairs, I decided, regretfully, to sit tight. Barring a citizen's arrest, which I couldn't pull off without proving the guy had broken the law, there was nothing I could do.

I did make note of what I could read of his license plate number. He was from Canada.

Sitting in the dark recesses of the lower deck and lulled by the slow heave and sway of the ferry, my mind began to wander through the maize of my life. The career part was good. My new position at the paper was alright - it at least held some promise of future adventures and interesting events. And the stress level, if not less than the old job, was at least different.

It was the rest of my life that bugged me. Not that it was so bad....just boring. I hadn't had a real date in almost a year and my apartment seemed empty. As if it were still waiting for the REAL family to move in. I sighed, shivering against the cold gloom.

Something else was bothering me. The kid who called me at the office mentioned a guy I supposedly wrote about in the paper. It haunted me as I went over and over every word and inflection of that conversation. It was his name. She'd said it wasn't mentioned. How could I have written about a man without mentioning his name?

The girl could be lying - but not about being scared. Someone could have threatened her. They could have been there in the room when she called and for some reason, she was afraid to repeat the dead man's name.

One thing was for sure. The fear in her voice had incited my instincts. *Something was wrong.*

CHAPTER TWO

Some thirty minutes later the ferry docked in Kingston. I barrelled up the ferry lane, past a few restaurants and gift shops, and headed up Highway 104. At the Y in the road I hesitated. To the left was a straight shot into Suquamish.

To the right, a more scenic drive to Big Valley and the family home. I didn't have time to go by there now, but after the interview, I'd call Mom and elicit an invitation to a late supper and an offer to spend the night. I decided to stay to the right and at least do a slow rumble past Lofall Park - remembering those painful, pubescent years when my bicycle had been my best and sometimes my only friend in grade-school.

The red bomb could cruise around 60 all day long. I down shifted at the Port Gamble speed sign, the backfire of the huge engine booming through the old mill town - all four blocks of it. Then whisked up the highway on the other side. Finally I passed the crumbling remains of the old Four Corners store, glancing quickly to the left as I whisked past the turn towards Mom and the scores of childhood memories still living there with her. Five minutes later, I past the road to the Lofall Ferry.

The ferry didn't run there any more. Years ago, long before my time, the ferry was the only way to get across the bay to Port Townsend. It was a marina now, fenced off and used only by the yacht club members and the very rich.

It had also been my Uncle's paper route. At fourteen, he had sold newspapers to the people waiting in line for the ferry to dock. Every Christmas at the family dinner, since I'd first plucked a spoon from my highchair tray to shove a wad of Pablum into my toothless mouth, he'd told us this same story. And every year the wind got colder, the customers grew more stingy, and Uncle Johnny's paper route became an even better example of the Great American Dream. He also nagged at me every chance he got. To get married, stop my foolishness - which I had to guess meant living an independent life - and settle down.

Ten minutes later I drove through Poulsbo, my old hometown and high school. The town had changed. It had once been a real fishing town, populated by mostly Scandinavian immigrants. Its best feature then was a bakery with its own brand of nutty bread on display in the window.

I would have liked to stop, but there wasn't time. The main street of town was already packed with rush-hour traffic and I was eager to find the reservation before dark.

14

I had to make contact with the girl who'd called me to make sure this wasn't a complete fluke. With my luck, her dad will have come home by now, tired from a long, couple of days commercial fishing on the bay, cranky that his daughter had over-reacted and exaggerated his disappearance.

Normally I prefer to get much more information before I leave the office. But, since she'd hung up so abruptly, that wasn't possible. I hoped the whole trip didn't turn out to be a scam - forcing me to slink back to the office next week, depressed and embarrassed over having made the knee-jerk decision to come out here.

Within ten minutes I made Lemolo and the edge of the Suquamish reservation. A sign to the right pointed to the museum and I turned into the parking lot.

It was vacant. Without so much as a last name or an address, I had no idea where to begin looking for her. I locked my car and looked for some sign of life around me. All I could see was trees and brush.

The air smelled of sea water and dead fish. The beach couldn't be too far away. With any luck at all, I could spot a house from down there or run into someone who knew her.

I got back into the car and changed from my heels into a pair of old tennis shoes. Retrieving my raincoat from the back seat, I put it on over my jacket and headed for the shoreline. A well-used path disappeared down a gravel bank and I ended up sliding most of the way down on my butt.

The tide was out, uncovering yards of muddy beach as I stretched my legs in a fast-paced walk. Skirting a tangle of seaweed, a family of tiny crabs panicked at my approach and made wild, side-scuttling darts for the water.

On my left, small waves slapped the pilings of an old wooden dock, creaking from the constant give and shove of the current. Next to that, a half-sunken rowboat grated on the gravel bottom, the tattered end of a rope still tied to its bow. Farther out, a lone duck bobbed up from a dip.

After hiking a lonely half mile, I spotted a set of wooden stairs set into the high bank with a flimsy hand rail. A storm had stacked driftwood in front as high as the second step. Picking my way among the bleached-out logs, I crawled over the largest piece and began to climb.

The healing salt air and the sounds of the surf had a calming effect on my frazzled nerves. Some of the boards on the rickety steps were loose and I took care to step over them. Soon, with the biting stench of the bay mingling with that of the rich earth and rotting wood, I was puffing and blowing up the steep bank. The lap of the waves was behind me, the cry of the gulls overhead.

Dopey from the cold, a few honeybees circled the wild flowers, dive-bombing some Scotch Bloom. Suddenly, a yellowjacket grazed my cheek.

I swatted it, jerking my head back instinctively. A quick gasp, I felt myself falling...

I thrust both hands behind me.

Nothing there. Nothing but air...
I balanced, scared sick. Then, hard wood scraped against my hand. The rail. Quickly I grabbed it, heard it groan from the sudden weight. My nails gouged into the wood.

As I bent trembling knees to sit on the step, a warm, strong hand gripped my arm. "Miss O'Shaunessey? Is that you? Kathleen O'Shaunessey?"

"Yes. Who are you?" Heartbeat booming in my ears, I tugged at my raincoat, snugging the front panels closed under my chin. My shoulders hunched against the cool bay breeze.

"Oh, I'm so glad to see you," she said. "I knew you were coming."

"Are you the one who called me?"

"Uh huh," she said, perched two steps above me. "You wanna go to the house? We can talk there." A toothy smile swept across her face and flashed in her dark eyes. "My dad's still gone, but now that you're here, they won't dare try anything."

They? I made a mental note to sort out the whole story later on and some distance away from this cliff. I nodded and let her help me to my feet, already winded by the climb and the sudden fright.

We topped the stairs and went directly to a small path between the trees. Hidden in the quiet depths of the forest, the kid relaxed a little and seemed more willing to talk. "Is that your car? The red one? You'd already left when I saw it. It's really a neat car. It's a Porsche, isn't it?"

This time I smiled, hoping my bad mood wasn't being perceived as unfriendly. She was young and obviously Indian - pretty in a naive sort of way, with bright black eyes, a short nose, and what grandma used to call 'those child-bearing hips.' The boys probably teased her a lot. With no make-up on, she first appeared about fourteen. Then I realized how long it had been since I'd seen a seventeen year-old who wasn't trying to look twenty four. She wore a fuchsia pink and purple ski jacket, topping a pair of tight jeans and red ankle warmers.

There was something vaguely familiar about her...

"Have I ever met you before?" I stopped, supposedly in the interest of communication. Actually, if the truth be known, I was winded and still shaky. Surely, the oxygen up here was much too thin for anything without feathers and a little twitchy tail.

I've got to get back into shape. Starting next week.

The girl shook her head. "I don't think so. Just on the phone, earlier."

"No, I mean, have I ever met you. In person."

"Huh uh. Not unless you've come to my school or something."

Wryly, I grinned - remembering the old alma mater.

She skipped ahead a little ways, running backwards in front of me. Her mood had obviously improved since this afternoon. "Daddy reads your paper all the time. Can you say something in there from me? Kind of ask people to look out for him? And if he can, tell him to call or come home?"

I shrugged, "I'll see what I can do."

She opened the door to one of the oldest houses I'd'ever seen still standing, and said, "Come on in."

The moss on the roof seemed bent on devouring the shingles - there wasn't much left. The plank walls, painted at one time a ghastly robin's egg blue, had dulled over the years to a depressing grey. I followed her inside and squeaked the door closed behind me.

Someone had done their best. It was immaculate.

The kitchen floor had been scrubbed raw. The tracks in the old linoleum were worn through to the wood and smelled of soap. An ancient wood cookstove crouched in one corner with several pots bubbling in the back. Gingerly, she lowered a small chrome door to expose a lump of red-hot coals and inserted a few lengths of log.

The windows were covered with strips of an old sheet, washed, ironed, and edged with red rick-rack. The window-sill lacked a curtain rod but a line of nails secured the makeshift curtain to the top. In the center of the ceiling one lonely light bulb swayed from its frayed black cord, casting dark, moving shadows to the space under the cupboards and across the chipped enamel sink.

Overall, there was a stench of rot and decay - thick enough to clog my sinuses and soak into my skin like a sponge. It seemed as if Old Mother earth had lent out her wood long enough. It was time to give it back.

"Would you like some soup?" she asked, using two rags for potholders as she lifted the largest aluminum pot from the back of the stove. "It's just beans and a can of tomatoes. I didn't have any bacon." She filled two mismatched bowls with an old-fashioned ladle and pulled a pan of homemade biscuits out of the oven. She then plunked them on the table and said, "Dig in."

The soup was surprisingly good - delicately flavored with some herbs I couldn't quite place. "Its good," I said. "There's a different flavor to it I can't quite place."

Her face brightened. "Wild onion. My mother brought some starters from..," she paused, touching her forehead. "...where was it she came from? Daddy told me once." Then she shrugged, turned her palm up in a 'how do I know' gesture, and said, "Anyways, she planted a patch up on the meadow, a long time ago." Returning to her soup, she tipped the bowl on edge and scraped the bottom. "They still grow there, just above us on a little rise. It's kinda funny. They won't grow anywhere else."

"Your mother's not home?"

"My mother's not alive."

Her blunt honesty startled me. "Oh. I'm sorry. I...didn't know."

In a downward cast of eyes, she replaced the empty bowls with a saucer and said, "That's all right. She died when I was born. I never knew her." Then in a charming lack of sophistication, she plopped an opened biscuit on my plate, spread it with a knife of margarine and spooned some fresh, hot applesauce on it. "This is my favorite dessert. I hope you like it."

"Uhm, on the phone, you told me..." Suddenly I remembered something else. "You know, I don't even know your name."

"Camille."

"I mean your last name."

"Cloud. Camille Cloud." This time, her quick, friendly smile didn't quite reach her eyes. But she was trying. "My great-grandfather's name was Dancing Cloud. Isn't that neat?"

"Yes. Yes, it is."

"I wish we still did that. Don't you think so? I mean, like have a name that means something. A sort of...personality thing. Now, its just Joe or Jack or Robert. And Suzy. Don't you hate the name Suzy?"

"Uh, yes. Now, on the phone, you said..."

"I mean, I like your name. Kathleen O'Shaunessey. It tells who you are. When I read it, right off the bat I knew what you were like."

"You said your Dad was missing?"

She slid back into her chair. "Yes, he is. When I got home from school, he was gone. He's still gone."

"When was that? What day?"

"Let's see, I guess it was last Monday. Five days ago."

"On the phone, you said he was taken. Do you mean abducted?"

She shrugged one shoulder and nodded. I continued my line of questioning. "Do you have any idea who did it? Did you see anyone? Does he have any enemies, anyone who might want to harm him?"

She sniffed and pushed her plate to one side. "Well, if you ask me, I think I know who did it. In fact, I'm sure he did it." Watching her closely, I saw her pick through the clutter of her thoughts. "There's this guy. A white guy...he lives in Poulsbo. He came to the elders awhile back, wanting to lease some of our land. Reservation land. Promised them all kinds of money, and this big...place. Went around telling everyone they could go there and drink for free, anytime they wanted. My Dad said NO. That we shouldn't trust him and they didn't need their bellies full of white-man liquor. But, the other guys, they needed the jobs and...they argued with Daddy."

"Do you think they're the ones?"

"Oh, no. They argue a lot and push each other around, you know, like in fun. But they'd never really hurt anyone."

"Then, who.... I guess I don't understand what you're trying to tell me."

"It's that white guy, Miss Shaunessey. He wants our land. And if we don't give it to him, he's going to take it."

"Can he do that? Aren't there treaties to protect the Indians from this sort of thing?"

"Treaties?" She grimaced. "Yea, sure there are. And every one of them broken by the white man, at least once."

This was beginning to sound a bit farfetched. *Camille just may have more imagination than she needs.* "Oh. Well, he can't just come in here and take it. There are laws, even on reservation land, building codes and all kinds of restrictions to prevent this sort of thing. Not to mention the environmentalists."

"But if the Tribal Council agrees, if more of them vote for it than against it, they can lease it to him. Like for fifty or a hundred years, or something."

"I see. And your dad..."

"He's the chairman and doesn't usually vote. You see, it's all kind of political. The council represents the whole tribe, by having one member of each family sit on it. Our family has been involved in these things ever since anyone can remember. Which means that being from a powerful family, Daddy carries a lot of weight when it comes to the others making up their minds. And he's one of the few that's against it.....on paper anyway."

I let that 'paper' comment pass. For now. "I'll do what I can," I said. She was visibly upset, and seemed reluctant to unburden a lot of personal problems to a complete stranger. I decided the rest of my questions could wait, or even be answered by someone else. "I'll need to talk to these other men - I think you called them elders?"

She smiled, and said, "They're all down at the Pow Wow. You wanna go? I can introduce you to most everybody, tonight."

"Pow wow? Do you still do that kind of thing?"

"Sure. Every Friday. Usually, it's just our own tribe. Only this time we've got visitors - because of everything that's been going on. One couple came all the way from Montana. They probably crossed over on the same ferry as you did." Camille sprang out of her chair and placed the dirty dishes in the sink. "You know, some of the tribes do some really neat stuff - like 'walking the stick.' Have you ever seen it before?"

"I don't believe I have."

"Come on. You'll like it."

I'd always wondered just how much of what I'd heard about Indian folklore was real and how much was superstition. I grabbed my coat on the way out.

The path was barely discernible in the dark. As we walked, brush whipped at my legs. Far above our heads, the trees had intertwined their branches like locked horns. I wrapped my arm around hers, hating the feeling of dependency, hating more the rustling of little creatures, unseen.

"Has your father ever disappeared like this before?" I asked, the sound of my own voice somewhat comforting.

"Oh, no. Daddy would never just take off like that. He might go out in the woods and sort of... prepare himself for the meeting. Maybe fast for a couple of days. But he wouldn't just leave and not come back. Not without telling me he was going."

Something flew over my head - *God, let it be a bird* - rustling some leaves in a tree. We walked on. She pointed with her free arm, the silky cloth of her jacket making a hissing sound. "Over there's where we meet."

19

We entered a brightly lit hall filled with the humid smell of warm, earthy bodies and a slight whiff of beer. The loud jovial voices we had heard as we came in, hushed now to a murmur. Twenty five to thirty faces turned and gawked.

Self-consciously I smoothed my wild and kinky hair, wishing I'd tamed it with a scarf. I hadn't planned on being the ONLY white person here.

Feeling her tug on my arm, I turned to Camille just as someone greeted her. She introduced me. "Hi, Mike. Betty. This is Kathleen O'Shaunessey, from the Seattle Gazette. I asked her to come." To me, she said, "Mike Hampton. He's the tribe's attorney and been doing all the legal stuff on this development."

He was an older man - gruff and built like an oversized panda bear. He shook my hand, saying, "Pleased to meet you. This is my wife Betty." She and I exchanged pleasantries, then Hampton leaned towards me, and half-whispered, "I'd like to see you before you leave." He handed me a card. "Call me, would you?"

It was quiet in the hall. Too quiet, with each ear tuned to our every word. "I'll try," I said, then smiled demurely and excused myself. With as much poise as I possessed, I strolled behind Camille to a spot on the bench lining the wall. I sat next to her, feeling like a cross between a celebrity and a warden, resisting the urge to clutch my purse beneath my breasts. All but one of the faces were unfamiliar. The other I had seen just hours before at the Edmonds ferry.

The bruiser in the Buick was back.

CHAPTER THREE

An old woman, sitting on a stool at one side of the room, started a simple beat on a drum. Measured and intensifying with each thump, it hypnotized the crowd with a single-minded purpose. The chattering subdued and finally stopped. Within minutes, two more drums picked up the beat and began to throb with the same heart-beating rhythm.

A huge bonfire had been built on an earthen mound in the center of the floor. The flames crackled and snapped, radiating heat and the smell of burning wood. Two teenage boys emerged from the bleachers and threw some fresh sections of log on the fire - scattering pieces of hot coals. Sparks flew as the smoke curled up to the ceiling and escaped through slits, purposely made for this purpose, in the roof.

Looking terribly self-conscious, the boys began to hum and jiggle around the fire - first on one foot and then on another. Two or three at a time, a dozen or more men also appeared on the floor, chanting in a high-pitched whine. I don't know what I had expected. But I didn't think they'd be so earnest - that the dance would be this important.

Camille was watching me. Realizing my mouth was hanging open, I snapped it shut and wiped at the corners with two fingers. With a chuckle she nudged my arm. "This is how our ancestors called on their guardian spirits. It's a kind of prayer where they asked for help in hunting or in healing. A man who had a spirit that would bring him game or chase fish into his net was considered wealthy."

The rhythmic drums and the chanting grew even more intense. Mesmerizing - almost sensual - it swept through the room with an electrifying force.

I glanced over at Camille. Her head had lolled back and her face almost glowed with a rapt expression. I couldn't help but think that they had something....something valuable... *At least they're convinced they do, which is almost as good.* And as far as I could tell, they weren't stoned.

The intensity climbed to a fever pitch. The heat from the raging fire shimmered on the many brown bodies, slick from sweat. A middle-aged man huffed out to the middle of the floor and with an wolf-like howl he placed a long cedar stick on the floor. This simple act seemed to be a popular one as the others cranked up their singing, sending the dancers into a rabid frenzy. It was impossible not to react. Shadows leapt and pranced on the walls from the flickering light of the fire and the dancers wild passion. Primitive and savage, it touched that part of me that I preferred to keep hidden.

In the excitement, I almost missed Camille's cue. She waved one hand to the side in a way that one might clear a space in a cloud of bubbles. And as if her hand were a magic wand, the few people standing in front of us saw it and moved to each side - making a path, deferring to her will.

She wanted to see the stick.

Who is this kid? And why is the guy with the Buick staring at her?

A cloud of suffocating smoke rolled into the bleachers, massing around my head and stinging my eyes. Seized with a spasm of choking and coughing, I got up.

I need some fresh air.

In the next moment, I saw the Buick guy stumble out the side door. *Hold on, Fat Boy. I don't like this 'thing' you have for teenage girls.* I looked over at Camille. She had told me on the phone, she'd felt threatened. But for now, weaving and muttering on the bench, she seemed to be in another world. At least she'd be safe. Probably safer, here with her friends and tribe members, than at home by herself or even with me.

I followed Fat boy out the door, hoping he hadn't recognized me and wondering if there might be a connection between this brute and Cloud's disappearance. Some kind of a lead is better than nothing and I certainly couldn't talk to any of the Indians tonight.

Glancing back to see if my leave-taking had made an impression, I blinked - then spun back around and scurried out the door.

God help me. There's no way I'll ever see it in print, but sure as my name is Kathleen O'Shaunessey I swear I saw that damn stick move - all by itself.

Once outside, I looked around for Fat Boy. Aha. He was staggering toward his Buick. *Oh, gross.* He was leaning across his fender, vomiting.

My Porsche was at the edge of the lot where I parked it. *This creep has got to have done something illegal.* I decided to follow him.

The Buick nosed out of its space, the muffler dangling noisily by a bolt and blasting loud, black smoke. I fumbled in my purse for my car keys and unlocked the little red door. Holding my breath, I turned the key in the ignition.

Come on, car - START.

It worked. The engine turned over on the first click and throbbed almost evenly as I geared into reverse.

The Buick had turned onto the highway, headed toward town. I did the same, staying about ten car lengths behind him. Roaring through the black night, my headlights hurled to the fields and to the clear-cut logging areas with their dead and blackened stumps standing like charred ghosts in a graveyard.

His car weaved across the road, throwing gravel at the shoulder. At one point, he narrowly missed a huge ditch. After that, he straightened out and slowed down to about forty.

Finally - the town of Suquamish. The streets were deserted, except for a few taverns. On the corner and down the block, bright, neon signs blinked *Budweiser* and the open doors blared the sounds of a live band.

I shortened the gap between our cars, keeping him in view. At the flashing red street light, he turned right. Down two blocks, another right turn, and he eased into the Dungeness Inn's entrance, pulling into a numbered space.

I drove by, careful not to show my brake lights until I was out of his line of vision. At the end of that block, I doused my headlights, made a U turn and switched off the engine. Coasting the last few yards on a down-hill grade, I jockeyed the car into a service station lot next to the motel and parked over on the side.

The motel was a string of old cabins, fenced with a high rock wall. Too high to jump over. *Damn.* There was only one entrance. All he'd have to do is watch out his window, to see me approach.

What, besides the woman and kids, could he have in that room? He must have that runaway girl locked up - why else wouldn't he bring them to the Pow-wow?

With my head ducked down behind the wall, I circled towards the back lot, counting the rooms - theirs was the third from the end. I checked to make sure I had the right one.

A slice of light beckoned from the back door window, a dull glow seen through the shabby curtain. *Good. They're still up and moving around.* A head, disquieting in the gloom, moved from my left to the right.

Creeping about twenty feet, I skirted a large bush and stumbled over a sack of old lawn-mower cuttings and litter. My hands plunged into cold goo as I fell. Too late, I noticed the bare light from a half-moon glinting off the wet plastic and little puddles of dew on the top.

The huge rounded humps were stacked knee-high against the mortared rock fence, discharging dank smells of rotted grass and empty beer cans. I used the stack as leverage and hiked up over the rock wall, landing with a grunt on the other side. Running doubled over, I counted cabins until I reached the one with the light. Checking the side, I noticed that the Buick had been parked in a lean-to garage off the side I guessed to be the kitchen.

The cabins were old, probably made from pre-WWII lumber. A rickety porch spanned the length of the back wall, the three steps covered with moss and rotting leaves. I tiptoed to the wall, next to the back door. Holding my breath, I flattened my ear against a large knot-hole.

Voices muttered from the other room. "....she was zonked out - like in some kind of trance," he said, and coughed wetly.

Someone else, obviously a woman, said, "I knew one of them would be gifted."

"Yea, well you got the wrong one. All this'n here does, is eat and bawl about one thing n' another. And I'm gettin' tired a' chasin' after the little brat."

"Get off my ass, Frank." Then quieter, with the thunk of an object hitting the floor and the rustle of a paper sack, she continued, "Look. It'll still work. They really look alike?"

"Yea. Can't tell 'em apart. When I saw her last night, I thought Carie had run away again. I was just about ready to grab the little snot and chuck 'er back in the car. Next time she does that shit, I'll tie 'er up and ferget where I put 'er."

I was right. He IS holding that kid prisoner.

Feeling my way along the wall, I tried getting closer to the window. *If I could just see...* Suddenly, from under the porch - a shriek shattered the quiet night, sliding eerily down the scale. Like a crazed woman, it wailed - clawing at the boards beneath my feet.

Good God. What's this?.

A violent scramble, I could feel the floor hump up. Before I could hide, some boards cracked open on the end of the porch. A force flung it to the ground. Something dashed out of the hole, then another - streaking into the night.

Oh, for crying out loud. It's two alley cats fighting.

I leaned back against the outside wall, my heart racing painfully. I waited...not daring to breathe. But, this time, I was lucky. Fat boy mumbled but didn't seem alarmed.

Now then. What's he done with that kid?

I stepped to the back door window, peering through a gap in the curtain. But as I moved, my foot scraped sand on the rough planks and bumped an empty beer can. It clinked and tipped over, the pull-tab rattling around inside as it rolled. I jumped back and grimaced - knowing what was next.

A hand snatched the curtain aside, exposing a face in the window. *Fat boy.* "What the hell?" he said, fumbling with the lock and banging the door open. "Who's out there?" he shouted, and stepped out onto the porch.

CHAPTER FOUR

I swiveled and lunged for the yard. But my foot slipped, sliding sideways in the green algae on the old porch steps. My face hit hard ground with a jarring thud. I wanted to scream - I could hear the angry echoes in my head - but the sounds couldn't come out. The blow to my chest when it smacked the earth, had knocked the wind out of me. I felt woozy, sliding in and out of consciousness.

I coughed, fighting for air, to stay awake, to make the awful spinning stop. Something - it tasted nasty and gritty in my mouth - gagged me. Dirt. My mouth was full of dirt.

I hawked it out, then painfully gasped air back in. With each exhale, I spit and wiped my tongue on my sleeve. As my body filled with its much needed oxygen, the fuzzy, indistinct shapes behind me took on the hard edge of reality.

My vision locked onto Fat boy's shoe. *I'm doomed.* I was still on the ground - weak and defenseless. He stepped up next to my face, - gravel crunching under his feet. Rough hands on my arm wrestled me onto my back.

"What the hell are you doing here?" he hollered.

Weak from shock and a wash of terror, I tried to struggle - to fight back. But he seemed unable to feel the few blows I rained on his head and shoulders.

He pulled me to my feet, easily, as I floundered like a fresh-caught fish. His arm snaked under my bosom - snugging my back up against his belly. His wet palm covered my mouth. For a moment, my body hung from his moist hands.

Then taking his hand between my teeth, I bit down - hard as I could - grating my teeth together like a vise. Blood, his blood, oozed onto my tongue. "Damn bitch," he said, jerking his hand away and examining it.

Heaving my leg up and back, I laid into his grasp and bashed the tip of my shoe to his ear. He cursed again and grabbed my foot.

I turned and dug my claws into his cheek, just missing his eye. "Leave me alone." He backhanded me - a painful blow to the same cheek where I'd fell.

We stumbled onto the porch. As my feet landed on solid board, my knee came up. He was expecting it. He jumped back, keeping his crotch out of reach. *I've got to get away from him.* With the last bits of my dwindling strength, I scrambled and kicked...

He chuckled. "Knock it off, girlie. You're comin' with me." Clamping my mouth shut, he muscled my arms behind me and gripped my wrists together. Mashed against his dirty T shirt, his bear-like chest hair smothering yet cushioning my face, I couldn't breathe. Fighting for air, I heaved and wheezed - ignoring the nauseous smell of his sweat.

He dragged me across the porch and up to the back door. Dangling like a rag doll, I kicked at his shins. "No. Let me go." One hand came free. I grabbed at and caught the trim on the doorway.

He yanked my hand away, breaking my fingernails to the quick. "Knock it off," he growled.

I stumbled and almost fell into the cabin. Inside the tiny kitchenette, cigarette smoke billowed around the woman's head like a shroud. The same one I'd seen with him in Edmonds. She eyed me for a moment, grinding yet another butt into an ashtray and stood up. Waving a hand at me, she said, "What are you doing here? Good Christ, Frank, get her out of here. What'd you think you're up to?"

"The nosy bitch was listening outside the door." He slung me into a straight-back wooden chair using his bulk to keep me there. A fat finger jabbed into my chest. "Now, I wanna know who the hell you are and what makes you think you got the right to spy on us. And no funny stuff."

How dare you. "I don't have to tell you anything, you fat scum bag."

His ringing slap dulled the sickening crack of skull against wall. My skull, their wall. That same chuckle, throaty now - almost sensual. "I can see right off," he said. "I'm going to have to teach you some manners."

The woman spoke up. "Frank, knock it off. You're going to land us in jail, yet."

"Shut up old woman. I'm running this show. If you don't like it, take a hike. Get the hell out."

"And leave you with my kid? Forget it."

While they argued, I worked on ridding the fog from my brain. *I've got to concentrate.* My sore head throbbed like the drums of ten toy soldiers. I tried rolling it to the left. *Not too bad. A few cymbals and a flute, and I'd have a full fife and core band.* I blinked, twice.

Fat boy was still here.

"Damn you, old woman," he snarled. "Here I am, trying ta take care of business. And on top of that, I got to fight you too." To me he said, "I want your name and what you were doing on my porch. And I want it NOW!"

I had to think. *Thank goodness I didn't have my purse with my I.D. in it.* "I thought I was coming in my own cabins' back door. I'd gone for a little walk over to the coke machine and didn't bother locking up before I left."

"What coke machine?"

"The one over at the service station."

He sneered and hooked his thumbs in his belt. "They ain't got one. You're lying." He looked over at the woman and said, "We'll have to get rid of her."

The woman shook her head as she jiggled another cigarette out of its package. "Now, wait just a damn minute," she said. Flame shot up from a yellow-green lighter in her hand, revealing round, coffee-with-cream-colored cheeks and black, unreadable eyes. She lit the cigarette, dragging in smoke with a vengeance. "If she's got something to say, let her say it." She glanced at Frank, her features seeming to be set in stone, then nodded in my direction. "Go ahead. Speak your piece."

"I uh, went to the service station, just taking it for granted that they'd have a coke machine. Most of them do. When I couldn't find one there, I walked over to the tavern." I motioned in the direction of the street with my chin, "The one over on the corner."

His grin exposed a repulsive jag of cavities. "You mean the Blue Goose? A young lady like you, just sallied on in there?" He frowned and scratched his two-day stubble. "Who waited on you? Who was behind the bar?"

"Uhm, I don't know. It was too crowded. I sat down at a small table just inside the door, and some woman came up to wait on me."

"A woman? You mean, like a waitress? In the Blue Goose? Now I know you're lying."

This would have to be good. "No. Really. Uhm, they were real busy. Come to think of it, she did seem kind of confused."

"What'd you mean, confused."

"You know. Like she wasn't sure what they had." I mentally blocked out the fear of another hit. "She had to ask the barkeep where they kept the bottled sodas." I smiled, feeling my lip crack where he'd hit it, tasting the warm paste of my own drying blood. "I ended up having my coke in a glass with a sack of cashews."

"That busy, huh? Well, it's Friday night. Could of been them guys working on that new highway job up in Hansville. Hauls their trailers around with them." He stretched as if to shrug off his self-doubt. "You say a woman waited on you? A waitress?"

"Yes. Uhm, she didn't seem to be...you know, very knowledgeable about the place. Didn't even know whether I could buy a can of coke or if it came out of the tap. She had to go ask someone."

"Who was there?"

"I couldn't say. Just a bunch of guys - rowdy men, goofing around." *I have to be convincing.* "One of them kept hassling me, asking me to dance."

A sneer tugged at the corner of his lips. "See anybody playing pool? Who was winning?"

"I...couldn't tell from where I sat." I took a chance and said, "They were playing darts, though. Whooping and hollering - I thought there was going to be a fight, there for awhile."

"Yeah. Well, that's 'cause the pool table's broke. Can't get the guy out here from Seattle to fix it." He peered longingly out the back door window in the direction of the street. "I don't know. Maybe you're telling the truth, maybe you ain't. But I can't let you go, till I go over and ask." He grabbed a cigarette from Margaret's pack and snapped her lighter open. The whites of his eyes were marbled with red. "Thought you was one of them peeping toms or somethin'."

"Why not let me go now? Then you wouldn't have to come back. You could just...enjoy yourself. Otherwise, if you keep me here too long..."

"Yeah, and what if I do? What're you gonna do about it?"

"Nothing! I won't do anything."

Watching his burly arm draw back, ready to strike, I steeled myself for another hit. "I'll make you a deal, though. If you let me go, right now, I'll go on home and we'll all just forget about what happened."

"And if I don't?"

"Then," I grimaced, waiting, "...I can't be responsible for what happens."

"What'd you mean? Like what? What's gonna happen?"

"Well, my boyfriend will...come looking for me. I'm sure he's already concerned."

"Oh, hell. You gotta boyfriend over there? You never said before."

"You didn't ask." I paused, letting my new lie sink in. "I'm sure he's quite worried by now. He was awake when I left, and told me to hurry back."

"Oh, hell. What's gonna happen if he sees you all bloodied up and everything? I don't need no jerks coming over here."

"Then let me go. I'll say there was a scuffle at the tavern and I got in the way. Otherwise, if he calls the police...I don't know what to tell you."

"Wait a minute. You went to the tavern alone, with your boyfriend asleep in the cabin? What's he gonna say about that?"

"Obviously, he's not going to like it. He'll definitely be angry. The question is, do you want him angry at me or at yourself? It's up to you."

"How do I know I can trust you?"

"You've got no choice. It's now or later on with the cops." Frank flopped into a chair across from Margaret, blew a puff of smoke to the side and mashed the cigarette into the ashtray. "Yech," he said, frowning at her. "Menthols. You know how I hate menthols. Damn things turn my stomach. If you're gonna spend good money on cigarettes, buy something a man can smoke."

"And you can buy your own," she snapped, and snatched the pack off the table. Up until now, Margaret had been watching him with a quiet but bright-eyed interest. She rose to dump the ashtray into a wastecan under the sink then turned to face him. "I don't like you getting me involved in your schemes, Frank. I told you about that, before."

"What'd you mean by that? 'My schemes.'"

She jerked her head in my direction. "I don't need no more trouble, Frank. You better let her go."

"All right, all right." He looked at me and thumbed at the door. "Get the hell out. Just don't come snooping around here anymore."

I rose to leave, setting loose a new set of jack hammers in my head. Dizzy for a moment, I leaned on the counter head down. The woman lifted me up and shuffled me toward the door. "If you gotta puke, do it outside," she said. "I got enough to do, cleaning up after him."

"I'm going." *Come on Kath. A few more steps....* Behind us, I heard a door open from one of the back rooms and sensed someone else entering the kitchen. She spoke, *did she say Mamma?* The outside door knob was in my hand, the pain blasting away in my brain. I willed my hand to pull the door open and glanced at the figure as I stepped onto the porch.

Poised in the doorway, I blinked, rubbed my eyes and reopened them. *This cannot be real.*

The pain deepened. I wanted to cry. *I should leave* - but I knew I couldn't. A name blew up in my head and popped out of my mouth. "Camille." This was impossible. I had just left her at the Pow Wow. "What are you doing here? I left you back at the...."

Fat boy moved faster than I ever would have thought. "You are lying, ya Bitch. Get in here. Margaret, close the door and lock it."

CHAPTER FIVE

The back of the chair dug into my back as he shoved me into it.
Margaret was livid. "Now you've done it, Frank. She knows. What'll
we do with her?"

"Shut up and let me think."

Timidly, the girl peered at me from the bedroom doorway.
Good grief. That's not Camille. But she looks so much like her.

"Who's Camille?" she asked me.

*Oh, God, if I could only tell you. You've got a sister Honey. Just a
few miles down the road. And I promise I'll tell you all about it some
day. But not now. It'll get us both killed.*

When I didn't answer, she turned to Margaret. "Mamma? What's going
on? How come that lady called me Camille?"

"Never mind, Cerese. Go back to bed." Margaret waved at the girl to
go back in the bedroom. "Frank. We can't just leave this woman here.
It's too dangerous."

That's it. They're twins. They've got to be twins.

"Mamma? What are you doing with that lady?"

"I said, never mind. Go back to bed." *I wonder if she knows she has
a twin. My God, the resemblance is astonishing.*

Fat boy rattled the old refrigerator door open and snatched a can of
beer from the top shelf. "Christ, it'll be morning before we know it."
He took a long swig, staring at me from around the can. "I just figured
out something'," he said. "You're that newspaper lady, ain't cha?" To
Margaret's questioning glare, he replied, "I heard there was some reporter come in from Seattle. I told them I didn't like it - didn't make no
sense having some broad come snooping around, poking her nose in
where it don't belong. But I never figured she'd be coming to the Pow-
Wow."

I hated him. Hated all the things he stood for and what I feared he
was doing to that girl. But I couldn't help her or myself in this position.
Trying on my most placid expression, I kept my gaze on the floor. *I'd
better not say anything. He doesn't know who else I've told about this.*

He belched and tongued one of his back molars. "Tie her up. I'll have
to go tell the boss." While Margaret used an old rayon scarf to bind my
wrists, Frank hitched up his pants and jiggled his car keys. He looked
around as if he'd forgotten something, until his eyes lit on the girl.
Descending on her, he grabbed a handful of hair and bent her head
over to the side. "And you..." he growled. "You keep your big mouth
closed. Comprende?"

"Let go of my hair. I haven't done nothing."

"Frank!" With a deft move, Margaret wedged herself between them. Her face just inches from his, she snarled, "Leave my daughter alone!"

Daughter? I don't think so.

His fist fell open and he released the girl. "I ain't hurting the little brat." Drawing back his burly arm, he feinted a strike at Margaret. Obviously thinking better of it, he turned back to the girl. "Not one single word. You hear me? Keep your trap shut."

"I'm not saying nothing to nobody. Just don't pull my hair."

Petting the girl's head like a pet dog, Margaret eased her back to the bedroom. I could see her wait for the soft click of the lock before she moved away.

Frank was pulling on his jacket. To Margaret, he said, "Boss's gonna be pissed."

"Don't blame it on me," she replied. "Wasn't my idea to drag that woman in here."

"Keep an eye on these two. I'll be back after I talk to Dave."

"Don't give me that shit. You're going out drinking and sticking me with yer dumb mistakes."

"Look, old woman. I don't want any more of your lip."

"And what do I do with her?" She thumbed in my direction.

Frank balled his fist, the car keys sticking out from between his fingers. "I already told you. Just keep her tied up till I talk to the boss. I'll be back," and with a window-rattling slam, he left.

Margaret looked at me. "I'm sorry, lady. I never meant for things to go this far. But this is our business. You should have stayed out of it."

"What you're doing here is illegal."

"I know that. But there's nothing I can do about it."

"You could let me go. With no kidnapping and false imprisonment charges, they'd probably let you go with a small fine."

"And let Cerese grow up poor like the rest of us? Hopeless and uneducated? No. It's too late. This is our ticket outta this hell-hole and I ain't gonna give it up."

"If all you want is an education for her, there's better ways to get it than this."

She turned on me like a rabid dog. "Yea, sure. And all of those ways takes money. I want her to have a decent life. She's Indian. Which means she's to remember her place is on the reservation, keep her mouth shut, and accept whatever crumbs the white man's government decides to sprinkle at her feet." She stared at me as if she were waiting for me to contradict, to prove her statement to be false...

What do I say to that?

She sighed, wedging a pillow between my head and the wall. "I'm gonna try and get some sleep. I suggest you do the same."

His hands woke me up, unnecessarily rough, pulling my arms up in the back where they'd been tied. I moaned from the pain, hoping he wouldn't break them. "That's it," he barked. "Get on outta here."

31

"Whaaa...," He'd untied me. I cleared my throat. "What're you doing?"

"I told ya already. Get outta here, before I change my mind."

I remembered not to argue. I had no idea why he let me go or even why he'd kept me, but the door was open and it was time I left. Stumbling on rubbery legs, I concentrated on getting out of the cabin, off the porch, and out of his yard.

Once outside, I headed towards the entrance. I'd never get over the rock wall in this condition. A brisk breeze whisked by me, rattling some dried leaves by my feet. Limping down the old hard-top street, I laid my head back, breathing in clean, free air. The sky above me was warming to the day. A thin, pink sunrise seeped into the haze, much like spilled ink into a blotter. I pretended it was just for me as I made my way to my car.

I needn't have bothered.

The car was not going to start. In fact, it was never going to start again in its present condition. Frank had been here. Brightly colored wires drooped from under the dashboard - gutted by a pair of fat, moist hands. I was really starting to dislike that man. *Where's my pocketbook?* I gasped and began to search - pawing under and behind the seats, sticking my hand in the crevices, rummaging through the glove compartment. No keys, no credit cards....and no money. He'd taken everything but a single quarter - lodged between the mat and the side wall.

This was too much. Too tired to cry, I slumped onto the driver's seat. Car door swinging wide, feet propped up on the door jam, my weary head drooped to my knees. I felt violated - molested in places the beating had not reached.

An old hopped-up, repainted pick-up, rumbled into the parking lot. A young man with *Jack* embroidered on the right shoulder of his coveralls threw me a questioning look as he unlocked the bay door. I didn't blame him, I probably looked like hell warmed over. At least I had the good luck of parking outside a service station. But - with no way to pay, how would I get him to fix it?

An old pay phone leaned wearily against the light pole by the road, its accordion door swinging from a single hinge. I walked over, knees wobbling and wanting to buckle. It was an old phone and I'd have to use my quarter.

Listening to the metallic tinkle, I dialed an 800 number. *Lord, let him be there early. Just this once, let him show up for work early.*

A grouchy voice grumbled from the other side of the bay...*that wonderful city of street lights and patrolling police cars...* "Seattle Gazette," he said.

"Oh, God. Tom. I'm so glad you're here. There. I mean..." Damn. I can't talk when I'm crying. Never could.

"Kathy? Is that you? Kathy! Talk to me. What's wrong?"

"Tom? Can I charge a repair job for my car to the office, until I get paid?"

"What?"

"I'm broke and my car's incapacitated. It won't start. It'll never start again."

His voice boomed in my ear, "Where are you? Kathy. Don't cry, for God's sakes. Calm down and talk to me. Tell me where you are. Are you still in Suquamish?"

"Yes." I sniffled, looked around for a kleenex and started crying again. They were in my pocketbook.

"Where in Suquamish? In town?"

"At a service station. A Texaco, I think."

"Are you all right? Have you been hurt...? Kathy, stop crying and tell me if you're hurt. Talk to me Kath. Do you need anything?"

"I have to blow my nose."

"You have to what?" He sighed, audibly. "OK. Let's start over again. Your car's broke down, you're out of money, and you have to blow your nose. Is there anything else? Is there someone there to fix the car? Can he give you a loaner? Talk to me, Kath."

"I don't have any keys either. Or any money, or a driver's license. Nothing, Tom. They were all in my pocketbook."

"So where's your pocketbook?"

"He stole it when he cut the wires."

"Who's he? What wires? Kathy, what the hell is going on? Are you sure this guy stole it? And if so, have you reported it to the police?" I could tell Tom had his fat lips screwed down in that irritating way he had of dealing with women who, he felt, were being 'difficult.'

Too bad. I had good reason to be upset.

"Tom, the pig beat me, tied me up, and trashed my car. I don't think he'd be struck dumb from a guilty conscience by stealing a lady's pocketbook. Now, are you going to help me or not?"

"Whaaa - well of course I'm going to help you. Someone beat you? Well, for Christsakes. Why didn't you tell me? Who was it? I'll kill him. Are you all right?

"Just shook up is all. I didn't mean to turn the faucets loose. I'm OK, Tom. Really I am."

"No - it's me who's sorry." Contrite now, his guilt oozed through the phone receiver, thick enough to spoon. "Kathy. Honey. What can I do? I know, let me come after you. In fact, stay there. You say the Texaco station? I'm leaving right now."

I held the ear piece where I could see it. *This is not the Tom I know. I liked him better grouchy.*

"No, Tom. Never mind."

"Kath, I can't just leave you there."

"Thanks, but I'm OK. Just tell this little guy, this mechanic, to fix it. Right away. Tell him to charge it. And keys. Tell him to fetch a locksmith to make me a set of keys."

"You got it, Sugar. I'll take care of everything. Have him call me here, I'll vouch for the repairs and anything else you need. How bad are you hurt? Do you need a doctor?"

"No, I'm all right. Just tell this guy here, to fix my car. That's all I need. Just fix my damn car."

"Consider it done. Just...take care of yourself."

"I will. Thanks Tom. I'll see you later."

"Later? How soon? Aren't you coming back?"

"After I finish my story. I'll talk to you later, Tom."

"Kath?"

"Bye now. Be sure to call that mechanic. The Texaco station on Third and...." I stretched my neck to read the old street sign, "...looks like 'Bay Road'."

"Texaco on Third and Bay Road. Kath, will you call me back? Keep in touch?"

"Bye, Tom," I said, and quickly hung up. I had to talk to Camille. *Wait until she hears about her twin sister.* I wonder if....No. She couldn't possibly know. That old woman did, though. Ole' Margaret.

It was morning and the sun was up. After making arrangements for the repairs and hearing he had no loaner - nothing there for me to drive, I started walking back to Camille's. After a weary twenty minutes, my mushy brain started to clear. *There's gotta be a better way.* Behind me on the highway, I heard a car slow down as it approached. Although I hadn't hitchhiked since the eighth grade - I'd missed the bus that took us home from the homecoming football game - this was no time to quibble. I lifted my thumb in the glare of their headlights and jerked it in their direction. The car passed and stopped a few yards in front of me.

What luck! I hurried past the slick back fender, heard the muffled click of an automatic lock, and watched the back door of a silver-grey, Lincoln limousine swing open. Exhausted, and slightly numb from shock, I got in.

CHAPTER SIX

The glove leather of the back seat felt smooth as a second skin as I slid into the limo. Dyed a slate gray, the thick padding matched the Japanese silk drapes and carpet perfectly, setting off the black teakwood bar. It looked great - but the guy at the other end of the seat looked even better.

He seemed tall, even when sitting down. "You look like you could use a drink," he said, reaching to undo the lid to the wet bar. Hefting an expensively-shaped bottle of Shnaaps, his hand all but covered the writing on the label. The words below his fingers looked odd. I concentrated, focusing my gaze on them... Aha. It was all in German. I meant to ask him if he'd brought it back from there himself when my attention was diverted. His tailored, light wool suit sleeve nudged back just enough to expose the wink and glitter of an emerald cuff link as big as a cat's eye.

I took the offered glass, surprised that I was shaking. The liquor felt warm going down, soothing out my high-strung stomach. I tried to say "Thanks", but when it came out more of a squeak than a spoken word, I let it go as a nod. It was embarrassing. In between sips, I stared at my feet. "Feeling better?" he asked, his brow creased with what seemed to be genuine concern.

"Yes, uhm, I do. Thank you very much."

He gave directions to his driver through a levered opening in the thick glass divider, then settled in his corner. His right arm crooked over the back of his seat as he sat watching me. What his brandy didn't warm, his gaze did.

I wiped my the palms of my hands on my slacks, consciously keeping my knees together. "I must look a fright," I stammered, cleaning the corners of my mouth with thumb and first finger.

He crossed his legs, rustling the perfectly creased pants. "You look like a beautiful woman who's had a hard night," he said, sending through me the odd urge to nestle my rump to the seat. There was something about him, aside from his obscene wealth...

"Ready for a refill?" he asked. When I blinked stupidly, he pointed at my empty glass.

"Oh, no." I said. "One more of these and I'd be stretched out flat." I crimsoned at my awkward words, wondering....

"You need food and a chance to clean up," he said. I sat mute, unable to argue with the obvious. "Do you mind going to my condo?"

"Oh. No, thanks. My mother doesn't live far from here - if you wouldn't mind taking me..." I must have stared at him.

He laughed, hands held in a mock hold-up. "No strings, no hanky-panky. I promise. If it's home you want, then home it is. But you're more than welcome to shower at my place while I make some phone calls."

I shrugged, "Well, maybe next time. I'll just go on to my house for now. Or, my old house. I mean, I don't really live there anymore, uh...." *Good going, Kate. Nothing like an electrifying delivery of wits and candor to charm a man silly.*

Eyeing the portable phone on his side of the limo wall, I considered calling the police to report my run-in on the reservation. I'd have to lean across his lap to reach it... Naw. Every other paper in town would have my story before I had a chance to write it. All I really knew was that an obnoxious Indian had one girl who looked like another and that he'd caught a prowler, (meaning me) outside his cabin door. I could push an assault case and maybe illegal imprisonment but no more. The rest was all conjecture.

I gave the driver directions to my mother's house. He answered with a quick nod. Turning to the handsome hunk beside me, I said, "This is going to sound really dumb, but I swear you look and sound terribly familiar."

"Could be. I was on the board for city development in Seattle recently. I helped put together a project for The International Trade and Commerce for the Pacific Coast Division."

"That's it," I squealed. "You're David Abrahamson. One of our journalists interviewed you for the Business section and I tagged along. That's been, what? Three, four months ago? "

"Yes. I think I do remember. How could anyone forget those flirty brown eyes of yours? In fact, I think I asked you to lunch at the Arboretum."

"Kind of. You were going to call me at the office and never did." For the rest of the ride, the grey limo snaked through the turns and dips of the familiar, country road as we huddled, making small talk, mellowing out.

He preferred to talk about me. "Are you still at the Gazette? I'd think a beautiful woman like yourself could do better than pounding the sidewalk for a living."

"Oh, it's alright," I stammered. "But I doubt that I'm very beautiful at the moment." My lip was getting puffy and I sounded like I'd been to the dentist. I touched my right cheekbone and winced. It was very sore.

"Nothing that won't heal in a few days," he said. Then, as if he had a sudden idea, he began to rummage around under the portable sink. Pulling out a plastic baggy, he filled it with ice and handed it to me. "Here. Put this on your lip. It'll help stop the swelling."

"Thanks," I said, touching it to my fat lip and then on my cheek. It didn't seem to help. I shook my head and gave it back to him. Without a word, he placed it in the tiny sink of the portable bar. He then leaned back and studied me, as if he would memorize my every contour, remember my every move. "You haven't answered my question," he said. "What brings you to Suquamish in the wee hours of the morning?"

I wanted to ask him the same thing, but couldn't do anything with my hands. Finally, I locked my fingers over my knee and said, "I'm here on assignment. Doing a story on the Indians. I should be getting back..."

"Hey. That Gazette's not going anywhere. This is Saturday. Why not relax a little, get some rest? A journalist needs to be on her toes. By Monday morning, you'll be bright and cheery - ready to knock their socks off." He splashed another inch of liquor in my glass, his face brushing the dried ends of my hair. "By the way, I'm sorry to say I've forgotten your name."

"Kathleen O'Shaunessey."

With a studied look from out of hazel-brown eyes, he clinked his goblet against mine in a toast. "An Irish lass in Poulsbo? Hope they're ready for it." I shrugged one shoulder and gave him my best smile, hoping my lip wouldn't crack. His gaze swept the length of me, saying, "Or better yet, I hope I'm ready for it."

"I think you can handle most anything you take on."

His answer was in the flare of his narrow-bridged nose, the curve of his discerning smile. He finished his drink and snapped the bar lid closed over our used glasses just as the limo slowed to a stop and parked.

The chauffeur, a small Asian, unlocked the door from the front with some kind of a switch and ran around to my side to help me get out. David and I said our goodbyes and exchanged business cards.

Walking up the driveway, I never thought I'd be so glad to be back at the old farm. To my left, a small pasture with a few ancient apple trees, sat strangely vacant. Weeds and grass had grown hip-high with no cow or sheep to keep them gnawed down. The weather-beaten barn, brown and rickety with rot, continued to defy the gravity that would one day, send it crumbling to the ground.

The old farmhouse was to my right, sporting new, white window shutters and a coat of bright yellow paint. There weren't any lights on, and I'd given up my key long ago. I'd have to wake Mom up.

After a few knocks, I followed my mother's journey from the bedroom to the back porch door, with the progression of lights being switched on. Her little dog Timmy, the product of a one night stand between his pedigreed Shin-Tsu mother and a neighborhood mutt, followed at her heels and barking in alarm.

"Timmy," Mamma scolded. "Hush." In the porch now, I could hear the quick tap of the dog's tiny toenails on the tile floor and Mamma's heavier steps. She called out in an uneasy squeak. "Who is it?"

"Mamma. It's me. Kathy."

"Well, what in the world...." she said, opening the door and ushering me quickly inside. "Kathleen! What are you doing here this time of night? Are you alright? I didn't hear your car...."

"I didn't drive here in my car." Timmy recognized me immediately. He began to jump up, yapping excitedly and scratching my leg with his sharp claws. I reached down to scratch him behind the ear as he leapt, wiggling joyously, into my arms. He weighed all of 12 pounds and half of that was hair - tan hair with black and brown splotches and at least 4 inches long. Underneath all of that, he was a jumble of squirming, kinetic energy and large, soulful-black eyes.

Mamma blinked sleepily, and drew her pink-flowered robe closer about her neck. "Well, come in here where I can see you." she said, and motioned me through the back porch and over to the kitchen table. "I don't have my glasses on."

"Mom, it's okay. I'm sorry to wake you up. My car broke down not far from here, and I needed a place to sleep."

My relationship with my mother had always been a kind of affectionate tryst. We loved each other dearly as long as we weren't in the same room long enough to argue - a period of time which seldom lasted more than five minutes. We left the darkened porch and entered the brightly-lit kitchen, Mamma in front and I following her. She turned, got her first good look at my face, and gasped. "Good grief, Kathleen. What happened? You look terrible. Did you have a wreck?"

"Thanks, Mom. I needed that." Timmy whined at my feet, begging for attention. He knew something was wrong. I picked him up and immediately his little tongue darted out to lick the scratched spot on my cheek and my bloody lip.

"Well, you know what I mean. Oh, my poor baby girl. Just look at you. You're all battered up and your clothing's dirty and torn. I haven't seen you look this bad, in years."

"I've had a pretty rough night. Let me clean up a minute and we'll talk." I put Timmy back on the floor and patted his head. With one moist kiss to the back of my hand, he trotted off to his breakfast bowl.

After a quick wash-up in the bathroom and running a comb through my snarled mass of curls, I sat down at the table and watched my mother bustle around the sink. Timmy eased under the rungs of my chair and curled up, nose to tail, directly under me. Mamma filled the coffee maker with cold water from the tap and grounds from a large can. Every now and then, she'd eye the side of my face where Fat Man had hit me, but she seemed to be willing to wait. If not already, I'd have a black eye and a bruise by morning.

She set heavy mugs on the table with a container of coffee cream and a package of cookies. Timmy was tossed a doggy biscuit, which kept him busy for the moment. "Are you hungry? I can fix you some eggs if you like. And sausage. I've got some I bought from the Indians. Venison, mixed in with beef and pork. It's really good."

I shook my head *no*, within the support of my upturned hands.

Sliding into a chair next to mine, she touched the sore place on my cheek, making me wince and jerk my head out of reach. "You're all puffy and baggy eyed," she said. "And your lip is bleeding. Are you ready to talk about it? What in the world happened?"

"I told you, Mom. I'm OK. Really, I am. I didn't mean to scare you." I raised up and glanced at the counter. "Is that coffee ready yet?"

38

Her eyes roamed over my face as if her gaze alone could heal the wounds and cure all of my pains and disappointments. And although I would have a tough time admitting it, her loving care was exactly what I needed and I honestly felt better. "You know, that sausage does sound good. Is it spicy?"

Pleased that there was something she could do, Mamma bounced up, poured our coffee, and plucked a package out of the freezer compartment. "Not hot, like with peppers. But it's got lots of sage and garlic in it. I think it's good." With a large, sawing-type knife, she hacked at it, trying to cut half-inch rounds off the end.

I checked an impulse to overreact, my head full of advice as to the use of modern conveniences. Instead, I stayed in my seat and covered my mouth with my hand in pretense of stifling a cough. After a minute of leaning on the hard-frozen meat with all of her weight, she clucked her tongue and put the knife down with a disgusted thud.

Every now and then, over the years, our thought waves have flowed together in a way that we'd know what the other one was thinking. As I focused on the cupboard door, she looked up at the same spot, and said, "What am I thinking of." She plucked a plate from the shelf and put the sausage roll on it. "I always forget about this thing." Setting the sausage in the micro-wave on defrost, she plopped onto the chair next to me, saying, "Okay. Now will you please explain, what in the world happened?"

"I'm on a story, Mom. I got a call to investigate a disappearance on the reservation. I looked around a bit, talked to a few people, and wandered into the wrong cabin. My mistake, they thought I was a burglar."

"That's it?"

"In a nutshell, yes." The details, such as the twins and the possible abduction of Cerese, would have to be filled in later. For now, I was too tired and there was no need for her to be more worried than she already was. "I'll be giving a full report to the police tomorrow." I looked at my watch. "Or rather, today. It's already six-thirty."

To change the subject and because I noticed she seemed a little more distracted than usual, I asked her a few questions. "So, Mom, what have you been up to, lately?" Our last conversation had been about a new diet she'd found at the health food store. Guaranteed, she'd said, to trim the fat from even her 52-year-old behind. "You look good. Have you lost any weight? And a new hair-do, too? Sexy, sexy. You better watch out. You'll get so hot, the guys will be standing in line."

To my surprise, she blushed and began to stammer. "Oh. It's nothing, really. Just dinner a couple of times. And.. something about some tickets to the ballet. The Nutcracker starts showing the second week of December. Oh, how I'd love to see that again. And he wants to go to Hawaii in January for my birthday. But that's definitely not...uhm, it's not certain yet. I'm not sure..."

"You're kidding. The Nutcracker? Hawaii? Mom. What're you saying? And who's this 'he?' Are you really dating someone?"

"Oh. I thought you knew."

"Know what? Mom, are you really dating someone?"

"Well, yes, uh, I guess you could say that. I have uh, been seeing someone on occasion. Uh, you know, now with you kids gone, I have to admit that..."

"Well, I know that, Mom. Just tell me..."

"... I do get lonely out here. And, it's nice to have the attentions of, uh..."

"Who is this guy, Mom? Do I know him?"

"Well, he's a gentleman. He's been very nice, and we have a lot of fun together."

"I do know him, don't I?"

"I can't really say. You may remember him from your high school days. Although, he certainly wasn't a... what you'd call a...regular visitor to our home, then. But you might recall hearing his name."

For years after my parents divorced, I'd been telling her to go out. Have some fun. But now that she seemed to be doing just that, and she still hadn't told me who with, I felt sick inside. Although determined to hide it, there was a growing sadness in the pit of my stomach. "Who is it, Mom? If you say he's one of my old teachers, I'll croak."

"Oh, no. Nothing like that. I, uh, I don't believe Teddy has ever been a teacher."

"Teddy? Do I know a Teddy?"

"You'll probably recognize him by the name, Sheriff Belltower."

"The Sheriff? You mean old Bucket Belly? It's a joke, right? You're not serious?"

She looked at me for the longest time, forcing me to feel her disapproval. Finally, she stroked my cheek with the back of her finger, and said, "I'm sorry, Dear. I'm sure this must be a terrible shock."

"I'm not shocked, Mom. I mean, I'm a big girl now. I understand that you have....that you get lonely out here by yourself. And I'm glad that you're...seeing someone. I'm sure it helps those long evenings go by." I stretched my neck to loosen the thickness in my throat. "Well, you know what, this may even be a blessing in disguise. I needed to talk to the Sheriff anyway. If you'll lend me your car, I can stop in on my way through town and congratulate him on his, his new romance."

"OH. You don't need to do that, Dear. I mean, he told me last night, that he'd be coming over this morning, anyway. In fact, he should be here soon. I'll have to run take a shower. Are you worried about your car? Maybe we should have it towed? I'm sure Teddy would help us..."

"No, Mom. My car doesn't need to be towed." Later I would wish I had shut up. But for now, my mouth seemed to have acquired its own engine and was racing out of control. "I need to report a crook. It seems, that while you were making out with the local fuzz, some scum bag imprisoned me and beat me up. He then wrecked my car and stole my purse. And...I believe he has kidnapped at least one child. A teenager. About the same age I was when Daddy ran off." She blanched and drew back away from me. Her eyes began to moisten.

"Mom," I stammered. "I didn't mean..."

"I was afraid of this. I knew you were hurt. Thought you must have had a fender-bender and didn't want to admit it. Why didn't you tell me about this? You'll recall, I asked you several times."

I was already mentally kicking myself for my show of immaturity and trying to form a decent apology. *Will I ever learn to keep my trap shut?* She then probed my inner depths with that same fixed gaze that had discovered my every sin and secret since I was born. "I'm going to tell you something, I want you to always remember," she said. "No one, including this man, will ever mean more to me than my children - no matter how old we all become. You and your sisters are my life. My whole life. And I never want you to forget it."

"I know, Mom. I'm sorry. That was an asinine thing for me to say."

For one tense moment, she studied me without comment. The wrinkles on each side of her mouth, that had begun many years ago as laugh lines were now etched in permanent creases and her skin was drier than I had ever remembered. I was beginning to wonder if she might not accept my apology. "I'm glad you're having a good time," I said, my belly churning. "Really, I am."

Then, after checking me over and clucking over the swelling, she said, "You're going to be black and blue for awhile, but I doubt anything's broken. Does it hurt?" I shrugged, still feeling guilty about my burst of temper. She finally surrounded with a parental hug and stroked my back. For a few minutes, neither one of us spoke. I hadn't realized how much I had missed her. Then she said, "There's Tylenol and an ice bag in the bathroom closet. Put some ice on that little face of yours, while I go get dressed."

CHAPTER SEVEN

By the time Mamma had finished dressing, the sausage had turned a crispy brown in the pan and I'd whipped a half-dozen eggs for an omelet. Timmy bounced and yapped beside me, nose lifted to the scent of the frying meat. The wag of his long hairy tail swept half-circles in the dust on the kitchen floor as he tried every trick he'd ever learned to beg a bit of sausage. I tossed a slice on a saucer and set it on the floor in the corner. Leaving him to gulp it down in ferocious concentration, I switched on the oven to heat and fumbled through the cupboard for a box of Bisquick.

Mamma emerged from the bedroom in a crisp, linen-look dress, full make-up, and new pumps. "MMM, doesn't that smell good?" she said. Every few minutes, she darted glances out of the kitchen window at a spot where she could see a mile up the road.

"Hope so. Is there any of that blackberry jam left you made last summer?" As she reached over my head into a top cupboard, another smell wafted through the kitchen, overpowering the sausage. "Isn't that the perfume I gave you for Christmas two years ago?"

"Why, yes. I suppose it is. OH. There comes Teddy, now. And I want you to be nice to him, OK? Show him what a lovely lady you've grown up to be."

Sheriff Belltower pulled up the driveway in a black and white, four-doored Ford cruiser with a North-Kitsap Sheriff's department emblem blazed across the door in big, navy blue lettering. I backed away from the window so he wouldn't catch me watching. The Sheriff I remembered had always been a well-meaning if somewhat sanctimonious old goat, but he had a reputation in town for honesty and more than a few families credited him for keeping their teenage sons in school and out of jail. Belltower knocked politely, setting Timmy off in a wild, yapping scramble to the door. Mamma called to the dog, "Hush, Timmy." But Timmy felt the strain in her voice and reacted in pure doggy fashion. He lunged at the door, barking with a ferocious abandon.

Mamma smoothed her skirt and moved swiftly to let the Sheriff in, keeping one raised foot between the dog and the Sheriff's ankle. They murmured briefly, and in a raised voice strictly for my benefit, I heard Mamma say, "Come on in, Ted. You're just in time for breakfast." Inside the kitchen, she introduced us by saying, "I'm not sure if you've met my daughter, Kathleen."

I instantly flashed the friendliest smile my sore cheeks could produce and stuck out my hand for a firm shake. "Nice to meet you, Sheriff. I don't think we ever formally met but I remember seeing you at the football games and dances."

"Nothing wrong with that," he said, a little louder and a lot more gregarious than the occasion called for. He looked older than I'd expected, a little haggard around the eyes, and was dressed in 'civvies' - a light blue satin windbreaker with *Huskies* emblazed across the back over a white open-necked shirt and tan, western-style slacks. "Not being on speaking acquaintance with the Sheriff usually means you never been in trouble."

I let that go by without comment.

Mamma plopped a coffee cup in front of him, flushing prettily as she filled it and placed the cream and sugar within his easy reach. "Kathleen had some problems she wanted to talk to you about."

"Mamma, I..."

"Well, tell him, dear. About your car, and that awful man."

"What happened?" The Sheriff said, seeming to relax with the more familiar role of investigating crooks and evildoers. "You have an accident? Somebody rough you up, or what?"

The Tylenol was beginning to take the edge off my headache as I related the whole event from the first phone call at the office. The Sheriff interrupted only once, in the beginning. He brought out a mini-tape recorder, placed it on the table in front of me, and said, "Just for my own use."

I told him all I remembered, leaving out the scene at the Edmonds Ferry dock with the runaway girl I now knew as Cerese, and her comment at the cabin. Neither did I mention my suspicions about her being Camille's twin. I wasn't about to just hand him the entire case on a silver platter, while he spent his time romanticizing my mother.

Belltower didn't miss much. He eyed my bruises and my fat lip, and said, "What made you follow the guy in the first place? Somebody tip you off?"

"I didn't like the way he was staring at the kid." The Sheriff didn't budge or make a sound, but I could tell he wasn't convinced. "Hey," I said, angry that he'd all but called me a liar. "It hasn't been that many years since I was that age and being leered at by some lecherous old poop. And it's not much fun, let me tell you. Especially, when no one believes you."

Glancing over at Mamma, he shrugged and tried to look virtuous. "Yeah," he said. "I'm sure it ain't easy, being a teenage girl. No fun at all. Anything else you want to say? Any hunches? First impressions? Woman's intuitions?"

"He's definitely a crook, of some kind. But, the most puzzling part of all, was how he let me go. Just like that, he untied me and said to get out. The only thing I can think of, was that when he called his boss or whoever he answers to, he was told to let me go. Which would explain why he's stayed out of jail this long."

The sheriff reared back, ready to take offense at my suggestion that a criminal walked his streets unrestrained and that he, the Sheriff, remained blithely unaware of it.

"The guy is a slice short of a sandwich," I said, calming his ruffled ego. "He'd have been locked up long ago, without someone else to call the shots. A boss-man that knew how to stay above the law. I had the feeling that this guy was a hood and had been a hood for a long time."

"Did you get a gander at his license plate?"

"I tried. But it was too muddy. Other than seeing he had Canadian plates, I couldn't read it."

"Well," he said, clearing his throat and smiling in a way that hid his chipped front tooth - the results of a long-ago fight. "I guess that's all we can do today. You'll need to make out a report at the station. Just tell them the same thing you told me. I promised your Mamma I'd take her to Seattle today, but I'll get right on it soon's I get back." He looked fully at Mamma then, transforming on the spot to a big, happy teddybear. "You're looking awful pretty this morning," he said to her. "About ready to go?"

"Yes," she said, hurriedly clearing the table of dirty dishes.

"Never mind, Mom. I'll get those. You two go on and have a good time."

"Alright then. I'll just get my coat."

It was five miles into town and I still needed some wheels. And once again, Mamma seemed to hear my thoughts before I said them. "The Nissan is in the garage, Dear. Keys are on the peg, here by the door. Will you promise me you'll stay away from those people? Let the authorities handle it?"

"Of course. Believe me, I'm not about to go back there."

"I believe you, Dear," she said, touching me cheek to cheek with a one-arm hug. "Be sure to lock the house up, when you leave."

"Oh, you don't want to drive around in the Sheriff's squad car. You go on and take your car. Do you mind if I borrow the old GMC? Just until my car's ready?"

"Of course." She thumped the painted wooden placque with one finger, where keys to everything she owned swayed and tinkled from the cold draft coming through the open doorway. "Help yourself. Timmy will need to go out. I'll let you do that. Keep him on a leash or he'll try to follow us and get lost."

"Your Mamma's right," the Sheriff warned as he stepped outside. "I wouldn't go messin' around them guys if I were you. Next time, they might not let you go so easy. You could get hurt. Hurt bad."

As he hustled Mamma off to the detached garage, I saw her glance back at me. And for one moment, there on the lawn, she hesitated and her eyes widened with fear.

CHAPTER EIGHT

I needed to rest, but I couldn't. Hyped up on coffee, my head swirled with images from last night's events, repeating over and over again like summer reruns. I decided to get on with the investigation and come back later when I thought I could sleep.

The old three-quarter-ton pick-up had been parked under a lean-to, off the side of the tool shed. The original blue paint had faded and rust had sealed the door shut. I kicked at the handle and along the bottom edge, breaking it loose. Finally it opened with a loud squawk.

I adjusted the seat as far up as it would go and brushed a layer of dust off the seat and the dashboard. It had been a long time since I'd driven this ancient heap.

Surprisingly, it started right up. It had to be a good 20 years old by now but just as dependable as ever. The huge engine roared to life, banging and popping out the back. I checked the gauges for gas and oil, thumping them with my finger for accuracy. Convinced it would hold together at least until I reached town, I backed the truck into the driveway, shifted into first, and eased it down to the road.

For the first couple of miles, it rattled and shook with a fearsome and irregular knock. But, it finally warmed up - chugging down the road at a whopping 45 mph.

The old barrel felt good under me and brought back fond memories. Daddy had bought it in Montana, right after his discharge from the Army. In a freak mid-June storm - the worst one in a decade - he drove it due West through Idaho and over Blewetts Pass in the Rocky Mountains, pulling our 17-foot travel trailer. It had climbed that icy slope as surely as a mountain goat, passing everything else on the road and retrieving an occasional stranded vehicle out of a road-side snowbank.

I switched the radio on and wasn't a bit surprised when it was still tuned to a country western station. I even rocked my shoulders a little and sang along when Hank Williams belted out, "Your cheatin' heart....will tell on you. You'll cry and cry..."

The song also reminded me of Daddy - an earlier and younger version. Those few years before I was old enough to know the difference between what was and what should be - before Viet Nam had sickened his mind and made him impossible to live with for Mamma and my sisters. But not for me. Him and I had been involved in our own little personal war, long before the Hanoi Hilton and the Ho Chi Minh Trail.

I clicked the radio back off and stared at the road ahead. My hands had curled around the thick steering wheel so tightly that the muscles in my arms were beginning to ache and my head and the bruised side of my face throbbed with pain. I wished I'd brought Mamma's Tylenol with me.

The truck lumbered into the parking lot of the Poulsbo Police Station. I parked it around back, suddenly self-conscious of the antiquated old tank, and found a rear entrance.

The Sergeant on duty had propped his heels on a scarred wooden desk and had dived, nose-deep into a true-crime magazine. I waited for the count of five at the counter. A quick count of five. He didn't budge or look up. Feeling my anger mount at his rudeness, I reached over and plunked the button on an office bell.

"Yes, Ma'am," he growled, letting his boots fall to the floor. "Can I help you?"

"I need to make out a report. Assault and battery."

Normally, I would have been much more patient and have been known to be charming if the occasion called for it. But, I was extremely tired, must have looked like a witch on a fresh-meat hunt, and everything I had, hurt. I could see him mentally pull on a mask of polite deference, nod, and rise to his feet. In the three steps to the counter, he managed to touch the pistol on his hip to make sure it was still mounted, adjust himself in his trousers to make sure everything else was still mounted, rake me up and down with an I-know-a-fugitive-when-I-see-one look, and thoroughly piss me off. He flicked the spring latch that opened the waist-high door at the end of the counter and said, "Take a seat Ma'am, here at the desk."

I didn't tell him I'd already spoken to the Sheriff at my Mom's house. I did give him the same information I'd given Belltower, once more leaving out the part about Cerese and my suspicions of her being Camille's twin. I left the best part until last - the fact that I worked at the Seattle Gazette. "I need to find out who owns that old Buick," I said. "I don't have the license number."

"If it was purchased in this county, you can check over at the court-house on Monday. Otherwise, I can't help you."

"I have no idea where he purchased it. He's got Canadian plates."

"Then you might as well give up."

"How about checking to see if there are any tickets or warrants out on someone who answers to his description?"

"Don't have enough information to do that. An old Buick and a fat man by the name of Frank, just ain't going to work on a computer. And even if it did, I couldn't give that information out to a civilian."

"Why not? How many warrants can you have?"

"Can't tell you that, either. Go on home, Lady. The department will call you, when they get something."

By then, I was steaming mad. I decided to leave before I landed myself in the pokey. On the way out, I passed a pay phone in the hall. *I'd better check on Camille.* I rummaged through my purse, looking for a quarter. While I dialed, a business card fell from a side pocket onto the floor. As I bent to pick it up, Camille answered, "Hello?"

"Hi. It's me - Kathleen. I wanted to see if anything else has happened since I left last night."

"After you left? Uh, no, not that I can think of."

She probably wondered where I'd gone, but I didn't want to frighten her even more. "Have you heard anything from your Dad?"

"Daddy? Huh uh. Have you?"

"Nothing yet. Uh, one more thing. There was a guy there at the Pow Wow, who drives an old blue Buick. He's staying at a cabin in Suquamish and hangs out at the Blue Goose Tavern." I knew as soon as I asked, there was no way a young girl could answer such a question. "You don't know who it would be, would you?"

"A Buick? The Blue Goose Tavern? No....I don't think so."

"All right. Just checking. You're sure, you haven't heard anything about your father, from anyone, since he left or seen his abductors?"

"Oh. Yes, I saw that one guy from Canada at the Pow Wow. I don't know what kind of car he drives or what tavern he goes to, but he was with the white guy that night when they came to the house. The night before Daddy left. I thought you knew."

"Hold it," I said, my heart quickening at the thought I may be getting somewhere. "Let's back up a minute. You said, the guy who helped abduct your father was at the Pow Wow. And you thought that I already knew about it. Why? I mean...what would make you think that I knew this guy? Did you hear or see something?"

"Well, yeah. Some of the people saw him when he left. They said you jumped up off the bench and followed him out." Her voice was beginning to quiver. "We figured he'd be in jail by now. Didn't you know it was him?"

"I do now. Look. I want you to sit tight, and don't let anybody in till I get there."

"You mean, nobody can come in? Not even my friends?"

"NO. Unless, lets say, you've known and trusted them for at least...a couple of years. I'll be out there by tonight. OK? If you have any more trouble, call the Sheriff." I thought about that statement for a minute, then said, "If that doesn't work, is there someone, there on the reservation, you'd normally go to in this sort of circumstance?"

"Uh, yeah. I'd probably call Mr. Hampton. He's that attorney you met last night. Or I'd call one of the elders."

"Sounds great. I doubt that you're in any really serious danger, but do call them if you need help. Don't make any waves, and I'll see you later."

"Ok," she said, seeming to sound relieved. "I'll be here."

I got back in the truck, crossed my arms over the steering wheel, and dropped my head down for a moment of rest. I was exhausted, frustrated by a Saturday morning bureaucracy, tormented by numerous aches and pains, and cranky as hell.

I needed a nap.

I nosed the truck into the sparse traffic and turned right toward the family home. At the top of the hill, a glint of silvery sunlight caught my eye. It wasn't much - with this headache, I didn't need much - just a flash of gray metal between two buildings. I'd seen it before - that unmistakable curve of a Lincoln limousine's back fender. Just a few hours ago, in fact. It belonged to the most incredibly handsome, hopefully single, and probably filthy-rich hunk I'd ever shared a back seat with.

Just to be sure, I dug the business card I'd retrieved from the police station floor, out of my pocket. Yep. *This is it.* A quick cup of coffee wouldn't hurt. After all, he *had* invited me to stop in.

I parked the truck in a vacant lot across the street and checked my make-up and hair in the rear view mirror. Not too bad. I had showered before I left, camouflaged the bruises with make-up, and wrestled into some jeans and a sweat shirt left over from my high school years. Shabby and worn at the knees, but they were clean and seemed to match my mood of the day.

His condo was in a converted church building, painted white wooden planks complete with steeple on top - the type usually reserved for Christmas cards. I walked across the street and up into the glassed-in porch which served as an entry way. From that vantage point, I could see into the parking garage and the whole back-half of the limo. Beating back a wash of indecision and a panic attack, I saw a red call button on the wall and pushed it.

That same low baritone was recognizable, even over the squawk of the intercom. "Yes?"

"Hi," I said into the little square box. "It's me, uh, Kathleen. Remember? Your friendly hitch-hiker...from last night?"

"Of course I remember. Come on up." Another buzz signaled the yawning doors of an elevator. It soon closed with a whisper and surged up to the second floor.

I don't know what I expected inside. Hadn't really thought about it. A couple of bedrooms maybe, a well-stocked kitchen, jacuzzi tubes sprouting from the tub... What I got was an expansive living room, all done in shades of creamy-white and teal blue, accented by a touch of scarlet. An Austrian crystal chandelier glittered with a kaleidoscope effect, bouncing light and colors from the window to the surrounding walls. I could hear their musical tinkle from the draft down the hall.

"I hope I haven't come at a bad time," I said, my senses heightened, ready to detect the presence of another woman and the suggestion that I shouldn't be there.

"No," he said, smiling. "Come in. You're just in time for coffee and a late breakfast."

He was even taller than I'd thought he'd be, looking like a male-model in his jade-green silk shirt with matching sweater vest over a pair of perfectly pressed and tailored oyster-colored slacks.

"Look," I said, trying not to sound defensive. "I realize my face looks like it kissed the front bumper of a semi on a down-hill run. But I hoped I could ask you a few questions."

Instead of responding, I noticed he was reading, amusedly, the cartoon and tacky verse on the front of my sweat shirt.

"It's something I drug out of the upstairs closet," I stammered, knowing my face would flush and hating it. "Why is it, I always seem to look like a motherless waif around you? I really do have clothes. I just don't have any with me."

David laughed then. Not a deep, rolling guffaw, his laugh was a little stilted, as if he had almost forgotten how. But he laughed and said, "That's the easy part. Come this way." He then led me to a small bedroom. And before I could mouth the words, *no thank you, I really couldn't*, he gestured open-handedly to a closet stuffed with women's clothes and said, "There's more here than will ever be used. Help yourself to anything you want while I make some phone calls."

I sorted through the array of slacks, dresses, suits and shirts. No middle of the line for this guy. These were top dollar, best-of-the-line clothes. The come-down from the stress, combined with my lack of sleep, had me disoriented and unhinged. I *was* tempted. But, I hadn't come here as a charity case.

The two top drawers held an array of lipsticks, creams and powders - all in the same brand. Four kinds of perfumes, including the gold tasseled atomizers, adorned a gilded tray. Whoever this guy is, he was sure used to having company. Female company. I did use some French *Guerlain*, squeezing it on all my warmest places, which included behind my ear. I then adjusted my old sweat shirt over my jeans, cocked my head at a virtuous angle, and glided out to the kitchen.

The table was set with a cloth I could have sworn was real Irish linen and a charming bone china, hand-painted in apple blossoms. He seemed to be quite adept with a stove and a spatula. "There you are," he said, flipping an omelet onto a platter. A basket of croissants and marmalade set next to a tray of fresh melon slices. "I hope you're hungry."

"A little." I didn't mention I'd just had a big meal. He held the chair ready, without commenting on the fact that I hadn't changed. So that he wouldn't think I was either rude or just plain stupid, I said, "There's a lot of nice clothes in there. Looks like a dress factory."

"As a matter of fact, I do own a small ladies-wear chain. They're made in Taiwan," he said, flashing a warm, bronzy-eyed look.

I was admiring a vase of fresh-cut, white Mums mixed with some blue Dutch Iris, when I noticed his eyes. They had changed. Lost in his own thoughts, the hazel had been brought out by the greenery of the flowers. Curiosity perked, I wondered if he'd made his phone call.

My second breakfast of the day was delicious even though I couldn't eat very much of it. As we dawdled over coffee, David pushed his saucer aside and said, "If you're not too tired, we could go for a ride on my boat. Would you like that? There's a great little beach I can show you. It's secluded, quiet, and not that far."

I debated - there was that little matter of a story to get out, a nasty man with a kid in a cabin, Camille... But a few more hours with some well thought-out questions, could be time well spent. "Yes," I said. "Yes. I'd like that."

CHAPTER NINE

There was just enough wind to fill the sails. Under David's expert hands, the boat sliced through the water, the sound of it magnified by the absence of a motor. Waves sloshed up the sides, hitting us full face with their spray. I pulled ropes when told to, dodged the beam when it swung, and felt the pinch of the cold mist on my cheek.

With quick, confident moves, David set the boat in a tight, left hand turn while I scrambled to hang on. His seahawk stare raked every inch of moving water around us. Nothing went unnoticed - a floating log, an oncoming cruiser, a clanging buoy that warned of a dangerous sandbar.

The wind changed direction. He immediately pulled a rope, wound a winch, and another sail popped up on the prow - narrower and easier to steer.

I mentally drew a line on a map, from where we'd left to where we were going. "Isn't that where I..."

He grinned in appreciation. "Sure is." Hands busy with the sail, he pointed with his chin. "There's Suquamish. And that bunch of houses is Lemolo. I picked you up about a half-mile out of town."

The island lay just off the coast of Kitsap Peninsula. About 30 acres in all, it was heavily wooded and surrounded by a rocky beach. Circling around to the southeast side, David and I lowered the sails and drifted into a natural little harbor where we anchored.

Once we were ready to go ashore, David and I boarded a little plastic rowboat that had been bobbing along behind us on a rope. Perched in the front, I curled my fingers around the side railing and checked out the scenery while David rowed us to shore.

A worry, too fleeting to grasp, nagged at the edge of my mind. Like a news bulletin, it flashed once - too fast to read - and then was gone. *Oh, well. I'll think better later on, when I'm not so hyped.*

The rowboat scraped bottom and David jumped the last few feet. Balancing on the seat for less than a moment, I hopped onto a raised, slightly rounded rock.

A high, solid rock bank rose up from the rocky beach. It appeared impenetrable. It wasn't until I had walked a few feet, my shoes crunching in the loose gravel, that I saw the wedge-like opening in the rock wall. A trail had been gouged, between some huge boulders.

David tied the boat to a large piece of driftwood. He turned and asked, "Are you ready?" His eyes followed the trail to the top. "It's a bit of a climb. But not too far."

"I guess so," I said. "What an incredible place!"

Stepping up ahead of me, he reached back to grab my hand and pull me over the high spots. "I haven't put the stairs in yet. Don't want my cabin to be too accessible."

Cabin? This was the first I'd heard about a cabin. We continued to climb.

David's *cabin* was a two-story affair in white-pine log with a sweeping upper-deck balcony and floor to ceiling windows. He opened the door with a series of keys and dead bolts, going quickly to a wall panel to switch off an electric alarm.

Real pine paneling lined the entry wall and what I could see of the living room. Rustic wooden light fixtures blended nicely with the hardwood floors and overstuffed furniture. The dining table and hutch was an excellent bird's eye maple, setting just off the well-organized kitchen.

"Are you cold?" he asked me. "Care for a hot toddy?"

"No thanks. Nothing for now." I ambled over to a large window, overlooking the bay. "It's a great view. You know, there's something about the sea - it's never the same. One minute it'll be calm. But let the air pressure change and wow - instant storm."

"Mmm hum," he murmured from behind. "Reminds me of a woman." Enclosing me in his arms, his chin rested easily on the top of my head. "Cold and distant at first," he said, cuddling the crevice of my shoulder, "...but once you get the feel of her..." His breath warm on my neck, he nibbled my ear lobe. "...she's likely as not," his hands braver now, and searching, "...to go frothy with a downpour of passion."

Ignoring my wobbly knees, I moved away from him in a way that was not meant to say *no*, but rather *not right now.* "I...can't stay gone too long," I said. "I've still got an awful lot of work to do if I'm going to finish by Monday morning."

"I know," He said, touching my sore cheek with his thumb, and stroking my facial hairs in an odd, but extremely affectionate manner. "This isn't a good time, and you're probably exhausted. I...." Just then, the cellular phone buzzed. "Excuse me," he said, and walked briskly to the kitchen.

While he was busy, I took myself on a tour. Starting in the dining room, I eyed some ornate chinaware displayed in the hutch. A closer look revealed hand-painted foxes adorning the lid to a soup tureen. On another piece, an elongated fox body formed the handle of a tea pot.

The metal pull of a drawer handle jiggled when I leaned against it. Inside - *I really shouldn't be such a snoop* - I found exquisite hand-crocheted tablecloths and napkins. The bottom drawer was full of....

Oh, Migod.

Quickly, I slid it soundlessly shut, realizing I'd been holding my breath. Fat bundles of hundred dollar bills had been secured by old rubber bands and stacked under a thin layer of place mats.

I was back at the window blowing dust off the blinds, when I heard David's voice behind me. "I'm terribly sorry," he said, lightly rubbing the small of my back. "Some men are doing some work for me about a half-a-mile from here, and they've had some trouble. A man's been hurt.

I'll need to leave you here for awhile. About forty-five minutes. I hope you don't mind."

"I really do have to get back."

"I know. But, I'll need to take them a stretcher and see that they get him on a boat to the mainland. Help yourself to a glass of wine, and I'll be right back. I promise - no more than an hour."

There wasn't much else I could do but agree. I nodded, in spite of an ever-sinking feeling in the pit of my stomach.

He kissed the top of my head. "You've got to be exhausted. Go on upstairs and have a nap," he said, then grabbed a jacket and hurried out the door.

He was right about my being tired. The cords in the back of my neck were in knots and my head was beginning a crazy, nodding spin. I found the wine and filled a large glass. Padding up the stairs in stocking feet, I finished it at the window - watching as he climbed into a jeep and charged off across the hill. The view from there included a sweeping panorama of that half of the island and a large part of the Olympic Peninsula. I could even see them pull the injured man from a muddy pond. I then closed the drapes and went to bed.

The creeping twilight lay hushed in that moment, halfway between deep, dreamy sleep and the cold, hard facts of day. Through an open window I heard the soft rustle of a wind rushing the evergreens.

I was in bed. David's bed. But David wasn't there.

I blinked at the clock and groaned. 6:30 p.m. I'd slept most of the day. Stumbling to my feet, I immediately went in search of the bathroom. I showered again, letting the warm, pelting water massage my sore face and taut back muscles.

Pulling my clothes back on, I went in search of a kitchen and a cup of coffee. David wasn't back yet, but he had a coffee-maker on the kitchen counter and, next to it, some fresh grounds in a glass jar.

Unbidden, that same nagging worry I'd had in the boat, skipped across the edges of my mind. I tried to pull it in, to look at it and make a sensible judgement, but it was more of a dread than a well-formed thought. I shrugged, thinking that it probably had to do with my concern about Camille and her possibly-twin sister.

I needed to get back. *Come on, David. Where are you?*

I was also starved. Making myself a pot of coffee, I pawed through the refrigerator for a snack. Most of the packages were vacuum-packed and labeled in a foreign language. *That's odd...* Nothing in English. Not even the ingredients. I found an already opened wedge of cheese and sniffed. Camembert. Now for something to put it on.

There was nothing in the cupboard I could eat without cooking it. Didn't he have any junk food? Potato chips, cheezies, a lousy cracker?

I peered into a pantry. Aha. Bagels, sealed in soft foil and stamped in simulated gold with the star of David. Hmmm. Popular name. Ripping the package open with my teeth, I inserted some cheese into the top bun and took a whopping bite.

Closing the pantry back up, I pushed gently on the accordion door, a light wooden affair of tilted slats. It stuck. I jiggled it and noticed how the bottom part canted out of the groove.

OH, great! He's gonna think I'm a real klutz.

I kicked at the edge, hoping to fit it back in the runners along the floor. Still wouldn't close. In the half-light, my aim was poor and my foot slipped. I hit the shelf behind it and felt something give. *What in the world....*

Had I kicked a hole in the wall? Bending low, I ran my hand underneath and on the back wall, looking for any splinters or broken pieces. My shoulder brushed against a higher shelf and the whole pantry moved. Groceries, everything.

I nudged it a little farther and a light, automatically, came on.

Cowabunga!

Heart thumping, I peered around the corner. No one there. Carefully and quiet as a mouse, I entered.

What's this? A hidden room? Give me a break!

Along one wall, a cabinet held an assortment of ham radios with microphones attached, CB's, transmitters and receivers, a P.C. computer, telephones and modems, and several built-in T.V. screens.

Why would he....

A thumping outside frightened me. A quick gasp and I backed out - all the way through the pantry. Taking a chance, I lifted the flimsy pantry door and plunked it down, into the groove. It closed then, quite easily.

I dashed to the kitchen sink, looking frantically for something to do with my shaking hands. David strode into the kitchen, heavy boots thudding on the tile floor.

"Hi," I said, flipping the faucets on, pretending to rinse my cup. "You must think I'm a real lazybones."

His eyes moved restlessly around the kitchen, *thank goodness I got the stupid thing to close,* and came to rest on me. "Not in the least," he replied, brushing my forehead and the tip of my nose with pursed lips. "I think you're a bright, beautiful woman who needed a rest." He reached into the cupboard for a cup and saucer. "Sorry I'm late. How about a picnic? Would you like that?" His face seemed boyish, as if he was having fun and it surprised him. As if he hadn't had any real fun in a long while and I was reminding him how. "You must be hungry."

What should I say? "I, uh, I've got to get back. I'm really worried about someone."

Pouring himself a cup of coffee, he switched off the coffee-maker and placed the glass carafe in the sink. "Use my cellular phone. Tell her you'll be a little late. Here. I'll get you an open line."

I called Camille, hiding my frustration as best I could. "Hey gal," I said. "Are you alright? Anything happen since I left?"

"I'm fine," she said. "I still haven't heard from Daddy."

Uneasiness stirred in my stomach and started backing up my throat. Hiding it as best I could with a nonchalance I couldn't feel, I said to her, "Hang in there, Kiddo. I'll see you in a few hours."

Lost in a moment of fingernail-chewing thought, David surprised me with his good cheer. "So. Shall we?" At my wide-eyed blink, he said, "A quick sandwich on the beach. The picnic. Want to try it? I carried some dry wood to a great spot while you were asleep. We'll leave from there and I'll take us back to Poulsbo." He paused, seemed to sense my discomfort. "Or, if you really prefer, we can forget dinner and leave now. Immediately."

"I do need to get back. But....as long as we're here...." I shrugged, staying as pleasant as I could. "Just for a little while, though, I'll have to do some of the interviews yet tonight and see if the Sheriff has made any progress on tracking down that ape who beat me up." At the mention of the Sheriff, my mind turned to Mamma. And that same, nagging worry nibbled another corner of my mind. But, as before, there was still no shape to it.

David flipped open the refrigerator side door and loaded some frozen rolls into a basket brought in from the back porch. "They should defrost by the time we're ready to eat." Adding some bratwurst and brown mustard, he seemed to be looking for something...*probably the Camembert cheese...* When he couldn't find it, he plucked a bottle of wine from a rack and carefully laid some ripe bananas on top. Hefting a brightly striped blanket, we headed along the path in the direction of the beach.

A horseshoe-shaped stretch of sand, sprinkled through with crushed sea shells, cradled the natural harbor where we'd beached that morning. The sailboat, anchored some ten or twelve yards out, rocked gently in the waves. It's sails down and folded, the mast pointed nakedly toward the heavens. Behind us, the peeled trunk of a Madrona tree jutted out from the bank. In the last hour of daylight, its wind-whipped branches cast a moving shadow like long, broken fingers fumbling over a circle of blackened rocks and charcoal. Someone's old campfire site.

"I come down here at night sometimes...to think," he said, tossing the old pieces of charred wood into the water and restacking the rocks. He threw some dry wood into the circle and laid the dry twigs on top. I rose to gather more firewood, mentally forming my questions and waiting for the right moment to ask them.

A toppled fir tree drooped onto the beach, its naked roots gnarled and dark against the sunset. I snapped off the ends of its dried branches and laid them in easy reach of our campsite. David ripped into the trunk with an axe, chips flying with every whack. We added dried leaves and bits of bark to the dry wood and started the bonfire. Soon, it crackled and snapped, licking around the branches and the larger chunks of bark.

I spread the blanket on the sand, close enough to feel the warmth of the fire and sat down. The lap of the waves and the crackle of the flames lent a cozy and intimate touch to our little camp. I hugged my knees and stared into the flames.

After we ate, talking and laughing for a few hours - we were both 'old-movie' buffs, David waved an arm and indicated the hillside and the house above. "What do you think of it?" he asked. "From up there, looking this way," he pointed northeast "...you can see Whidbey Island. Over there, on a clear day, I can catch the high points of the San Juans. At night, from the south, there's a glow from the lights in Seattle."

"It's beautiful."

"It'll be even better when I'm through with it." He plucked a stray twig off the pile and drew shapes in the sand, a square...no, it's a house. A hotel?

I gestured towards the drawing, "Is that a new project?"

He nodded. "It's going in on the other side of the island." He waved an arm. "Over there. On the other side of the hill."

"Looks pretty big."

"It is." He sketched some more. "It'll lay like this." He paused, shooting an intense glance in my direction. "Can you keep a secret?"

"Of course I can keep a secret." I held my breath, my heart lurching to the dark sky. *He's taking me into his confidence. Maybe I was wrong. This guy is a highly respected, well-known businessman. I can't condemn the guy for being good at what he does. Besides, I could learn to really care for this man.* Out loud, I said, "Why do you ask?"

"It's like this. On the first floor we'll have a big hall, that can be sectioned off later. Eventually, we'll have blackjack tables, roulette wheels, the whole bit. And a row of one-armed bandits at each door. A big dining room here, a smaller coffee shop on this end with an office off to the side, and three floors above that. A total of 144 suites. There's a helicopter pad over here," he drew another round spot next to the building, "...and a dock with a small marina."

Well, there it was. A casino. I swallowed, hoping my face didn't show the turmoil inside me. My hopes were dashed, my worries confirmed. He had to be the 'white guy' Camille mentioned. And possibly the last one to see her father before he disappeared. Now what?

Tossing his stick away, he moved over next to me on the blanket, obviously mistaking my silence as awed approval. "Kathleen, I know this is a little abrupt, that we really haven't known each other that long. But, I want you here with me. I've never felt so good, being around anyone in my entire life. We could be a tremendous help to each other. Come work for me, and all of this," he swept his hand to include the entire island, "...would be your home, too. The condo, the limo, everything. What do you say?" Pulling me closer, he kissed the top of my head and tried to get me to look at him.

I allowed his one-armed hug while I stared into fire. I was surprised by his offer and, I had to admit, quite impressed with his wealth and power. It was tempting. But - my thoughts were centered on the real world.

Just across a short span of water from here, was an old, crumbly and rotting house where a young girl sat alone, waiting for her father to come home. Her twin sister, neither of them aware of each other, sat five miles away in a cheap motel room. Guarded by a pig with moist, cruel hands. And no matter how much I would have liked to stay and pursue my new options, this handsome hunk sitting next to me obviously had something to do with all of that.

I turned to the man of my dreams and said, "I have to admit, it'd be awfully easy to fall for you. In fact, I think I already have. But...I've got a story to write. I'm going to have to get back. Would you mind taking me?"

CHAPTER TEN

For the first minute, David didn't move. Then slowly he sat upright. He seemed to hesitate for a moment, then threw his drawing stick at the fire and bolted to his feet. One of the glasses cracked as he threw it at the basket. "I never thought you'd turn on me," he said. From the light of the campfire, I could see a mottled wash flooding his face, setting off a disturbing green in his eyes.

I grabbed my jacket and stood up. "Who the heck is turning on you? David, please. Don't do this. I'll be back in a day or two. I just need to take care of a few things."

He snatched the blanket out from under me. I stumbled, then moved out of his reach. Sand and all, he wadded the blanket under one arm then straightened, glaring at me. "You're a damn fool. Can't you see what you're doing?"

A piercing disappointment ripped through me. I hadn't wanted it to be like this. There for awhile, I had thought we really had a chance... I'd almost convinced myself I'd been wrong. Saddened by the hurt of yet another letdown, I forced my concentration back to the needs of the moment. "David, for God's sakes, don't you think you're over-reacting? I need to get back. Please. Don't be this way."

Head back, as if to beseech the heavens for the return of my sanity, he shouted, "How can you do this? Haven't I been good to you?" He grabbed my arm - squeezing it hard enough to hurt. "You better think this through, Kathleen, what I offered and what you're giving up. Before you run off and do something stupid."

That was the second time he'd called me a name. 'Damn fool', and now, 'stupid'. Jerking my arm out of his grasp, anger welled up in me strong enough to set off a buzzing in my ears. I said, "It won't work, David. Now or ever." Taking a deep breath, I forced my fury down to a manageable level. He was still my only way out of here. "I'm ready to go home, now. Why don't we go on back and talk about this tomorrow? After we've both calmed down. Just...please try not to call me stupid."

He whirled on me, lip lifted in contempt. "Why not? Who else but a dumb broad would turn down this kind of money and prestige?"

Enough was enough. I faced him, head on, the fear consumed by my burning rage. "I was right, wasn't I? This is Indian land. And you knew all about that beast Frank. That's why you didn't even bother asking me what happened when you picked me up in the limo. You already knew. I'll bet he even works for you."

"You are turning on me!" Pacing three to four steps to my left and back again to my right, he said, "Didn't I tell him, as soon as I heard, to let you go? Katie, we've got a good thing here. Why do you have to ruin it?"

"This is reservation land, David. It belongs to the Indians. It's their home."

"It's mine. You dingbat, have never heard of a lease?"

Swallowing a sour lump in my throat, I took a chance and said, "Yeah, I've heard of a lease. I've also heard of some questionable tactics on getting them to sign it. Where's those kids' father, David? What did you do with Mr. Cloud?"

"Don't corner me, Kate. I'm telling you. Don't corner me!"

Panting, his eyes reddened with his fury, he grabbed up the basket, still unpacked, and stormed up the path. I scrambled to keep up, pulling my way along by grabbing the brush and small branches. I barely had time to grab my truck keys before he locked the cabin and dashed back down to the beach.

The ride back in the boat was mostly quiet, only the gusty whoosh of the wind and an occasional clang of a buoy to break the silence. Every now and then, David ducked into the cabin. I could hear the squawk and static of the short-wave radio, his monotone voice mumbling and indistinct.

Finanly, the marina. We docked and I made ready to climb out.

"Not so fast," he growled.

"David, I'm sorry...we both said some things that neither one of us meant."

His anger seemed to have settled into a certain resolve. He tied the boat to the dock with deft, deliberate movements. It was even more scary than the outburst.

I hurriedly said, "If you're worried about me ratting on you in the paper, don't. We don't print anything we can't prove. That part about you and Mr. Cloud...was just a guess. A bad guess. I...I'll need to check with missing persons, ask around with some of his friends. Probably showed up by now, anyway. Tell you what. I'll bet you anything that Cloud's home right now eating supper." I lifted both shoulders in a cheerful 'wouldn't that be something' shrug. "The whole thing's probably a big mistake. Went on a four-day toot and he's there now, half asleep. Hungover and one sorry dude."

David's gaze swept the deck, the other boats, and the sky - at everything and everyone but me.

With one foot on the outside ladder of the sailboat, feeling the easy dip from my weight, I mentally gauged the distance of a walk through town to the pick-up. As I brought my other foot over, David stepped up on the rail - preparing to jump off. The boat did a definite yaw to that side and gently bumped an old rubber tire tied to the edge of dock. As the space widened between dock and boat, David jumped out ahead of me and grasped my hand - helping me leap the last foot and a half of water. "While I'm here," I said, trying to keep my voice from shaking.

"I thought I'd do a piece on the Northwest Indians that still reside on the Olympic Peninsula. You know, remnants of the Chief Seattle tribe. That sort of thing."

"I'll take you in the car."

It was the first time he'd spoke to me since we left. He still had hold of my hand, grasping it like a captured bird. "OH, uhm..." *How do I reply to that?* "That's really nice of you."

We began to walk - the length of the dock rocking under our feet. A chill ran up my back - every instinct I possessed urging me to run. His guiding hand, gentlemanly except for the grip, led me up the steps. We passed through the gate and out onto the concrete parking lot.

David's grasp tightened. Since his fast walk covered twice the ground as mine, I was forced to trot along beside him.

We reached his car - the BMW we'd come down in. David opened the passenger door with his key and half-helped, half-shoved me inside. Striding around the front, he jabbed a finger in my direction as if I were a poorly-trained pup who'd been ordered to sit and to stay.

Again, we didn't talk.

He drove like he did everything else. Expertly, single-mindedly, and in full control. Reaching the reservation and the Cloud residence, he braked hard in the driveway, the car sliding sideways in the loose gravel.

Camille met us on the porch. "Oh, Kathleen," she said. "I'm glad you're here. Are you alright?" The whites of her eyes showed around her round, black eyes as she watched David approach. She recognized him.

I clambered out of the car, amazed that only one day had passed since I'd last been here. "Yes. I'm OK, Camille. We've got a lot to catch up on." David's hand was gentler now, a firm nudge in the middle of my back to keep going - to get in the house.

To David, Camille said, "There's someone to see you. Said he was supposed to meet you here." With a questioning blink in my direction, she turned back to David and stepped aside from the doorway to let him and I inside.

Frank sat at the kitchen table, enjoying an applesauce dessert and a cup of Camille's coffee. An insolent grin for me, a respectful nod for David, and he said, "Looks like you got in some playtime, Boss. Nice tender little thing. She give you any lip?"

How could he have....*the radio on board the boat.* Swept by a wave of guilt, I stumbled on a kitchen tile. *I should have handled it better. Now I've endangered Camille's life, too.*

Quickly, I wiped at a tear - damned if he'd see me cry.

David marched me to the living room, leered over me while I sat on the couch. He smoothed his slick blond hair and looked at me without seeing, deep in thought.

Frank shoved aside his dirtied dishes and stood up. Sucking in his flabby belly, he asked, "What'll we do with 'em, Boss?" He tucked in his shirt and hiked up his trousers. "That newspaper dame already knows more than she ought to."

His suave veneer of gentility gone, David grimaced and pivoted on one heel. "Shut up," he snapped at Frank. "Just shut up." Back in control and all business, David peered out a few windows and snooped inside a closet, rifling through some linens.

Camille fluttered over to the couch and plopped down next to me, shivering as if she were cold.

David turned his full attention on her. "You got a basement to this place?"

She answered, "Sort of..." and glanced at me, trembling. "It's a root cellar, really. Not big enough for...."

David stomped to the kitchen. He kicked the throw rug aside and grunted when he spied the inlaid shape of a trap door built flush to the floor of the kitchen. He grasped a metal ring imbedded into the wood and pulled. The wooden door squealed on its rusty hinge as it flopped over to the side.

He stepped partway into the dank, musty darkness. "Do you have any lights down here?"

Camille shook her head. "No. There's a flashlight, though. In that cupboard." She ran to fetch it and handed it to David. "You can see, there's hardly any room...just some old bins. Daddy stores apples down there and sometimes he buys potatoes in fifty pound bags...and it's cold. And damp. Real damp." She stopped chattering to stare at David as he came back up, dusting the bottoms of his pants legs. When he didnt' return her frightened gape, she turned to me - shaking with a visible, growing dread.

I had no idea what to tell her. "I don't think....," I mumbled, wishing I could comfort her with something more than a half-hearted doubt. "He's not going to..."

Frank had been watching the scene, digging at his teeth with a toothpick. Ignoring him, I reached for Camille and hugged her as she cried softly on my silk blouse. "David," I said, daring him not to answer me. "She's just a child. For Christ's sake, leave her out of this."

He swiveled towards me, jaw muscles bunched from his look of sour distaste. "She's already in it."

Frank hovered within arms reach, waiting. David gestured to him with his thumb, "Put them down there for now, and lock it. Then wait here till you hear from me. You got your beeper on?"

Frank slapped the black box on his hip and checked to see if the red light was blinking. He nodded. "Got it. I'll take care of everything, Boss. You go on ahead."

Then David, the former Prince Valiant and Saver Of Damsels In Distress, turned on his heel and walked out.

CHAPTER ELEVEN

Camille was right. It was cold and damp and very dark. A decaying, moldy-apple stench surrounded us. On the way down the hole, I'd snatched the flashlight from the floor where he'd dropped it. I flashed it now on the rotting timbers, shrinking at a large spider.

Camille asked, "How long are they going to keep us here?"

"I don't know, Hon. Sorry I got you into this mess."

"That's all right, Miss Shaunessey."

"O'Shaunessey. Just...call me Kathleen."

"Oh, uh, Kathleen. You know, Kathleen, it's probably the other way around. It was me calling you that got us..." Her voice breaking, she tried bravely not to cry. "I didn't think this...I didn't know this was going to happen."

Her despair was heart-breaking. I could feel myself coming out of my own self-pity, responding to the need of the moment. "Of course you didn't." I said, and began to search the dark walls with my bare hands. "Don't worry about it." A tiny bit of light seeped through the trapdoor over our heads, just enough to see the outline of her head.

She paused, watching the flick of light. "What're you looking for?"

"For a way out of here." Thrusting upwards with both hands, I lunged against the trapdoor. It didn't budge. "There isn't any way out, Miss...uh, Kathleen. Just that trap door thing, and they've bolted it."

"Evidently." Shining the light on her face, I was glad to see she'd regained some of her composure. "Well," I said, propped on the lowest bin across from her. "At least we've got time to talk. I've got a lot to tell you if you're ready to hear it."

"I'm ready." She paused. "Is it bad news? Have you seen my father?"

"No, it's not bad news and I haven't seen your father. But I can tell you about another relative." I drew a deep breath, thinking, *I better be right,* and settled into the bin. "You may be surprised to find out, but it appears you've got a sister, Camille."

"You're kidding."

"No joke, kiddo. She's your twin sister and looks just like you. Can hardly tell the two of you apart."

Camille gasped. Even without the aid of my light, I knew she'd blanched and slapped her hand over her mouth. "How do you know? Did you see her, yourself?"

"Yes, I did. Friday, at the Edmonds Ferry, then again in Suquamish." I sensed her move through a full range of emotion, going from shock to anger. "Why didn't Daddy tell me?" Then disbelief. "No. That can't be right. Maybe you just thought some other girl was my sister, because she's Indian. Maybe we all look alike, huh?"

She doesn't believe that. Not really. I waited, quietly.

"Wouldn't that be something if I did have a sister? Wow. A twin sister. What'd she look like? I mean, yea, she probably looked like me, huh? What was she like, though? Did she say something to you?"

When she stopped and seemed to expect an answer, I said, "She didn't say much to me. She actually spoke mostly to her mother."

That set her off again. "Mother? How could she have a mother? My mother died, Kathleen, when I was born. And if she's my twin, that would be her mother too, wouldn't it?" She paused, taking a moment to process all of what I'd told her. Then, animatedly, her voice high-pitched and cracking, "Wait a minute. Wait just a minute. Maybe Mamma didn't die. Maybe after she had us, she wanted to leave Daddy - he told me himself that he used to drink a lot. Sort of carouse around with the guys." From the sound of her babbling, I could tell she had jumped up. A quick flick of the flashlight showed her hovering over me in the cramped space. "Maybe she left him, and...and since it wouldn't be fair to take both of his children away, she just took one. Whichever one was handiest at the time. You know how it is. You have to do, what you have to do kind of thing...."

This train of thought was taking us nowhere. "Camille," I said, finding her arm in the dark and pulled her back down on the seat. "When I said, 'mother', I meant stepmother or foster mother. Adoptive mother. Whatever. But I don't think the older woman's truly related to you or to Cerese."

"Oh. Well, at least there's her. Did you say, Cerese? Is that her name?"

"That's what they called her."

"Wow. Cerese. Don't ya see? Cerese and Camille." Another stretch of silence.

I thought she must be pondering her new status. She was a twin. Her originating ovarian egg had been split and duplicated. A living, breathing double lived - not far from here - unaware that she too, had a sister. Camille's breathing changed, a few big inhales, exhaling with heavy sighs. Then calmer, open-mouthed puffs.

Finally, in an oddly objective tone, she spoke. "You're right. I do have a twin. And...that is her name."

Well, now. Thank you for sharing that. Out loud, I remarked, keeping it casual, "All right, Camille. What just happened? Why are you so sure now?"

"My guides just told me. They say to trust you...that you're basically honest."

OH, boy. Here we go. "Your guides? Sorry, honey. There's no one here but us chickens."

"Oh, yes. Yes, there is. There's a presence here, now. Don't you feel it? He says that.." Camille then chuckled.

Right. Here we are, buried alive, a sack of moldy apples and three potatoes away from the Happy Hunting grounds and she thinks it's funny. Poor kid. It's been too much. She's....confused.

"My guide says that you make unwise, impulsive decisions at times and you can be quite judgmental. But you mean well...and you have our best interests in mind. He says that we should work together...and that he likes your smile."

How am I supposed to react? How would anybody react to that? My skin prickled along my shoulders, the back of my neck, and down my arms. *Judgmental? Who, me?*

Sounding more normal, she asked, "So. Where do we go from here?"

"Go? We're not going anywhere till somebody pries the lid off this tomb. But, since this is our first chance to really talk, tell me about your father. What did he think about this development project? Did he say anything to you? Could he be off, maybe, on a toot?"

"Daddy? Well, he used to drink. A lot. But he quit, Kathleen. A long time ago. A couple of the other guys had a problem, and they quit, too. For awhile. But, they didn't stick with the program. Quit going to the meetings. And after a little bit of that, you know what happens. Right back to the bottle. Daddy didn't though. After that one time, he never did drink again."

"That's great, Camille. Now tell me what he said about this situation. This...land development scheme. Did he..."

"Oh, yea. Daddy hated it. He was on the Council and always voted it down. Said they'd bring in sub-contractors for most of the building, and any new jobs it might create would be just the stuff no one else wanted to do. Besides, he was afraid the younger people would get the wrong idea about drinking and gambling."

"And there's this other thing. See, our family's one of the oldest families in the tribe. Daddy said he remembers his grandfather talking about a legend. There on that same island. Kathleen, that island is a place of fasting and visions. Long ago, a chief of our tribe and his young bride died of some awful disease - I think maybe it was smallpox - and they were buried there. She was pregnant with their first child. And well, to tell you the truth, they blamed the white man for it. They didn't have this disease before then. And if that grave is disturbed, especially by a white man, Daddy says these ancestral spirits will come back and wage war on them."

"What do you mean by that? Spirits can't go to war. Can they?"

"Well, they can cause all sorts of problems for them. Accidents and stuff. Make them see things that aren't there. Sort of drive them crazy."

I didn't comment or interrupt, but at her mention of accidents, the scene of David fishing the man out of the muddy pond flashed in my mind. A chilling kind of dread skipped up my spine and I shivered.

Camille was still talking. "But, what Daddy was mostly worried about was that if they build this casino on that island, our whole land, along with the last of our Indian heritage, would suffer terribly."

"I take it, his was the only dissenting voice on the Council?"

"A few others held out for awhile, but...they gave in. The money. They all want the money. Think they're going to get rich."

"And you? You don't care about the money?"

"Oh, I guess it'd be nice. But Daddy said there wouldn't be that much - not like they claimed there would be. Daddy told the Council at the last meeting that even if there was a lot of money made, these guys running the casino would be in control of the funds. We Indians would never see much of it. And after locking us up in the cellar like this, I tend to think he's right."

"Could be."

Her voice wavered. "Kathleen, are we ever going to find Daddy? I miss him so much."

"Hang in there, kid. We'll make it."

"I'm scared. He's never been gone this long before."

I reached for her shoulders, hugging her with one arm while she cried. "Sssh, now. It's OK. We'll find him as soon as we can. Soon as they lift the lid and let us out. They can't keep us here and they know it."

When she'd subdued to an occasional sniff and a hiccup, I leaned back, my head resting on the smelly boards behind me.

"There's something more," she said, "I haven't told you. I wasn't sure you'd understand."

I waited.

"...about two weeks ago, I had a vision. It was right after Daddy went to one of those council meetings. I saw these guys, white guys I think. One was really short. All I could see was their backs. They were bent over my Dad, beating him with clubs." More crying. "And they threw him in the water. It scared me so much I woke Daddy in the middle of the night, and told him."

"OK, try to be calm, now. Tell me what happened. What was your Dad's response to you?"

"He laughed at me. He'd never known me to have visions before. Thought I was making it all up. Trying to prove myself to be a shaman in the eyes of the tribe. You know, like a medicine man. My grandmother had prophetic powers. They started just about the age I am now."

I didn't interrupt. It was her story, her heritage.

Wouldn't want to be judgmental.

Camille inhaled jaggedly. She'd stopped crying. "Then one day, he'd been out on his boat all day, fishing. And when he came back, he went to the other members, rounding them up, all mad about something. He called an emergency council meeting down at the lodge. They talked for a long time and he didn't get home until after supper. He was moody - didn't want to talk, wouldn't hardly eat. That was the last time I saw him. The next day while I was in school, that was last Thursday, they came right in our house. They left muddy tracks all through the kitchen and cigarette smoke. They must have grabbed him then, I could see where they'd been wrestling and knocking stuff over. The day after that is when I called you."

I leaned back and gave a loose-lipped blow. She'd given me a lot to think about.

Overhead, footsteps thumped. There was a creak, and dust swirled in the vacuum as the trap door opened. A shaft of sunlight beamed through. I blinked, felt it warm on my face, and rubbed the sting from my eyes. When I could squint enough to see, I looked up through the hole.

Frank's face and neck covered most of it. "You can come up for awhile. Just don't try something stupid." There he goes again with the name calling. This time, I'd have to consider the source. Another set of shoes thudded close by. More measured, more self-controlled.

David.

Camille crowded in behind me as we climbed up the stairs, her head about hip-high to me. I wanted to bolt - but I didn't. I made sure Camille didn't either, by keeping her well behind me. We'd never get away and trying to run would only make things worse.

David lounged near the outside door, his greenish-brown eyes less like reflections on the edge of a clear lake and more like the mud at the bottom. That well-shaped jaw and neck was bunched now with corded muscles. I shivered when he said, "It's time we talked."

"Yes," I replied, hoping I sounded half as controlled as he did. "I guess it is."

CHAPTER TWELVE

We moved slowly to the living room, Camille shadowing my every step. We sat on the couch, as Frank positioned himself in the doorway between us and the kitchen. His paunch belly a-quiver, he still wore the same ugly shirt, the same obscene expression and the smell of stale sweat still lingered around him like smog.

His little pig-eyes flickered over the length of my thigh, up and then down again. I was preparing to say something about it and damn the consequences when David cleared his throat, ready to speak.

"Listen up," he said in clipped, purposeful tones. "I want that land and the right to build any damn thing I want on a ninety-nine year lease. The arrangements were almost completed. Then this kid," he aimed a first finger at Camille, thumb up as if to cock it, "combined with the disappearance of her father got the whole damn tribe spooked."

I felt her lean close and wedge in behind me, as if she were afraid his leveled finger would shoot. David frowned distastefully, and said, "They won't budge until they think their spirits and ancestors are going to be appeased." I watched as his lips, the same ones I had thought so well-bred, grimace to a pale slash. "So," he continued. "I'm giving you one last chance. You'll not only save your own hide, you'll also keep your informed pal here," he jerked a thumb at me, "from having a most unpleasant accident."

I wanted to slap that coolly handsome face, to strip that unruffled poise from him like last year's wallpaper and bare his black soul until he hurt at least a fraction as much as I did. I wanted to cry and make him tell me that it wasn't true - that none of this was real. That he was not the gangster he seemed to be. That this was all a horrid nightmare and I would soon wake up, still in the cabin, warm and snugly in his satin-sheeted bed, and find my woes and fears a quickly fading fabrication.

David did not oblige. He studied Camille a minute longer, sweeping the curve of her dusky-soft cheek, watching the frightened quiver of her bottom lip, and said, "Do as I ask, and you'll get your father back the same day."

In a thin wail, she started to ask, "What do I...," cleared her throat and started again. "What do I have to do?"

"Have a seance with all the council members present. Only this time, you convince them the Gods have given their blessings and they all think it's a great idea. You'll have to be convincing - it's all up to you."

She looked at me. Hoping, I supposed, to hear me say she wouldn't have to. While I in my stupidity, mouth agape, ready to shoot his insults full of holes, ready to blast him with rhetoric powerful enough to down a B22, I, Kathleen O'Shaunessey, ran out of ammunition. It was all just too absurd. I couldn't think of a thing to say.

She bravely attempted to war with him alone. "I can't do that. It just...isn't like that. You see, I don't have any control over it, over what they say. Or even whether anything happens. I'm just a kind of a vessel. Like a water pipe that they come through. They come when they're ready, and say what they want said."

"Then fake it. I'll see that you get a little purse for your trouble."

"What? You want me to fake it? For money? I'm sorry - my gifts are not for sale. I would never do that. Never."

I was still flapping my gums like a netted goldfish. I had to think - to help this kid out. "What're our other options," I squeaked.

"There aren't any. Either do it like I said, or..." he made a slicing motion across his throat.

My brain cells began to click. "Can I talk to her?" With a wag of my head, I indicated Frank. "Alone?"

David stood up and strode towards the kitchen, a sad resignation dogging his face and shoulders. As he passed by Frank, he muttered. "Throw 'em back in the hole."

Fat, moist hands curled around my arm. I struggled. "Can't you wait a minute?" He grinned with a cruel kind of glee.

Again, I tried to wrest my arm free to slap him. It wouldn't reach. "Let go of me, you ape." He twisted my arm to the back and up. I gasped from the pain.

I screamed - from anger and from frustration. "David. Don't do this." At the doorway, he paused - wavering, debating, then ducked his head and went out. I sobbed as I saw him go, pleading, "He's hurting me...David!"

Head yanked back by my hair, I couldn't see the steps. I fell, crying now, "David!" My left calf burned - skinned on the slimy-slick steps.

Terrorized, Camille tripped in behind me and crawled into the bottom bin. The top banged shut over our heads, the bolt slammed home. Four, hard, thudding steps...then nothing.

They were gone.

In the dead silence of the dark, I could hear a muffled, wheezy sob. "Camille? Are you all right?"

"Daddy's dead, isn't he." It was a statement. She didn't ask me to deny it. "They've killed him just like they're going to kill us." I reached for her - found her backed into a corner, trembling with terror. She lurched out of reach when I tried to touch her.

I would have preferred to lick the wounds of my own despair. To be allowed to grieve for that spark that had glowed so very briefly, then gone out. But my heartache would have to wait. There wasn't time. "Hey," I said. "It's all right, kid. Everything's going to be all right." Nudging her to sit up, I found her hands in the dark and held them.

"We're not dead, yet. Just locked up for awhile." Breathing deeply, I fought back my own panic. *I've got to think. Plan.* "Camille, Honey. Talk to me. We'll take what you know and what I think and see what we come up with."

"What do you want me to say? I already told you what I know."

"I want you to tell me everything that happened up to your call at the Gazette."

"I already did."

"Only from the time your Dad started to fight these guys. I want to know about the first contact, the first time this whole idea was ever mentioned."

"Well, let's see." I heard a little grunt, a sigh, and the sound of fabric sliding on wood. When she spoke again, the wail was gone. "I guess the first real contact we had was that day the meeting in the hall had just broken up. Daddy was all excited. It meant jobs, Kathleen, and money. More money than the people around here have had in a long time. And medical insurance. Our social services are gone, Kate. Whittled down to nothing." She took a deep breath. "They said some guy wanted a 99 year lease on a piece of one of the islands. This...David wanted a house built and some of the guys would get to work on it. A few months after it was finished, he came back and wanted the rest of the island. He sort of hedged around, never did say exactly what he wanted to build. Just something about a place for people to stay, 'to share the peace and beauty with others,' he said. And went on and on about how they can learn from us - our wise old elders, and he made a big deal about us being the first Americans." She sniffed and seemed to shiver. "Kathleen, the people here are just like any other men. Flatter them, offer them money, booze, and they're going to think you're the greatest ever. Then this David what's-his-name..."

"Abrahamson."

"This David Abrahamson brought over a contract. Daddy didn't like it. Said it was too vague. Said it gave the man Carte Blanche to the reservation. I think Daddy was more offended than anything else. That they might think that just because we're Indians, and maybe not educated like the others, that we're morons or something. And you know Daddy. No, I guess you didn't know..." In the dim afternoon light, filtered down through the cracks in the trap door, I could see her owl-eyed blink. She gasped, and stammered, "Oh, I didn't mean to say 'didn't.' I mean DON'T. You DON'T know Daddy. Present tense." She paused, swallowed down a sob. "Kathleen. I'm so worried about him. What're we gonna do?" More muffled sobs and loud sniffles.

"Shhh, now. We'll think of something. It's not over yet by a long shot. Shhht. Listen!" A familiar clump of shoes, the creak of a rusty hinge, and light. Bright, wonderful, life-giving light, streaming in from the open trap door, above.

Towering over the hole like a backwoods Buddha, Frank indicated with a waggle of fingers and a rude jerk of chin, that we should climb up. As we gingerly stepped out onto the kitchen floor, Frank loomed just out of arms reach and said, "The boss is on his way."

This time I was ready.

The three of us faced off in the kitchen as we waited. I spied my pocketbook next to the sink - an old one I'd borrowed from Mamma to carry a few necessities in. It had been rifled, its contents sprawled across the counter. Flashing a dirty look at Frank, I gathered up my brush and lipstick and rinsed my face from the cold water faucet.

I sensed him in the doorway even before I turned. Bending his 6'4" frame to squeeze through the 5'8" door, David strolled in. With an 'after you, ladies' gesture, he motioned that we might return to our seats on the couch. Clearing his throat and crossing one perfectly-creased pant leg over the other, David said, "May I assume you've discussed this matter and come to the conclusion that if you cooperate, we can all go home and leave this young girl in peace?"

I patted Camille's trembling hand and felt her slide closer. I then sat up, board straight, and answered, "Yes and no. First of all, I've got some questions."

David dropped his lids to half-mast. "I didn't come here to be interrogated."

"Well, hang on to your jock-strap, Asshole, because you obviously need us in your sick little game and we're not going to play until we know the rules, whereabouts, and the condition of the other contestants. Namely, Camille's father and her twin sister Cerese." Watching him for reaction, I noticed his high, refined cheekbones, his long expanse of thin, translucent skin, and remembered wanting to love him.

His piercing stare, this time, was directed at Frank, who was saying, "Might as well tell em, Boss. Cerese, the little bitch, has run off. An' I can't find her anywheres."

"Shut up, you dimwit."

Frank leaned back as if from the force of David's anger. He held out a beseeching paw. "But...Boss," he whined. "Pretty quick, they're gonna know, anyhow. Meeting's in little better than an hour." He nodded at Camille. "We'll have to use this one, after all."

So that's it. They had been going to masquerade Cerese as Camille, and have her take the Cloud seat at the council meeting.

"You just had to screw things up for me, didn't you? You big-mouthed jackass." David said. Then, exerting a fair amount of self-control, he paused and thoughtfully stretched his neck. I supposed he was doing some mental arithmetic, adding facts, subtracting people, hoping his final equation would come out to mean he wouldn't have to count on Camille. She'd already refused him once and was in no condition to hold court at the meeting.

My services were another story. I should have kept my mouth shut. After all that's happened, this tribe is probably going to end up with a some money and a few jobs - which is better than what they had before. *Who's going to miss an air-headed, kinky-blond journalist from Seattle? There'll be questions at work, but I doubted any real investigation. My mother would go immediately to the police, but even with her romantic involvement as a lever, she couldn't compete with the persuasive power of David's money. He can even claim the twins, now orphans, went with me.*

Looking older, David rose to his feet and headed outside. As he passed Frank, he snarled, "Do whatever you have to. Just don't mark her or the kid." Then he was gone.

Our attention switched back to Frank. Hitching his pants back up on his belly, he waddled closer. Remembering the pain he'd inflicted before and hating him for it, I edged up the back of the couch, shrieking, "Get away from me, you swine." Camille had dashed to the corner of the room out of his line of vision.

Feet planted and knees bent, Frank parried with me. He was obviously enjoying himself. "Boss says you need to be taught some manners."

I took a chance. In two swift strides, one on the couch seat and another off the arm rest, I hit the floor running. Faster than I expected, he blocked the door like a guard on a basketball court and waved his arms as if I might curl myself into a big ball and bounce over his head. From the corner of my eye, I noticed Camille pacing the small corner space, touching each familiar object, trailing one hand along the wall, as she crept closer and closer to the doorway.

I was keeping Frank busy - hoping to lure him away and give her the space she needed. Red-faced and panting, he feinted to the right and back - never quite leaving his post. Ready to claw my way out if I had to, I said, "It won't work, Frank. Give it up before you add kidnapping to your list. You're getting the dump, man. If you think David's taking the heat and tarnishing his lily-white reputation, you better think again." His pig-eyes jerked to Camille then back to me. He was sweating.

To divert his attention away from Camille, I said, "You're going to jail, Frank. They'll have you locked up so long you won't just forget what a woman looks like, you won't even care. Before you get out, you'll be an old fogy. We're talking elderly. Senior citizen. With a cane, a bald head, and a limp dick. That what you want? High-tail it, Frank. Get outta here, keep going, and don't look back. It's your only chance."

Frank's grin was gone - he'd stopped having fun. With plodding, bull-like steps, he came at me and took a meaty swing at my head.

I ducked, he missed. On the farther side of the room, I sensed more than saw Camille creep... closer, ever closer...

Another step, another grasping swing.

Just maybe, I can.... Thumbs in my ears, I jeered at him. I hopped, monkey-like, making a total fool of myself. "Old Fart Frank, hee-haw, hee-haw." He clawed the air, inches in front of me. "Old Limp-dick Frank. What cha gonna do, boy? Can't do nothin' with that puny thing."

Crazed with anger, he lunged - caught and wrapt his hand in my hair. As he twisted my head down, I saw Camille's back. She'd jumped for the doorway.

She was gone.

CHAPTER THIRTEEN

Camille disappeared around the corner. I started ticking off the seconds in my head. *A thousand one, a thousand two...*
Frank seethed with rage. "Limp dick, huh? We'll just see about that, you snotty, high-society bitch." Twirling me around, he took a roll of tape from his pocket, and taped my hands behind my back. "We'll see who's limp after I get through with you."
A thousand six, a thousand seven...
Dragging me over to the couch, he threw me on the seat. I immediately bounced off the back, changed direction, and flipped onto the floor. We scrambled, his sour breath hot in my face. He slapped me. Then, he was on top of me, wedging me between the couch and the floor.
A thousand ten...
Flesh grazed across my mouth and I bit down, hard as I could. He screamed and grabbed his cheek with one hand. An ounce of flesh in my teeth, I spit - hating the taste of him.
I was getting tired. Wheezing hard, I wrestled my elbow up, poked it in his neck up against his windpipe. Quickly, he jumped to his feet and threw me back on the couch. His knee ground painfully into my groin.
Where was I? *A thousand twenty....a thousand thirty...*
Frank flipped open the buckle on his pants. With my last strength, I arched my back...trying to wrench free. He stunned me with a jabbing undercut to my jaw. I turned my head to clear it, felt his hammerlock around my neck.
Finally, gasping for air, I stopped struggling. For about one minute, Frank watched me. When I didn't move, his paw went back to fumbling at his pants buckle.
"It's too late, Frank," I croaked. "Don't you see? It's too late."
"Whaddya mean?" he growled. "I'll show you who's limp..." Then he blinked. Behind the red streaked rage in his eyes, I saw a tiny flick.
"Didn't you forget something, Frank? What's the Boss gonna say, now? Both girls are gone. And you lost them. You lost both of them."
He looked up, glanced around the room and screamed, "Bitch! You did it on purpose." Then he slugged me. Hard. White-hot pain stabbed in through my nose, exploding in my brain. Fighting to stay conscious, I forced more words past cracked, puffy lips, "Sheriff ought to be here any minute." *He should be hard at work on the case by now, making brownie points with my Mamma.* My head flopped to the side.

I barely heard his growl, "...ain't no Sheriff coming. Nosey bastard. Wasn't told about the meeting." Then I slid into the swirling black of nothingness.

Gradually the whirling stopped. Like fog lifting, I became aware of an elapsed length of time, hearing voices, realizing I'd been listening to them for a matter of minutes.

Frank's voice, whining, "I kinda had to, Boss. You shoulda heard what she said to me."

David's. "You idiot! Is this what you call leaving them unmarked? Get dressed. And cover her up."

I cracked one eye, the light was piercing. *I'm alive.* It felt wonderful. Even the pain. It meant I could still feel, could still breathe. I tried moving...and couldn't. My hands and feet were bound, corner to corner, to the bedposts.

"Hey." Frank again. "Hey, Boss. I think she's waking up."

"Bring the kid in here."

Sounds of scuffling. A cry. *Camille.* "Let me go. You nasty brute. Let me go!"

Damn. She's been caught.

Frank grappled with her, leaned her over to look at me. "Recognize anybody?"

"Kathleen! Are you all right?"

Frank, talking to me. "Hey, Smart-Ass. What'cha got to say, now?"

Hacking, I tried clearing my throat. I wanted to speak. I wanted to punish David for what he'd done and to tell Frank how much I hated him. It sounded more like a moan.

Camille shrieked, "You beast! What have you done to her?"

I tried again to stay awake, to speak. Felt the pain, tasted my own vomit. Too weak for anything more, I turned my pounding head and managed a blubbering spit.

"Where ya going, Boss? I'll trim this brat's heels. You watch me."

David's angry reply. "I'm going down to the hall. See that this kid is ready to cooperate. You've got five minutes. Then bring her with you, ready for the meeting."

"I'll do it, Boss. You can count on me."

"Just see to it." Pause. "No more excuses, Frank. And no more run-a-ways. Get that kid ready to jump through hoops and bark like a dog if she's told to. Or you'll be next."

"She'll be there. I'll take care of it, Boss." Thudding steps, going out.

"Now. You ready, Sweetheart? Take a good look." Frank again, evidently to Camille. I couldn't see much of anything. "Would you like some of this?" He wheezed, wet and passionately.

She screamed, "No! Leave her alone."

The bed jounced, nauseating me. I cracked an eye lid, saw Camille struggling with Frank - saw him push her face close to mine. He was forcing her to watch his vileness - his evil torture. "You heard what the Boss said, Sweetheart. Maybe you'd like a little of this...?"

A sudden, incredibly sharp pain on my breast. Through tears, I saw Frank brandish a pair of pliers, squeezing blood from my nipple. A scream echoed in my ears. My throat burned.

It must be me....

Hysterically, Camille fought him - her thrashing lurched the bed. I had to vomit. "Don't," she begged. "Please don't. I'll do it. I'll say whatever you want. Just, please. Don't hurt her anymore."

"I outta try it on you, ya little brat," Frank panted. "They'd never see it under your clothes."

"I said I'd do it. I'll do anything you want. Just, stop it. Stop it!"

They left. Peace, blissful peace. Eagerly, I searched for the swirling black...found it...

and gratefully sank.

CHAPTER FOURTEEN

The sound of my name pulled at me, tugging me away from the murky dark.

"Kathleen? Kathleen! Wake up." A hand...touched me.

"No," I cried, yanking on the binding ropes. "No more. Don't. Please don't."

Again, I heard my name. "Kathleen. Wake up." The same hand, cool and gentle, the voice somehow familiar. "You poor thing. What have they done to you?" She touched my face, smoothed back my hair.

Beneath my buttocks, a cold, damp spot chilled me. It smelled of urine. I had wet myself during the beatings.

I squinted, the face was out of focus, the room dark. *It's not Camille.* "Who...who is it?" I squeaked. The pain was a live thing, a monster larger than me, mushrooming inside my body, threatening to split me down the sides.

"It's me. Cerese. Camille told me you were here." She said, fumbling at my wrists. I felt the ropes fall slack, my arms, then my legs, go free.

I can move. I tried rolling to one side, setting off more fireworks, awakening more monsters.

Raising me to a sitting position, Cerese said, "I know it must hurt something terrible, but we've got to go." She fumbled at my clothes, "let's put this coat on you...there you go. And your shoes...there. All ready to go. Can you stand?"

I was on my feet. I fought the oncoming darkness, forcing my eyes to focus. Cerese's arm was around my waist.

"Here," she said. "Lean on me. We'd better go now. Before they get back. I know of a spot, Camille told me about it. We'll hide there, for now. Can you walk? Okay. That's good. Here's the door."

The fresh air strengthened me. It was dusk. A stiff breeze rushed past me, ruffling my hair. Holding tightly to Cerese's shoulder, I half-leaned, half-walked along with her. "Don't worry, Miss. Everybody's gone to the meeting."

Hustling past the cars and the small clearing, we entered a stand of evergreens. "Here's the trail. Lean on me, that's all right. Thank goodness you're so little. We're gonna make it, Miss O'Shaunessey. We're gonna make it."

The ground felt spongy as we tramped through the old forest. I gulped huge amounts of air, tinged with the acrid smell of pine needles. A twig snapped under-foot, some birds twittered overhead. We trudged on.

Cerese panted under my weight. Every few steps, my knees would buckle and she'd pull me back up. She began to tell me how it all happened. "After Frank left, well, he'd been gone quite awhile, my Mom finally fell asleep. She's not my real Mom, you know. I never did feel like she was, you know what I mean? How sometimes you just feel things and you don't really know why or how? But you're just sure that you know something to be true? Anyways, Frank left and Mamma fell asleep - I'm just calling her that cause it seems like I always have and it'd feel funny not to. ANYWAYS, Mom went to sleep and I saw my chance to boogie on out of there. I mean, ever since Frank came on the scene with his big ideas about getting rich, something about developing a construction thing, I just couldn't see living in that house with him. Not one more day. Know what I mean...?"

We were out of the trees, pushing through the high grass of a meadow. Her excited chatter and the heightened exposure lent an urgency... My dead weight was getting heavy for her. Cerese had me stand still for a moment while she changed sides, holding me up now with her left arm. "So, here I am, sneaking through the woods, trying to find an unlocked car or something - anything to take me back to civilization, you know? I wasn't going to steal it. I ain't no damn car thief. Just hide in the back seat as far as town. I mean, I know I'm Indian and all, and that don't bother me a bit, but these guys, especially the ones like Frank, are just too much. I mean, they're like primitive, you know? So, here I am, sneaking through the woods, and you'll never guess what happened. Not in a million years. It was like, looking in the mirror or something. I mean, like the twilight zone already. I mean, GET REAL. And she says, 'Cerese?' And I go, '...uh, duh, yea. My name's Cerese. Who the hell are you?' Then she goes, 'Hey. I'm Camille. We're sisters. You know? Twin sisters, she says. I just couldn't believe it. After all these years. A twin sister. She said she knew I'd be on this path. Sort of saw me here in her mind. Must be a shaman or something. Can you beat that? ANYWAYS, she's going to settle this thing tonight. Some big kind of meeting of the whole tribe, and then she'll call the law on old Frank. She told me where to find you and to get you out so's we wouldn't have to worry they'd come back after you. Ain't that something'? With you safe up here in this old shack she knows about, she's going to stand right up there and tell the elders. All about what Frank and these other guys have been up to, and what they did to you. The reservation police are all there and we're gonna turn them in. She told me too, where I could get to a phone and call the Sheriff. My own sister. Ain't that something?"

I'd walked as far as I could. An old log lay across our path, too high to step over. The smell of wild onions wafted in the breeze.

It's their Mamma's old garden.

Cerese, too, was winded. "Here," she said. "Let's sit down a minute." Craning her neck, she looked in the direction we were headed. "You know, I believe that's it, over there. See that shack? That ought to be it."

After a few minutes, I noticed Cerese was getting nervous. Fidgety. *The pain be damned.* I nodded to her and we struggled to our feet.

When we reached the cabin, Cerese quickly unfolded a plastic garden lounge, the kind I'd seen millions of times on patios and by swimming pools. I'd never been so grateful to lie down. "Camille said you should wait here," Cerese whispered. "I'm going down and make sure everything's going along like we planned and Camille's OK. Don't worry. I'll just peep in the windows 'till I'm sure."

She stopped on the way out and twirled around. "Oh. I almost forgot. There's a guy down there, says he knows you from work. A Tom, Horse...or Hoss...something like that."

"Goss," I croaked. "Tom Goss."

"Yeah. That's it. Anyways, Camille says to tell you, he's down there. Raising a big stink, wanting to know where you are. That's when I snuck up and got you, while everybody was busy trying to shut him up. Camille's scared to say anything until she knows you're safe." She eyed me a minute longer, shrugged off her own jacket and covered my legs with it.

The worst of it over with, spasms of shivering wrenched my body. It was probably from shock. I clenched my teeth to keep them from clacking together.

Giving the jacket a closer tuck, she turned to go out. "I got to go back and tell Camille that you're OK. As soon as she sees me and I give her the old high sign..." With thumb and first finger, she demonstrated by making a circle, "...she's gonna lower the boom." She then giggled, waved, and was gone.

CHAPTER FIFTEEN

The creak of the wooden shack door woke me. It was Tom and the twins. Through the fog of my mental shock, I caught the gist of their jabbering. They assured me, over and over, all was back to normal.

Tom wouldn't hear of my walking back. Scooping me up in two hairy arms, he carried me with great, ground-thudding strides. Camille and Cerese ran alongside, chattering incessantly. "You should have seen Frank," Camille said. "When I stood up and told the police and the elders, all what he'd done," she demonstrated, her arm out - her finger thrusted forward. "He called me a liar. To my own tribe. Can you believe it? When that didn't work, he kind of melted into a big, quivering mass."

We stopped for a breather on the same log by the old onion patch. Camille pointed out to Cerese, the slender green tops wafting in the breeze amongst the quack grass and told her the story of their mother. Then of course, they had to run over, pluck one from the ground and sniff deeply of it and the surrounding earth.

Once we were back in the house, Camille began to rattle her pots and pans in preparation of a meal. She sent Cerese to the woodpile for bits of bark and kindling.

I was dumped, unceremoniously, on the couch. Propped up in the corner, I watched my exhausted news-buddy waddle over to plop in the easy chair. With a loud heave and a groan from the chair's springs, he flopped down and began his slow-blinking stare. "We're going to have to call the police," he wheezed. "See what the charges are and if they've booked either one of them. They'll probably need your statement first, Kath. I don't know what the protocol is here. Whether we call the sheriff or the Tribal police or both."

"Why not just dial 911 and see who answers," I said. "Let them sort it out."

Wearily, he rose to his feet, grumbling as he passed me on the way to the wall phone in the kitchen. "I've heard some horror stories before, about the lack of co-operation between these county sheriffs and the Tribal police. Let's hope...." he said, as he dialed.

I must have dozed in the interim. I woke up, dazed from a frightening dream. I'd been fleeing in terror from the ghosts of a thousand war-crazed Indians pounding down from the heavens on painted, fire-breathing ponies. Arrows and spears held aloft, they'd shrieked and howled horrible, blood-curdling death cries and it seemed I could still hear the echo. They'd descended upon Seattle's twenty-story skyscrapers and toppled them into the polluted bay.

I rubbed my face and the back of my neck. Camille's wood cookstove had been stoked to the hilt and the room was hot. Too hot. Kicking off the blankets and coats covering me, I noticed that my clothes were soaked through with perspiration. My good, red suit was ruined. Still wobbly, I sat up, fighting back the soreness in my chest and arms and the allure of oblivion in sleep.

Two patrolmen peered at me from the kitchen doorway. I recognized the scrape of their boots and the authoritative boom in their voices as the sounds that had awakened me. One of them approached, a stout, black-haired and flat-featured young man. His tailored uniform was set off with a wood-handled revolver that rocked on his hip in its black leather holster. A name tag that read *Highbear* was pinned on a shirt pocket and enough chevrons had been sewn on the sleeve to signify the rank of Deputy. "Ma'am," he ventured. "Do you feel up to answering a few questions?"

I answered questions, going over and over the same ground until I was exhausted. I needed a break. Pushing myself to a sitting position, he leapt to my side and supported one elbow when he saw I was struggling to stand.

From his corner, Tom hollered, "Cerese? Can you help Kate?"

Both girls immediately ran in from the kitchen. One on each side, they trundled me off to the bathroom while the Deputy stepped back and sheepishly tucked one hand in his back pocket.

I would rather have had a bath and gone to bed. But, and I understood this, the police would need all the help they could get. These were some wily crooks - aware of the laws and how to get around them. Frank was in custody but I would have to press charges. They hadn't felt there was enough evidence to arrest David and Margaret yet - nothing they could prove. I intended to rectify that with my testimony.

I washed my face and rinsed it with cold water, grimacing in the mirror at the wild, blond mop on my head then returned to my couch. Other than for his slow, thoughtful blink, Tom didn't move. He stayed in his corner, unusually quiet, and didn't interrupt.

Finally, the officer thanked me and prepared to leave, saying they'd do all they could to make a good case.

"And David," I reminded them. "He's the real criminal. This Frank is just working for him. Kind of a hired bully that does all of David's dirty work."

"Can't do anything about him, Ma'am. Out of our jurisdiction."

"What do you mean you can't do anything about him? He's the real crook...the mastermind. I mean, he's the head cheese. If you don't go after him, he can just hire someone else and we'll all get to go through this again and again."

He hesitated, glancing at his partner who was just coming into the room. To me, he said, "I realize that, Ma'am. But, the county sheriff will have to pick up that part of the investigation."

His partner had been in the bedroom. Tucking some plastic zip-lock bags into his pocket, he now began to take pictures of me. The extended zoom lens looked like a big, black eye as he shot some close-ups of my visible bruises. His name tag read *Bowman* but he had gathered a little more paraphernalia on his sleeve and collar. Probably a Sergeant.

Seeing the first man's confusion, Bowman stepped forward and said, "I think what Officer Highbear is trying to say, is that we, as members of the Tribal Law Enforcement, are only authorized to pursue and cap- ture Native Americans."

"In other words, since we're all on a reservation, you can only go after other Indians."

"That's about it, Ma'am. If, in the course of our duty, we do take a white man into custody, about all we could do would be to notify the county sheriff." The Sergeant was taller, slimmer, and much more con- fident. He wagged his head regretfully. "I'm sorry Ma'am. I wish I could go after them. But all they'd need to do is evade us long enough to get back into the county jurisdiction."

"And? Would the county sheriff take it from there and, as you put it, pursue and capture them?" In fact, the Sheriff should have been here by now. I decided not to tell the tribal police about my family's predic- ament. Mother's romance with this same Sheriff. Not until I knew exactly, just what my family predicament was at this moment.

"I...can't speak for them, Ma'am. I assume that would be the case."

This 'Ma'am' business was beginning to get on my nerves. I took a deep breath, resisting the impulse to be rude, and rested my head on the couch arm. "I'm...too tired for any more of this."

Tom rose to his feet, hitched up his trousers, and handed the officers a card, "This is the Gazette's phone number and the name of our attor- ney. Any more questions, I believe, should be asked in his presence." To me, he said, "I have to get back to the office. Kate - are you sure you won't let me drop you at the hospital? The Medical Center is only a 10 minute drive from here."

"No, Tom. I'd really rather not. I don't want a rape trial, anyway."

"I don't mean that, so much. Just...have them check those abrasions. See if there's anything else...."

"No, thanks Tom. Nothing's broken. I just need some sleep."

Just then, Camille brought me a bowl of hot, milky soup. "You've got to eat something," she said. "Come on. Just a taste." I grinned wryly, remembering our root cellar tomb and wondered from where she'd gotten the pluck to go down after the potatoes. The officers quietly excused themselves, leaving me to my dinner and the slurping thereof, from the spoon Camille kept jabbing at my mouth.

Tom ushered the officers out, then came back to place a wet kiss on my forehead and said, "Take care, Doll. I'll clear some time off for you with Gunner." He handed another card to Camille and instructed her to call him if she needed anything. He then left.

After they'd gone and I'd drunk two more cups of Camille's blackberry tea, I changed into a pair of her old sweats. She gave me some painkillers which I swallowed and was vaguely aware of her covering me with an old quilt and tucking it around my feet before I fell asleep.

The next morning, everything I owned, ached. I managed to grab a quick shower and wash my hair before the Deputy Sheriff arrived. He introduced himself as Officer Marconi. Again, I was amazed that Belltower himself hadn't come. We went through another round of questioning almost identical to the first. The rape charge wouldn't stick unless I went to the hospital for tests, which I was not about to do. I'd rather he be tried for attempted homicide and assault and battery. We'd have a lot better chance for a conviction.

Marconi was worried. He scratched his head a lot, his questions bordering on incredulity. He didn't like the idea that I was a journalist, dangerously close to dragging David through a political field of mud. It seems the Abrahamson name had become a symbol of power, his money having fueled many a campaign. Small signs demanding that the citizens support Sheriff Belltower's re-election dotted the landscape on every road in and out of town.

Camille and Cerese were both grilled, again and again, about what they saw and what they knew.

"Frank had Katie on Daddy's bed, tied to each corner of the bedpost. And he'd been beating her," Camille said.

The Deputy leaned towards her, his eyes a hard, cool blue. "How do you know he'd been beating her?"

"I saw him."

"Did you actually see anyone hit her?"

"Yes. And even worse." Terribly embarrassed, she described to him the torture of my breasts with the pliers.

"And what was Mr. Abrahamson doing all this time?"

"He came into the hallway and stood just outside of Daddy's door. He asked him if...."

Again, Marconi interrupted, "'...by 'him,' you mean this man by the name of Frank?"

"Yes. David was watching from the hall and he asked Frank if I had agreed to cooperate yet. Frank said no, I hadn't. Then David said, 'Do whatever you have to do. Just see to it that she, meaning me, is ready to say anything she's told to. Or something like that. I can't remember his exact words." She shuddered. "That's when Frank did...that thing...with the pliers to Kate."

"And you...?"

"I said yes, of course. I couldn't let him do that to her. It was awful. He's a beast, Sheriff. A total animal."

"Well, you're seventeen. Old enough to be held responsible for your own actions. Would you be willing to swear to this in court?"

"You better believe I would. Anytime."

"Remember now. If they prove that you're lying, you'd be tried for perjury and sentenced just like an adult."

"I'm not lying. I saw them with my own eyes."

I had to hand it to her. The Deputy Sheriff grilled her for another hour, but try as he might, he was not able to break her down or chisel any holes in her allegations.

Then he started on Cerese. She was more defiant, almost snotty. He finally gave up. After he left, I called Hampton, the man I'd met at the Pow-Wow, to bum a ride to the Texaco station and pick up my Porsche.

Hampton came in the house, sweeping the kitchen with his quick, noncommittal glance. He held out an arm to Camille. She ran to him and was hugged. He then spoke to Cerese, telling her how glad he was she'd been found. She smiled, tentatively, but kept her seat.

To me, he said, "Are you alright? I heard what happened. It's a terrible thing. Is there anything, anything at all...?"

"Just take me to my car. There's some things I have to do."

"Certainly."

After another five minutes of telling the twins what and what not to do, we all said our goodbyes and Hampton and I left for Suquamish. It was my chance, maybe my only chance, to speak my piece. "Hampton, you're the attorney for this tribe. I don't see why you can't do something to stop David from building this casino. You know, we have laws against this sort of thing. And besides, have you ever seen Vegas? Don't you realize that this beautiful place will grow to look just like that? The thugs and the gamblers and the crime... My God, Hampton. Do something."

"There's one thing you don't realize, young lady. This is not David's casino. He's only part owner and the mortgage broker. The casino actually belongs to the tribe." He sighed, loudly and resignedly. "Let me start by saying that we are more than an ethnic group. Most American Indian tribes, at least those who are recognized, exist as a sovereign nation. Which means, we make our own laws subject only to Congress' authority to regulate commerce. Congress has set down the rules for the operation of a casino and they are enforced by the Federal Bureau of Indian Affairs. We've followed them. And if we want gambling to be legal on the reservation, then that's the way it stands. The Tribal Council, with me as their chief negotiator, have been putting together an agreement with the State for some time now to build a hotel-casino. I hate to say this Kathleen, but your likes or dislikes really have nothing to do with it."

He paused to bunch his jaw muscles and swallow. "We're going to use this money for schools and health clinics. That's all that matters to us."

"But he's a crook. He's been..."

"Anything that's happened between you and David is inconclusive. It's your word against his and you'll have to settle it between yourselves and through your own courts. We've put him through the required background checks and nothing of any substantial moot has been shown to be disfavorable." We were passing through the clear cut area where a whole forest had been wiped out by clear-cut logging. As if by former agreement, Hampton and I both kept our eyes straight ahead while he drove around a stalled logging truck. He continued to explain his position, wisely keeping his comments to the matters at hand. "If Abrahamson is charged under white man law and convicted, then we definitely will not want to do business with him. In that case, we will simply find another source of funding."

"And this Frank? He's an Indian. What about him?"

"He's being held on a warrant. He'll be tried in our court by a Tribal Judge and, if he's found guilty, he will be banned from the reservation, incarcerated, or turned over to the Feds for further prosecution. But again, let me remind you. This will have no effect on the building or not building of a casino on Indian land."

I folded my arms and stared out the car window.

Well. We'll just see about that.

CHAPTER SIXTEEN

The garage mechanic was the same little guy by the name of Jack. I'd seen him that morning when I stumbled out of Frank's motel room. Jack's station was perched up on a knoll and I noticed that if I raised up on my toes and peered over the top of some bushes and the rock wall fence, I could see Frank's door. I pointed to it and asked Jack, "Have you ever noticed anything different in the third cabin to the left? Anyone going in and out? I mean, besides the people who live there?"

"Who, them folks over there?" he asked, handing me my keys. "Oh, yeah. You better believe it. There's always something going on over there. In school, we called people like that, 'party animals'."

"Do you remember seeing a real tall guy? Well dressed. Might have been in a grey limo or a BMW?"

"I've seen the grey limo around town. Nice set of wheels. Can you believe it? Engine that size, and could hardly hear it hum in first gear. Cherry, man."

"How about the man? Real tall, blond guy?"

"Uh, yeah. Come to think of it, maybe I did. One night when I was working late. Looked like he had a kid with him. Funny looking kid, maybe even a foreigner. Wasn't in the grey limo, though. He had a nice BMW. Car like that don't belong in no gravel lot, parked up next to some dilapidated shack."

Must have been David. But who had he been with? Could it have been Cerese? As one of today's teenagers, she could have been dressed in a way that belonged more in outer-space than this little town. I thanked him for his information and for fixing my car. I then left.

My little red car pulsated with life from its restoration at Jack's shop. Spitting a colorless exhaust at the old heaps behind us, it rumbled merrily back to Seattle where I kept the TV turned off and the phone unplugged for the next two days.

Wednesday morning, I went to work. Tom brightened when he saw me come in. "Did you see the weekend edition?" he asked, hefting the tri-colored first page of section C.

"No, I haven't." Taking it with me to my desk, I first noticed the picture he had taken of the pandemonium at the meeting.

It was all there. Camille with Cerese standing beside her, clamoring for justice and quoted as saying David was linked with the disappearance of her father. Frank, having been read his rights and handcuffed, stood slightly behind David. They both bore slack-jawed looks of terror. Deputy Highbear stood to their far right, his face noble and without expression.

It was second-best to my having been there.

The second thing I noticed was my own byline. Tom had carefully constructed an article from my notes and added a copy of my statement, I'd made with the Deputy Sheriff. It was a nice piece. He'd then slapped my name on it - taking no credit for himself. Just below, in an editor's script, mention was made of my part in reuniting the twins.

"Well," I mumbled to Tom. "At least something good came of the whole thing. Thanks. You're a good friend." He had squatted on a metal folding chair just outside my cubicle and leaned in the doorway. "They still haven't heard anything about the father?"

"Nope. After four days, the search party gave up. The kid said he used to drink a lot but he hadn't in a long time. And he'd never been known to leave for more than a day or two."

"Don't sound good for the old man." I nodded in agreement.

"Has anyone ever traced this guy? This Abrahamson? Who is he? Is he from here, originally?"

"I don't think so. He looked 'big city' to me. He's slick. Typical high-roller. Backed by big money."

Scratching a wobbly chin, Tom shook his head. "He wanted to build an island-retreat with a casino for rich movie-types and TV moguls? Here in Washington?"

"Seems so. Evidently, if the Indians really push it, they can usually gain the right to draft their own zoning and building codes. If the right to build a hotel with a marina and casino came down to a state-court interpretation of their status as a solvent nation, who knows? Each case is taken on an individual basis."

"But...the thing I can't figure, is why go to such an extreme measure? Using a minor? Doing this...this horrendous thing to you? I can't buy it."

"What'd you mean you can't buy it? He did it, Tom. He did it. The man orchestrated the whole project. Got most of the council all hyped up and disposed of the only man who was against it. And if I hadn't showed up, he would have pulled it off." Swiveling in my chair, I thumbed the switch on my computer and waited for it to warm up. "Now, let's talk about something else."

"But, Kate. This is a professional business man, hired to do a specific and legal job. It doesn't make sense."

"Tom. I DON'T want to hear about it." *One more word about that man and I'll scream.* Opening up to a blank screen, I typed in my name, stared at it, fingers poised above the keys... But I couldn't resist. I looked over at Tom and said, "Just what do you mean by that?"

"By what, Katie? Oh, I'm sorry. Did you say something?"

"You know damned well, *by what.* That comment about it not making sense. Of course it doesn't make sense. None of it does. That's what has made it so awful. But I don't see why you can't *buy it*, as you say."

"Well, if he's that successful, why risk it all on this one project? Pulling the wool over some Indians eyes, is unethical, sure. But, as long as it's legal, no one outside the reservation's going to care. This is different.

84

Getting involved in some diabolical scheme with a murder-one rap hanging over your head? Beating someone up who has your kind of access to the media? I don't think so."

"But, he did, Tom. That's what makes it so crazy. He *did*!"

"Of course he did, Katie. We know that. But why? What were his motives? This goes beyond pure and simple greed."

We were interrupted by the news editor's appearance. Gunner tossed a four-color copy of the Portland Star, our biggest competitor, on my desk. Blazed across the front page were side-by-side pictures of Camille and Cerese. Below that, a statement from several of the elders - and David - discounting the whole thing. He referred vaguely to my talent as an imaginative writer, quoting me as saying I preferred fiction.

"Channel 10's got the same story," said Gunner. "They're reporting live from Suquamish on the 5:00 news."

A minute ago I'd been close to crying. Now I was ready to rip the man's jugular with my teeth. "Damn, him. Look! Look what it says. He's accusing me of lying." Shoving back my long sleeves, I offered up my battered wrists. "Does this look a lie? Or maybe that's my imagination, too." The bruises had faded from a reddish-purple to a darkish yellow color.

Gunner hovered over my desk - tall, sixyish, and scowling darkly. "Do you feel like another ride? I'd like to know what this guy's up to. We'll need something substantial on that casino. Are there any blueprints floating around? Maybe some contractor's got one. This is a major project. Will it be up for bid? And see if you can get some background on these guys. Don't take any chances. Call in to Tom here, if you need help. And don't forget your camera."

Too angry to wait in line for the ferry, I ripped down I-5, headed south. At the bottom tip of the Puget Sound, I took the exit for Bremerton. Forty minutes later, my wheels crunched into Camille's front yard.

She'd seen the car and met me on the porch. "Hi, Kathy."

Cerese came bounding up behind her. "Did you hear about it? Man, there's been reporters crawling all over here. They got these big, honkin' camcorders and everything. We're gonna be on TV. Tonight, on the news."

I didn't want to ruin their fun. It'd been rough on them too, and it wasn't over yet. "Yeah," I said, hoping I looked the part. "That's great." I went inside and at Camille's insistence, ate a late breakfast of her hot fried bread and jelly.

Camille gently dusted an old photograph and held it up so I could look at it. "I've been showing Cerese some of Mamma's old things and telling her what little I know about her." In the picture, the woman was about these girls ages' now and, again, the resemblance was striking.

I filled my coffee cup from the metal pot on the stove and said, "You two must have a lot of catching up to do. Uh, I need to use your boat. My editor wants pictures. If you tell me how to start it and the directions to get to the island..."

"That's all right," Camille said, "I'll take you over. Cerese hasn't seen it, either. As long as we get back before the news is on. They said at five."

The boat ride was an outing for them, a reoccurring nightmare for me. Camille pointed out landmarks, shouting over the roar of the outboard motor. "There used to be a longhouse over there on that knoll. Long time ago. Daddy says our grandfather grew up there. And a bunch of our other ancestors. Big families, living together, all at one time. Like one family would sleep down at one end with another in the middle and the grandparents on the other side. It's all crumbly and fallen down now. But you can still see where they cut whole trees for beams with little axes and stuff." She paused, looking dreamily at the shore, the foggy sky. "I wish he'd get home, though. I'm still awfully worried. Man, is he ever going to be surprised to see you."

Cerese said, "You don't think he knows about me? You really think it'll be all right with him, that I showed up now after all these years? He won't be mad, will he?"

"Mad?" Camille clucked her tongue at such foolishness. "Why would he be mad at you? I mean, it's not like it's your fault or something. No. He'll just be really surprised. I'm sure if he knew about you, he would have told me long ago. He'll find how we got separated and go after the people who did it. You just wait. They're not going to get away with it."

The wind whipped cold past my ears and seemed to lodge in my sore arm sockets. Stretching the muscles helped. I hunched my shoulders and made small circles with my elbows as the boat swung into Liberty Bay. Hideaway Island loomed just ahead.

We beached at a point just below the house and looped the boat's rope around a large, upstanding rock. I said to the twins, "You guys stick close to the beach. The house should be over on the other side of those trees. It's best if you stay away from it. I don't want any more trouble. Let's go down a little ways so I can get a picture." The tide was out and made for easy walking. We went along the beach of Hideaway Island, Camille, Cerese, and I. Now and then, we'd hop out of the way of the occasional squirt of a large clam, as it shot water up through its neck from its sandy burrow. A brisk breeze made knots of my kinky curls. My head was a-buzz, reviewing the events of this last week.

The Gazette's attorney had contacted the Sheriff and run head-on into David's high-priced counterpart - the District Attorney. He'd casually mentioned he was calling from a golf tournament in Vegas. He and David were waiting, with the Governor, to get on the green. Our attorney had immediately slapped the files back on Gunner's desk and said something about not touching it with a ten-foot totem pole. When Gunner asked why, the attorney mentioned a fond attachment to his career, his home, and his family. As he was leaving, he bid us, "Lots of luck."

But at least David was out of town and I had an injunction against his, or any of his associates, going anywhere near the island or the reservation. Most of the charges were piled against Frank. Thank goodness, there wasn't much chance that even David's money could get that creep out for a long, long time.

I sighed, noticing I'd approached the spot where the rock wall split. The path going up to David's cabin started just behind its jagged niche. It was hidden well. Up ahead of me, Camille and Cerese had walked within four feet of it without a hint of its being there. *I'll just go up far enough to get a good shot of the outside.*

The beveled roof line of the two-storied log cabin made a saw-toothed silhouette against a grey, weepy sky. I used the zoom lens for the close-ups and could see a part of the fireplace through the window. A frame shot would probably work better for the paper. I could use the trees on each side to get a good perspective of the size of the house. A cool breeze raised the tiny hairs on the back of my neck.

That room hidden behind the pantry...lots of people have an office with computers and radios. Why was it all such a secret?

We'd better get back. I could see the twins a good distance away. They were still walking, their arms linked and gossipy heads bent together. The breeze deepened to a cold wind.

Smells like rain. Snuggling my jacket tighter around my hunched and sore shoulders, I crossed to the other side of a large cedar.

I'd wandered off the path.

Plowing through some low-lying brush, I started to look for it. I kicked at a bush and gasped... It flew three feet in the air. I kicked at another one. Same thing. They'd been lying loose on top of the ground. I peered closer. Most of the brush had been brought here from somewhere else and scattered around to look as if it grew there.

It's a cover. I nudged a huckleberry bush. All dried out by now, it had been ripped out by its roots from some distant and rotting cedar stump.

Scraping them all aside, I cleared a space about five feet across and found the path. The bushes had obviously been intended to hide it. A few more feet, a few more loose clumps of moss and branches.

The path led to a cliff wall.

That's strange. Why would anyone cover a path that leads up to a sheer rock wall? It's too steep to climb. And no signs of anyone going around it. Hmmm.

Running my hand over the rock, I fingered every little crevice I could reach, half expecting a door to emerge on the face of the twelve-ton boulder. But, there weren't any buttons to push and the boulder didn't budge. Feeling a little foolish, I turned to leave.

I'd better get a grip. Too many cartoons when I was a kid. Ali Baba and the Forty Thieves could have waved an arm and bellowed, OPEN SESAME. Kathleen O'Shaunessey can't.

Brushing some dried leaves from my good slack bottoms, I hoisted one foot to pluck a persistent briar from my shoe laces. From somewhere, came the rattle of sliding gravel. I glanced up above the rock wall, prepared to duck if necessary.

Nope. No gravel up there. Nothing but vegetation and moss. Besides, it sounded...different. Muffled. As if it were far away.

I stood poker straight, held my breath, and listened. All I could hear was the twins at the end of the beach - Cerese's high giggle and Camille's lower, more thoughtful laugh. After that, a crow cawed and a seagull screamed. But no more sliding gravel.

Time to go home.

Pushing aside the cedar branch, I ducked and prepared to go under it. But instead of coming out on the other side of the tree, I tripped. Smacked the hard ground with my chin.

"Unh!"

For the second time, the air was knocked from my lungs. It hurt. I writhed on the ground, my sore chest heaving.

Finally, breathing somewhat restored, I clambered to my knees - spitting cedar needles. "Damn it. I'm getting awfully tired of this." No blood, but my arms were skinned, my slacks ruined. I tried standing when I noticed my left foot was caught. Reaching back, I grabbed the thing that encircled my ankle. Wire! A group of five plastic-coated strands, normally used inside the walls of a house. Angrily, I yanked on it. There seemed to be no end. I kept pulling - it kept coming. *Where's this coming from?*

I looped the wire, hand to elbow, and wound it as I walked. Little dust puffs mushroomed up from the ground as I jerked the wire from just below the surface. A surface, which I could now see, had been purposely laid. Dirt and gravel mixed, several inches deep, had been dumped and layered on top of hard rock. It was then covered by limbs and cut bushes.

The wire disappeared into the cliff wall. The end of it had been thrust into a small, drilled hole, covered with brush. It was the same spot where I'd stood just moments before. I kicked aside the loose shrubs and examined the ground. There were my footprints.

Wait. What's this? Another print - a large man's shoe... Only one person I knew had a foot that big.

David.

I scraped the dirt aside. I was standing on a square piece of plywood, about three feet wide. In the corner was a small chunk of rope, looped like a handle. I stepped back onto the rock, hooked a finger in the loop, and pulled. *No wonder he seemed to know about Camille's trap door. He'd had this one all along.* As it opened, the gravel slid off and fell into, what appeared to be, one end of a tunnel. A ladder had been rigged to the side, going down.

Should I go in? Is it safe?

Peering through the trees, I could see Camille and Cerese at the end of the beach, skipping rocks on the bay's calm surface. I would have to shout to get their attention.... *Just one little peek. That wouldn't hurt anything. Just far enough to see where it goes.*

I left the trap door open for light.

The tunnel followed the line of the rock wall boulder, dipped, then headed in the direction I could only guess would be inland. Above my head, cut timbers shored up the loose rock.

Bent over so I wouldn't bop my head, I crept along - leaving the last bit of light behind me. My foot bumped a hard surface and I stumbled. Scraping the surface with my toe, I found a ridge and kneeled down to touch it. A rod of cold steel had been covered over with gravel and passed through, what looked like, the length of the tunnel. Another ran parallel to that some eighteen inches away.

Train tracks.

I crept further in, trusting to my fingers to tell me where the rock ended and the timbers began.

It's getting hard to breathe. I really should go back.

But I didn't.

The slope of the floor changed. I was climbing. The darkness lightened to a dull purple. Again, the slope steepened. Carefully, groping with my feet and hands, I found another set of stairs that creaked as I climbed them.

I didn't see the wall until I bumped it. Couldn't tell it from the murky dark I'd been walking in. Sliding one hand across the slick steel, my fingers fumbled around a hatch-handle similar to those I'd seen on the outside doors of piper cub airplanes and old war ships.

I pushed down on it - it wouldn't budge. I pushed harder, leaning with all my weight, and heard a click - felt it give way. The heavy, steel hatch swept inward. I knew what room it was before I entered.

Damn curiosity.

David had covered his tracks well, in a mammoth effort to hide something - something too incriminating to be found. Two more steps.

Yep. This is it. There's the...

Lights glared, blinding me. Hard, sudden pain cracked the back of my head. My body slumped, and inky, swirling black engulfed me.

CHAPTER SEVENTEEN

I'd been listening to an irritating tap for some time, becoming conscious by degrees. I was on the floor, trussed up like a thanksgiving turkey.

To my left was a padded office chair - the type that perched on a single steel pedestal and branched out at the bottom with small wheels on the floor. Placed in position between oak-fronted drawers, it occupied one end of a seemingly endless desk. My bound feet faced the wall. Above me and a little behind, I made out the outline of a door. Tap, tap, tap. Turning to look behind me, pain exploded in my head from the hit I'd taken when I came in. I wasn't alone.

Whoever hit me is still here.

Taking care to keep my breathing light as if I were still asleep, my listening tuned to a pin drop, I groggily attempted to determine who was in the room with me. I suddenly knew where I'd heard the tappity-tap before. *A computer keyboard. Like the one I used at the Gazette.*

And with that, the rest of the realization flooded into my aching head - the creeping down the dark tunnel and the day I'd seen this room before. I'd been high on love, hungry, and pawing through the shelves of a pantry. A ham radio had been spitting out a garbled message...

The tapping stopped. A chair creaked. The roll of small wheels on tiled floor - the shuffle of papers - all sounds familiar to an office gal. I hoped my pretense of a light snore was convincing. I concentrated...

Don't let the eyelids flutter!

"Kathleen. Are you awake?"

Who in the world...

A harder nudge, more of a kick. "Kathleen." A pause.

Margaret?

"Aw, what the hell. I must of hit 'er harder than I thought." The hiss and crackle of the radio broke the quiet of the room. A familiar voice said, "Grey Ghost to base. Grey Ghost to base. Come in, please."

Margaret thudded over to the receiver. "Come in, Grey Ghost."

"Is your...guest awake?"

"Naw, she's still resting."

"Don't let her go before we have our uh, conference."

"She's kind of tied up right now. She ain't going nowhere."

"Keep me posted on...any new events. You have the portable transmitor with you?"

"It's right here."

"Hide it in your purse and don't let anyone see you use it. I want you to watch the dock and around Suquamish for an old Ford pick-up and driver. Try some of the bars without being conspicuous. Check in about every hour. If I don't answer, wait a little while and try again."

"I'd like to get my daughter back. I heard she found her sister and been staying over there."

"She'll come home when she's ready. Don't try to force anything. When this is over with, I'll see what I can do. Over and out."

A minute later, I heard the clank of the steel hatch and her grunt as she opened it. Then - with a whoosh and a draft of cold air, she was gone. I held my breath, listening, stretching my intuition like an antennae - feeling, sensing, tasting.

Nothing. Only the wild thumping of my own heart beat. I chanced a one-eyed peek. It was the same impressive system I'd seen before. I wiggled and humped to a better position.

Viewing the room from the floor and through a resounding headache, it looked bigger than it probably was. To one side, a high-tech phone receiver cradled the IBM modem. A green 19 inch screen blipped, advising any friendly user that access to its Executive Writing program could be had by pressing any one of its keys.

My feet were bound with black electrical tape as were, I assumed, my hands behind me. Keeping one wary eye on the screen, I rolled onto my back, still listening, my scalp crawling with fear that I might be heard somehow or even watched. Kicking with both feet, I flipped the office chair up-side down. It landed with a crash. The seat popped off the pedestal, rolling crazily across the room.

Now we're getting somewhere. Squirming to position my back next to the exposed swivel mechanisms, I rubbed the tape on my wrists against the sharp edges. Several times, the metal spirals on the screw cut the soft skin on the inside of my arm. I ignored my pains and kept rubbing. Finally, my hands were free. Then my ankles. I righted the chair, pushed it back into place at the computer and sat down.

One of the keys opened the menu. Most of it was code-like abbreviations and half words. Mashing the down key, I made ready to pick, at random, a sample of David's correspondence. An unmarked file, noted only by a single dot, looked the most likely. I highlighted it and brought it up. Extended menu. Did I want to proceed?

You better damn well believe I wanna proceed.

I clicked Y for yes. I then down-keyed to the last of that list, my heart throbbing, stomach squeezed in anxiety. More code words, many of them merely numbers. The last one was the same single dot.

A demand flashed across the screen, PASSWORD NECESSARY FOR FILE DISCLOSURE. The cursor blipped at the beginning of a line where I was expected to type it in. *Shazam! What in the world would he use for a code word?*

Guessing wildly, I tried *Open Sesame.* The program didn't like it. Another message rolled across my vision - I was given thirty seconds to wise up or it was locking me out. A digital clock in the corner of the screen, counted the seconds off for me. I tried another - *Grey Ghost*. Another warning. Its wrath had been aroused. Twenty seconds left.

What would David have used? What did I know about him that most people wouldn't? What was that he said...?

In the last remaining seconds, I remembered our late night hours at the beach and giggling at him. We'd been discussing the upcoming Council meeting with the tribe's elders. Plied with a bottle of good wine, a warm woman, and lots of outdoor air, David had done a John Wayne impression - hilarious because it was so corny.

I had said, "Come sunrise, the Injuns'll be right in your lap, Partner." He'd replied with, "Well, Pilgrim. This is a man's job. And a man's gotta do what a man's gotta do." Strutting stiff-lipped and barrel-chested to my peals of laughter, he'd spun and holstered an imaginary pistol. "We'll wait till dark, then circle the wagons. Come first light, we'll pull out. You'd best stay with the horses, Ma'am. An don't you be a-forgettin' yer a lady." I sniffed...*we could have been...*

But for now, there wasn't time. Quickly, my computer clock running out, I typed in, *The Duke*. That was it. A new, smaller menu popped up. The last title said, 'Vegas.'

As the memos and notes filled the screen, I scanned them, noticing the dates began in May of last year. David had been looking for funding for a resort/hotel/casino. Someone by the name of Joseph Platt suggested a site in Reno and a few more west of there on the highway going into Bakersfield.

David had turned them all down - complaining they were too costly, too much red tape. On one letter he had angrily referred to the 'Vegas Mob', saying that they had all the decent spots tied up.

Here we go.

A memo said, 'I'm going north to Seattle.' Suddenly, before I could read it, an over-ride from God-knows-where, blipped, REQUEST TRANSMISSION.

I tapped Y for yes and waited. Joseph, taking it for granted he was communicating with David, sent a three page letter. I quickly pushed 'P' to print and watched while the high speed Epson chattered out the letter as quickly as it appeared. Good. A record of the whole thing. But it would take such a long while to print it all and a bit noisy. If anyone came into the house...

Suddenly inspired, I dialed the phone number at the Gazette. At his answer, I said, "Tom? Can you keep my PC line open? I'm sending some files over the modem."

"Kate? Are you all right? What's going on?"

"I'm not sure. See what you can make of it. I'll be back in a few hours."

Transmitting done, I closed the hidden files and went back to the main menu. At the 'help' command, I requested a fuller explanation of the titles. Learning that T-DR meant tunnel door, I brought it up, highlighted the box 'OPEN' and typed Y.

As the huge hatch swung inward, I ripped the Vegas letter off the printer and stuffed it in my pants pocket. Exiting out of the program so they couldn't be sure of what I had found or what I knew, I turned everything off and headed out the tunnel door.

The command to open the door had also turned on some lights. Bent over, the sour taste of fear lodged in my throat, I ran.

CHAPTER EIGHTEEN

Popping up like a prairie dog from its lair, I emerged from the tunnel. Dirt and gravel peppered my face and clung to my hair and clothes. It didn't matter. Breathing deeply and gratefully of the salty-fresh sea air, I clambered out onto the beach.

The incoming tide had crept almost up to the cliff wall and there was little space to walk in. The small boat we'd come in was afloat in the surf, knocking woodenly against the big rock it was tied to.

Time to go home. I had to find the twins. Hopefully, Margaret had gone in the other direction where her boat would have been tied. Had she seen Cerese, there could have been a big stink about her coming home. "Camille? Cerese? Where are you? Come on. Let's get out of here." Beyond the small inlet, somewhere amongst a pile of boulders, I heard but couldn't see them. Breathing a sigh of relief, I called, "Hey. Camille. Cerese. Let's go."

Damn. I know they heard me.

Picking my way around the cliff and over the driftwood, I vowed to wring their scrawny necks for not coming when called. After fifty feet or so, I stopped again and hollered, "Camille? What are you doing? Would you just come and get in the boat?"

Finally, I rounded the sandy inlet. Here, I could walk without fear of breaking a leg. The girls were just ahead.

They were sobbing.

Now what? Maybe Margaret did find them. Or maybe one of them is hurt. If I ever get out of this place, I will never...never, never, never...come back. Their backs were to me as I approached. "Hey. Camille? Cerese! Talk to me. What's the matter? Can't you at least answer me?" They still didn't budge. Didn't look up. "Hey. What's the deal, here? Really, girls. If this is the way you're going to behave... Hey. I'm talking to you. Why are you bending over like that... Oh, no. OH, NO. Oh. I'm so...terribly sorry."

With a long, heart-rending sigh, Camille wiped her nose. The pitiful look she gave me turned my knees to mush. She was kneeling on the edge of shore, shivering, a wave of cold salt water sloshing around her mid-thigh.

Cerese sat cross-legged in the sand. I didn't want to look. But I had to. As I dropped down beside her, she began to cry and wail.

Clamped to her bosom, was the dead and bloated body of their father. He'd been husky at one time. No more than 5 foot 9, his broad shoulders and sturdy frame had packed an extra 60 pounds, probably fairly well.

I noticed he'd needed a hair cut and his fingernails trimmed, before I looked away.

Curiosity is a strange thing. A traffic accident happens - maimed bodies await the approach of a screaming ambulance. And though the patrolmen wave us on, keeping the stream of cars moving, clearing the road for the medics, we feel compelled to stop.

Fighting back the nausea and a stabbing impulse to bolt back to civilization, I gripped Camille's shoulder. "I'm sorry, kids." I couldn't even let them grieve where they'd found him. "You can't stay here. We've got to get back. The authorities can...uh...take care of him."

Cerese stared, red-eyed and wild. "You want us to leave him here?" She started shaking. "Is that it? We're supposed to leave him here?"

Her interest perked by the verbal exchange, Camille's sobbing reduced to a snuffle. Nodding emotionally, first at her sister and then at me, she hunched down, protectively, over the dead body. "No, Kate. Cerese's right. I, uh, we can't just leave him here." She straightened his wet polo shirt and flicked at a tiny crab scuttling through the matted belly hair. She started crying again. "It's him, Kathleen. It's Daddy. We can't just leave...."

The ride back was grim. The greenish-grey body lay crosswise on the bottom of the boat, between the two girls. I steeled myself, my face turned into the breeze - away from the stench. The outboard motor under my grip drowned out most of their wailing as I went through the arduous motions of getting us back to the house, vomiting every now and then over the side.

It was cold, wet, and getting dark. Navigating through each channel and around each point, I passed one landmark after another, grateful that I'd found it, scared to death I wouldn't see the next. Camille was very little help mostly because I didn't have the heart to ask her.

Somehow, we reached the pier. Hampton saw us come in and helped to get the body and the girls into the house. We laid it on the bed and left the twins there, talking softly between sobs. Hampton came out to the kitchen where I sat drinking coffee. "Kathleen," he said. "Please, this is difficult for all of us. I know you want me to butt out of your investigation. But this has gone too far. Your life is in danger, not to mention these two girls..."

"I can look out for myself, Hampton."

"I'm sure you can. But Kathleen...I'm your friend. I'm on your side. Really."

I pierced him with my best stare. "If you were on my side, you wouldn't be doing business with that man. If you're that set on building a casino, for Christsakes Hampton, find another broker."

"I take it, you mean Abrahamson. Do you know for sure, that he was involved in Cloud's death?"

"I think he was, yes."

"No guessing, Kathleen. Do you have proof? Or at least a theory to establish a reasonable conclusion of his motives?"

"No, I don't. Nothing good enough to bear the badgering of a good defense attorney."

"Then I implore you, to stop by my office. Please. We've got to talk about this."

I looked for some sign of insincerity in his eyes or his manner. I couldn't find any. "I'll try. Right now, I'm too worried about these kids." By the sound of Cerese's cries, she was almost hysterical.

His black eyes met mine, glare for glare. "As we all are, Kathleen. As we all are. Cloud and I grew up together. Our families have been friends for generations." He watched me for another minute, then said, "I will make the final arrangements. If you'll confine your investigation until after the tribe has had a chance to grieve, I'd be grateful."

"Of course. Hampton, I'm not here to make light of your position or take away your right to ferret out Cloud's murderer. But whether you believe me or not, someone is trying to kill me and possibly one or both of those girls. I can't just drop everything and go home. They could very well decide to follow me back to Seattle and finish me off in the streets. I'm sure you'd like to handle everything yourself and not let any 'white people' in on it. But you have to understand, I'm already in on it. A man is dead. His daughter came to me for help. And the culprit, as far as I can see, is another hated white man, living outside the jurisdiction of Indian law. I will not - let me repeat that - I will NOT abandon the case or Camille and Cerese now." That said, I turned to the sink and filled the coffee pot with water from the tap. Hampton closed the door quietly behind himself when he left.

Within hours, most of the tribal members had gathered at Camille's house. They had lost the chairman to their council and a long-time friend. Grief-stricken, they mourned him until the little house thundered from their groans. Then they spilled outside into the yard.

They gathered there, in small groups of three to five, which ultimately welded into a larger whole. They brought small drums, hand-made from cured elk-hide stretched over wooden frames - bearing symbolic paintings of salmon and eagles which glared unblinkingly, from their taut, leather surface. The tormented sound of their sorrow was enough to give me nightmares for a week, not to mention the drum-beating which seemed to be keeping time to the thump and stagger of a broken and bleeding heart.

Services were held at a little white church, next to the memorial for Chief Seattle. I felt I'd interrupted their lives enough and decided not to go. After the burial, some of them disbursed for their own homes, the others came back with the girls. For four days, small crowds gathered in and around the Cloud residence, including friends from neighboring tribes.

Hoping to find what clues I could, I mostly drove around Suquamish and Hansville, looking for those few who were willing to talk to me. Very few of them were. From what I could find out, Cloud had been as stalwart a citizen as they come. He didn't drink, he worked hard, and always paid his bills on time.

On the fifth day, the members of the tribe began to whisper. No longer could they afford pure, demonstrable grief. A single word winged from group to group, showing itself in the roll of an eye and the wring of a moist, nervous hand.

Killed.

The cause of his death was questioned by most of the tribe. He was an excellent swimmer, too strong to have drowned from a fall off the dock. Plus, the current would never have carried him in the direction of that island.

I would have loved to be able to go home. A scented bath, some clean pajamas and familiar surroundings would have started me on my own road to recovery. The tribal members obviously would have preferred to have one of their own look into it. But, I couldn't trust David to leave the girls alone and no one else believed how dangerous he really was.

At midnight, the girls and I were still huddled in the kitchen. Coffee gone cold, we said good-night and turned our tear-streaked faces toward bed. I sank wearily to the couch, the same one with the stifling puffs of dust where I'd battled it out with Frank.

For now, a few hours sleep. I had an idea I'd need it for tomorrow.

CHAPTER NINETEEN

A prodding couch spring gouged into my hip, awaking me early. I tiptoed outside, stretching my legs in a brisk walk. The fresh air felt good. Salt air was supposed to be healing. If that was true, both my body and my spirit could use a bundle.

Following the familiar path down to the beach, a bluejay scolded me from the top of a large spruce as the first rays of sunrise glinted from his strikingly colored feathers. Striding past the clubhouse where the pow-wow and my first introduction to the tribe had taken place - was that really less than a week ago? - a movement at the front door caught my eye.

Standing under the awning, a man flipped a cigarette butt into the gravel. His slim hips were encased in snug levis with the bottoms stuffed into high-topped cowboy boots. Seeing me, he squared his shoulders and faced me directly. Jutting his chin as if I were the one who was making him wait, he palmed the side of his temple - his light brown hair still wet from combing. Chewing the inside of my lip so he couldn't see me grin, I sauntered in his direction.

Thumbing at the front door, he said, "I hope you got a key to this joint. Where the hell is everybody, anyway?" His nose flared as he watched me approach.

I'd seen that same stance before, that same snotty attitude as if he were royalty and the rest of us bumbling peasants. "Bobby?" I asked. "Bobby Johansson, is that you?"

It took awhile. Nothing, not even the recognition of an old girlfriend, could travel quickly the sluggish depths of a head that thick. "Kathy? Well. For crying out loud. Kathleen...uh..."

"O'Shaunessey."

"That's it," he squealed, as if happy that I, myself, had remembered. "Where the hell you been, girl? It's been ages since..."

"...since the Senior High School prom," I interjected. *If he thinks I've forgotten what he did, even after these ten years, he's got another think coming.* I wanted to ask if those silly boots had ever seen the business end of a horse, but I decided to be nice.

"Lordy, Lordy. Would you just lookie here. It's good to see you, Kath. Damn good."

"Thanks. You look....pretty swell, yourself." Bobby and I had been 'an item' most of our high school years. At about half-way through the tenth grade and all of the eleventh and twelfth, I'd suffered his heavy panting in my ear and vows of his eternal love every Friday night and all of

98

football season. Finally, on the weekend before the last dance of our senior year and in the back seat of his Chevy Bel Air convertible, I relinquished my virginity - partly from curiosity, a good bit from my own exploding hormones, but mostly to shut him up.

He seemed to like what I gave him. Two hours into the prom, I found him looking for more. He was in the same car seat, drunk, pouring a can of coke and whiskey down the gullet of Irene Sundlund - a skinny, flat-chested freshman that everyone knew had never let a single boy get as far as first base.

Today, he was heavier, the heaviness that comes from lifting weights and gobbling steroids. He had a neck as wide as his jaw and biceps the size of a smokestack. I crossed my arms and said, "So, Bobby. What brings you here?"

"I got an appointment with that dude that's putting up the big hotel out here. Hey. That's right - you didn't know. I got my own business, Kath. Flooring. Carpets, tiles, linoleum, whatever you want to walk on, we got it."

"That dude... You mean, David Abrahamson?"

"That's right. You know him? Hell of a nice guy. All business. Professional."

"You might say that." I was happier to see Bobby than I would have wanted to admit. Sure, he'd been a royal pain that last year of high school and I was fit to be tied that night of the prom. But, boys will be boys and Bobby's weaknesses were at least familiar. And so were his strengths. The guy was too much of a meathead to be intimidated and he'd never backed down from a fight in his life.

I hooked my arm through his while he plopped a wet kiss on my forehead. "Bobby, before you go signing a contract with David, uh, Abrahamson, there's something you should know."

"Yeah? What's that?" With a finger under my chin, he raised my face up to the point of eye contact. "Hey, Kathy. You all right?"

"I'm fine," I snapped. Immediately sorry, I patted him affectionately, straightened my back, and met his gaze. I'd been leaning on his arm more than I realized. "Really, I am. I'm fine."

He pursed his lips in a poor imitation of me, and in a high, tinny squeak, he mimicked, "'I'm fine,' she says. She looks like shit, but the lady says she's fine." He peered at me, his light blue eyes wide, his eyebrows flying up to create a band of thirtyish wrinkles. "Kate, either the years have played hell with my best girl or there's something wrong. Some bad shit going down that you don't want to talk about." Gently smoothing my kinky hair back for a better view of my downcast face, he said, "Now, granted, it ain't any of my business and if you want me to butt out, it's just to say so." He paused, waiting. When I didn't answer he continued, "But, you don't grow up with somebody, crazy in love, without knowing something about them. About what makes them tick. And the old Katie I remember, would have died and gone to hell and back before she'd ever admit she had a problem bigger than she was, and she needed some help." He shoved my chin up again, forcing me to look squarely at him. "So, what's going on, here? Either tell me what it is or tell me I'm a stupid old poop that ought to get out of your life and stay out."

I had to giggle. There wasn't much else you could do with Bobby. "Why don't you come up to the house and we'll talk." I grasped his arm again as we walked along, rehashing some of the old times and catching up on some of the new gossip. Since Bobby had never left the old stomping grounds, he not only remembered more than I did, he had also seen the rest of our class grow up and enter the real world. He knew the girls that had formed our most popular clique, the same ones that somehow were appointed every year with the highest honors a high school class could produce - Homecoming Queen, class president, and the lead role for the play put on by our drama club, *Midsummer Nights' Dream*. I'd always wondered just exactly what their tactics were and if it had anything to do with their most obvious attributes - those very visible endowments kept snugly wrapped in tight sweaters and pencil skirts. They never failed to snub the rest of us unmercifully.

I asked Bobby, "Whatever happened to that witch Silvia? God, I hated her."

"Silvia Swenson? Ah, she turned out to be a real bow-wow. Got herself knocked up the first year out of school. Said it belonged to Donny MacInroy but he denied it. Went to her parents and everything, and swore on all that is holy, that he hadn't touched her since the Vikings district playoff with Silverdale in their junior year. Her mamma had fits to hear she'd been putting out. Boy, if Mamma Swenson only knew. Then word got out that Silvia'd been slinking off to that big dance hall in Bremerton, all the while lying to her parents and saying she was sleeping over with Angie Baker. Remember her? We used to call her Big Boobs Baker? Man, she'd do it with anybody. Well, come to find out, it was rumored that her and Silvia was caught with their pants down, and I mean that literal, necking with some sailors off one of them big airplane carriers."

By now, I was laughing hard enough to be in danger of wetting my pants. But I had hear the rest of it. "So, what happened?"

"Well, she spent the first year, sitting home with her baby, arguing with her daddy and getting fat. Then one day, she just up and takes off, leaving her kid there for her mamma to raise. Woren't gone more'n a couple a months and comes sniveling back. Broke, knocked up again, and with a bad drinking habit. Last I seen her, she was working part-time at the McDonalds, slinging burgers. Said she was getting her life straightened out pretty good, but you sure couldn't prove it by me."

We were approaching Camille's small house. I could see either her or her sister in the window. Outside, more mourners had gathered around an old pick-up, leaning or sitting on it, their stone faces pointedly turned away from me and my blond friend.

Hampton came out onto the porch from the kitchen. Deep in what looked like an intense conversation with a new man I hadn't seen before, Bobby and I were on the steps and ready to go in before he saw us.

"Morning, Kathleen," he said. He nodded to Bobby, "Hey there, Johansson. I see you two have met." He thrust out a calloused hand. "What brings you out here?" Bobby shook with him and also the other man. The new man was introduced as Sims, a carpenter and a contractor. I liked him. Taller than most of the other tribe I'd seen, his dark, longish hair was pulled back at the neck in a pony-tail and his fiercely etched cheekbones could be a portrait painter's dream. His eyes were lighter than usual, a surprisingly light golden brown, and there·was a keen, exciting presence about him.

Bobby said, "I'm out here for the same reason you are, Hampton. Looking to make an honest dollar." To Sims, Bobby said, "You bidding on the framing?"

Feeling the exhaustion of the last week, I slid past the two men towards the kitchen, commenting, "Looks like you're both out of luck."

They both swiveled and stared at me. "Why's that?" asked Sims.

"Well, because. It's been shut down."

Sims drew back and blinked. "The last I heard, the project was still on. Do you...have you heard something I haven't?"

Bobby laid a hand on my shoulder and nudged me to look at him, obviously wanting an explanation.

I answered both of them by saying, "Well, you know yourself what's happened. He's been shown to be a downright crook! Look what he did to these kids. To me. To your people, for crying out loud. I mean...really, Sims."

Sims interrupted. "Now, hold on there Kathleen. There's no proof whatsoever that David Abrahamson had anything at all to do with that. Looks to me like it was that other guy. Frank was his name."

Bobby was beside himself with curiosity. "What the hell? What's going on, Kath? Sims? What's this all about?"

"Not right now, Bobby. I'll explain later." Holding my arms stiff against my sides to keep them from shaking, I faced Sims and said, "You know damn well that, that cretin Frank would never be able to pull this stunt off by himself. I can't believe you're still going through with this project."

"Look, Kathleen whatever-your-name is, you came here to get a story. OK. You got it. Now, I highly suggest you go on back to where you belong and let the authorities take care of this." He made a reactionary gesture toward the road leading off the reservation.

Evidently, Bobby found the jerk of Sim's thumb, threatening. I felt him move up to stand beside and a little in front of me. "Careful there, Sims. This is a lady you're talking to and an old friend of mine. You might want to remember that."

"Hey, Bobby. I've got nothing but respect for Kathleen. She knows that. It just worries me, her digging into this Frank's shenanigans. She's already been hurt once. Next time, she might not be so lucky. Now, that Frank, that's one mean son-of-a-bitch. I'd testify to that, any day. But far as David Abrahamson being mixed up with him...? All I can do at this point is to take his word for it."

DEADLY DECEPTIONS

I felt a sick disappointment - not only in his attitude, but in my own inability to recognize character, or the lack thereof, when I saw it. Twice now, I'd been fooled - once with David and now again with Sims. *It won't happen again. Next time, I'll look - really LOOK - and even then I'll wait for awhile. Watch. Get to know them. Find evidence of their character and some back history, long before I begin to trust them.*

Staring at him, trying to keep my voice and my anger under control, I said, "That's a damn lie. You heard what he did, here in this very same house, and I'm sure you've also seen the police report."

Hampton had been strangely quiet. I turned on him now, with the unthinking ferocity that exhaustion can produce. "Tell him, Hampton. You were there. These men are wanted by the law."

He shook his head. "There's no warrant. He's wanted for questioning. That's all." He paused, stroking his double-chinned neck. "Without going into a lot of legal jargon, the best I can tell you is that it's still his word against yours. And until we get some kind of proof, something besides a biased statement from an emotional, inexperienced woman known to be his ex-lover, then it's business as usual."

I was flabbergasted. "Ex-lover? Is that what he's telling everyone? No wonder no one will listen to me. It's a lie, Hampton. A damn, dirty lie."

"Kathleen," Hampton said. "Don't you see? It doesn't matter. It won't keep you from getting hurt. Now, I'll plead with you once more. Let the authorities handle it."

Beside me, Bobby had bristled at his comments. But, I had to hand it to him. He didn't back off or interrupt. Then, with a nodded goodbye to the both of us, Hampton went down the steps to his car. Sims also left, striding across the porch in a single long-legged step and past the scowling group hanging around the pick-up. One of the men lounging against the back wheel, seemed to thumb a signal at Sims as he marched by - the barest of movements and noticeable only because he wore a heavy gold ring on that hand.

I found it, never the less, infuriating. I walked, as confidently as I could, in his direction. The huddled group had been muttering between themselves. As I flounced within earshot, the discussion stopped. The men were reduced to scratching their toes in the dirt or staring at a blank sky.

Addressing the one with the ring, I said, "Evidently, this development deal is going through, like it or not."

No answer.

"Is that true?"

Nothing.

"For crying out loud," I howled, thrusting a finger theatrically toward the house, "The father of these girls, DIED for what he believed in. That this land, the home of his father - YOUR forefathers - should remain unspoiled. You can't ignore that. Not now!"

The bunching of muscles at his jaw didn't prepare me for his seething reply. "Only thing around here we're ignoring, or at least trying to, is you. You been told and told again, woman. Go home. You don't belong

102

here. You got no business telling us about our own people and our land."

Taken aback, my hands flopped at my sides. I was still an outsider. Glancing at the other faces and seeing the same steely, black-eyed wall, I stomped back to the porch and into the kitchen.

I grudgingly permitted Bobby's hand on my shoulder. He meant well, thinking he had kept them from hurting me. But, it was my problem and I soon shrugged him away.

Camille had been at the window, wringing her hands. Her face was bloated and streaked from crying. A stab of guilt swept through me, wobbling my knees. I plopped down on a chair next to her. "You okay, hon? Don't worry about those apes out there. Come over and sit down. I want you to meet Bobby. He's an old friend of mine from High School."

Flushing to her roots, Camille perched primly on the edge of her chair, and said to her lap, "Nice to meet you."

"Hey, Camille. I guess you're the one who found her twin sister, huh? Ain't that something'? After all these years. Right out of the blue, too. Somebody comes up and says, 'Hi. I'm your twin sister'." Slapping his thigh soundly, Bobby shook his head in awe.

Camille's mouth twisted in a wry little smile, obviously thinking that Bobby's performance was meant to be entertaining. I was glad to see her tears dry as she watched to see what foolish thing he might say next. As for myself, I'd known Bobby a long time, and I would have bet good money he was sincere. Any time Bobby actually tried to be funny, he came off so corny he was nauseating.

But, Bobby being Bobby, couldn't let it rest. "I hear your Daddy kicked the bucket awhile back. Sorry to hear it. He wasn't a bad ole boy. Should'a told you about your sister, though. Instead of letting you find out like you did. Don't seem right to me."

"Bobby," I said, "Would you put a sock in it? She doesn't need this right now."

"Well, you know as well as I do, Kath. It ain't right."

"He didn't do it!" I howled. "We don't know who did, but it wasn't Mr. Cloud who separated those twins and we don't know why he didn't tell Camille or if he even knew. Now, will you please shut up?"

Sobbing anew, Camille ducked her head in her hands and in a squeaky little wail, she said, "Don't be mad at Bobby. It doesn't even matter anymore. Cerese's gone. She must have left sometime last night."

Still snorting and breathing fire at Bobby, I was secretly thinking through the possibilities surrounding the abduction of that baby. Camille's choking cries startled me.

She was saying, "It must have been a really awful homecoming. I mean, finding Da...uh," This was hard for her to say. "...finding Daddy dead and everything. Oh, Kathleen. I'm so scared."

I reached for her. "Hey, there," I crooned. It was awkward at first since we were both sitting down. I ended up scooting her chair over next to mine, the groaning screech of its wooden legs scraping against the old linoleum floor and sending shivers of ache through my teeth.

I patted her back, saying, "She'll be back. Don't worry. She has a history of running away. Poor kid. It's the only way she knows how to handle this kind of stress." I patted some more. "She'll be back. After things have cooled off a little." Hearing her snuffle wetly on my blouse, I looked around wildly for a kleenex.

Bobby grinned brightly and produced a huge white hanky from his back pocket. "But," she wailed, "you don't understand. I guess I should have told you right away but I was too scared. Those men, the ones who came after Daddy...they came by while I was still on the phone with you, and...," trembling hysterically, she spoke in little pinched squeaks. "...Kathleen, they said if I didn't keep my mouth shut, and told anybody, anybody at all, that...that I was gonna be next." With that, she tore into her bedroom and slammed the door.

I gave her a moment, then knocked quietly. "Camille, honey. Who was it? Please. Tell me their names. I'll call the Tribal Police and we can have them locked up immediately."

"No! Didn't you hear me? I don't dare. They're coming, Kathleen. I know they are. I don't dare tell anyone. Not even you."

I looked at Bobby. He was gaping dumbstruck in the direction Camille had flown - obviously without a clue as to the handling of hysterical females.

Not tell anyone? Good Christ, we're telling the world. Surely, Tom would have a follow-up article on the front page describing how he'd found me, his friend and co-worker, and my version of the rape. Huge waves of guilt washed over me as I considered my next move. There was no more room for mistakes. I checked my watch for the time. The copy boys would already have the lay-out ready. Blaring headlines would be rolling through the press within the hour.

Quickly, I snatched the wall phone off its hook and punched out a number. "Tom? I want you to stop the story."

His baritone boomed through the phone lines. "What? Kathy, I can't do that. Gunner'll serve up my arse like a spit-broiled lamb." Holding the receiver away from my ear, I tapped my foot, waiting for his complaints to peter out.

"I'll explain when I get there. Just don't let them print that story."

"But, Kath! The deadline was hours ago. How can I stop it, now?"

"I don't know! Sit on them, tell them it's all lies, break something...whatever, Tom. I'm counting on you. Enough people have died." I hung up in the midst of his sputtering demands to be told who had threatened me and turned to Bobby.

"You're going to have to stay here with the kid. Don't let her out and don't let anyone in, other than her sister." I scratched the number of the Gazette on a napkin. "Call that if something comes up. If I'm not there, ask for Tom. And whatever you do, don't leave Camille alone." Gathering up my purse and jacket, I grumbled as I went out the door, "And watch what you say to people. The Indians here have been hurt enough."

CHAPTER TWENTY

I started my old Porsche. Gravel flew and peppered the car's under-belly as I spun backwards in a half-circle and geared into low. The huge engine roared with life as I barrelled through the tight turns, streaking past large farms and dairies. The smell of gooey barnyards with cows mucked up to their knees wafted into my car windows.

At the southern tip of the Hood Canal I swung up to a take-out window and ordered a box of Kentucky Fried and a large coke. Alternately gulping and munching with one hand, I cruised into Seattle, past Airport Way and exited off I-5 at Meridian. At the entrance to the Gazette's underground garage on Spring Street, I jounced over the hump of sidewalk in the rush, scraped the car's tailpipe on the cement, and cursed.

Inside, I spotted the only empty parking place on the floor. The executive editor was gone, leaving his prime spot awaiting his return. I swung into it, cut the engine, and dashed for the elevator.

The doors opened with a whisper on the tenth floor. I whisked down the hall and through the swinging glass doors of the editorial room. With a secret wink to the receptionist, I kept my rolling gait all the way to my desk. Tom, having eyeballed my grand entrance, seesawed his way through the maize of clacking typewriters, humming computers, and buzzing phones. "Wait just a minute, young lady," he grumbled. I hurried into my own cubicle, flopped in my desk chair and watched him approach. If they had to rag on me, they'd have to do it on my turf.

Huffing and panting, his belly set a-quiver from the mild exertion, Tom leaned on the chin-high partition that boxed off my space from the rest of the horde. "Give, Kathleen," he wheezed. "And it better be good. My butt is on the block over this."

"So let them take a hunk. You can afford it."

Tom went livid, his face flushing to a bright purple. He sputtered angrily, "Is that the best you've got? If so, you're gonna be in some deep shit pretty soon and you're gonna be in it alone."

Quickly, I said, "You're right. I'm sorry Tom. I didn't mean that. Really. I am sorry." Dragging in a chair from the adjoining cubicle, I gestured grandly, "Here. Sit down." I breathed deeply and squared off, facing my indignant friend. "It's getting scary, Tom. They found Mr. Cloud. Drowned. His body washed up on that same island I called you from. Which reminds me," I swung to the computer screen and switched it on. "Did all those files I sent get here?"

He nodded, "Yeah, they're here. They don't tell us a whole lot we didn't all ready know. This dude Abrahamson was looking for a site to build a casino either in or near Vegas. Someone else had all the buildable locations tied up. He makes a play for Washington reservation land and hires a couple of muscle-heads to do his dirty work. The rest is history." He folded his short arms across his chest and scowled. "It's your turn. We scratched a perfectly good story. Front page. We want a better one."

Out of the corner of my eye, I'd been watching for Gunner.

He was coming.

Towering at least a head over everyone else, his adams apple bobbing furiously, the editor forged around the other desks in his funny, goosestepping stride. He came to a stop on the other side of the half-wall of my cubicle behind Tom.

In times past Gunner had reminded me of an old Disney movie with Ichibod Crane and the Headless Horseman. Even now, with stress causing my emotions to blurt out in ways I didn't mean and my imagination to conjure up images I didn't need, I felt the twinge of a snicker tug the corner of my mouth. Gunner's baleful glare brought me back to the world of realistic and rude people. "Give," he demanded.

I answered, "The kids' dad is dead. Drowned. She thinks she's next."

"Homicide?"

"I think so. Can't prove it yet. I hope to."

He fingered his short, pointy beard. "Is there any substantial reason for this kid to believe that? Or is she just..."

Interrupting him, I said, "The strong arms that muscled her father out of his own home and ultimately delivered him to the briny deep, threatened her with the same treatment if she didn't keep her trap shut. She defied them by calling me, here at the paper, and trusted me to handle it. That includes keeping her out of their grimy clutches and getting her father back. Unscathed. On that point, I've failed." I thrummed my fingers for emphasis. "I don't intend to lose her too."

"What about the sister? Didn't she have a twin come breezing in? Separated at birth? Are you sure? It's all beginning to sound terribly handy."

"Sad, but true," I said. "But look at the facts, Gunner. Someone killed Mr. Cloud - the one voice against David's big money schemes. With him out of the way and Camille's twin sister set to fake a message from the spirit world, they had the tribe ready up for a multi-million dollar rip-off of their land. Who knows what else they have planned out there. Think about it. Free and open access to the Pacific Ocean and all that lies beyond. Drugs, shipped in by ships, boats, and barges. Money shipped out in the same manner. No law, since the tribal enforcement officers can't really touch them out there. A five-star hotel where the rich uppercrusts can stuff their snoots with powder without a worry. An absolute haven for criminal activity."

Gunner fumed for a moment, then said, "That doesn't excuse your actions on that story. You should have found out about this and reported it days ago. If you want to continue to be a reporter on this paper, I'll expect a more professional attitude and less hysterics." While I steamed with subdued rage, he turned to Tom and said, "Do you share her conclusions and her fears for those kids?"

Tom nodded, "Pretty close. There are some awesome possibilities out there. Let me work on it for awhile, and I'll get back to you in another hour or so."

"Do that," he growled. "And check with the local cops. Last time I heard, this protection business was their job. Not some frizzy blonde."

I gaped after him, aghast. "Frizzy blonde? That over-bearing, pompous, sexist son-of-a..."

Jabbing me back to my chair before I could clear the seat, Tom said, "Let it go, Kathy. You embarrassed him in the eyes of the board members and you cost him some money. Now, let it go." Tom sat like a fat toad, his bulged eyes watching me warily. I knew from experience it was his natural expression when deep in thought and resisted the impulse to goad him into a flying leap.

"So now what, Tom? If we had run that story, you know very well they'd be after that kid with a vengeance. She's practically an eyewitness." Smoothing my hair back as I talked, I realized it had bushed out in a kind of forty-inch afro as if in empathy with my frayed nerves. The ends were terribly dry. I drew a handful of hair to one side as I talked and with slightly shaking hands, fashioned a loose braid just under my right ear. "And if we don't print it, they'll figure we've chickened out and go after her anyway. Just to make sure she never squawks again." Flipping the braid to the hair back, I squeezed my hands between my knees and shivered. "And there's something else. The Sheriff hasn't returned a single phone call and my Mom doesn't seem to be home."

In the middle of a slow blink, Tom said, "Don't worry about them right now."

"But, you see..."

Tom interrupted by saying, "I've got an idea." He elbowed up to my desk and tapped a key on my computer keyboard, bringing up the files I'd sent over from David's office. "On one of these memos, this guy Joseph mentioned that since the free feed at the S & L's was all over, it didn't look likely that your pal here could suckle another loan guarantee out of Uncle Sam. He suggested some San Francisco company with a branch office in Seattle that might put up some private funds. Here it is. Capital Mortgage and Trust. I'll be damned. It's just two blocks over in the new First National Bank building. Top floor." I snatched my purse off the floor and hung its long strap on my shoulder. Tom asked, "Where're you going? Kate? Now, don't be running off half cocked."

"Just paying our new neighbors a friendly visit." I sidled past his huge bulk, saying, "This guy's mine, Tom. He owes me."

"I understand that. But keep the paper's name out of it." Seeing my teeth clench, Tom hurriedly added, "For your own good. If they know you're from the media, you'll run into one brick wall after another. Make up something. Something reasonable - a logical response to a business exchange."

"Hey. I'll take care of it, O.K?" Seeing him sulk, I said, "I can handle it, Tom. I'll get back to you, here." I flounced through the office and out the door before he could stop me.

I retrieved my car and backed out of the head editor's slot, just in time to let his midnight blue Lincoln pull in. I gunned the Porsche up the hill, passed under the freeway, and drove home.

The Queen Anne district had once been a stately area where the shipping magnates of the 1920's and 30's thrived. Towering over the bayside and the loading docks, the view at that time - unmarred from today's crowded slums - must have been phenomenal.

Northwest lumber had been plentiful then and easily barged to the mouth of the Pacific Ocean. From there, the entire west coast was made accessible as were the foreign markets. Some of that lumber went into building wonderful four-storied houses for these self-made millionaires. They also brought the best architectural geniuses of their day over from Europe and set them loose to design archetypes worthy of this new world.

My apartment building had been one of them at one time, long since quartered into individual living spaces. But it still retained the original portholes, captain's walk, and latticed windows. It was now trimmed in a sea-going blue against a background of plank walls painted, numerous times, in a creamy white.

I collected my mail from the metal boxes out front and opened the lobby door with my key. The small elevator door gaped open, a scarred kitchen chair braced against the automatic closure. Written on the sheet of paper covering the up-button, were the words, *out of order*.

Sighing, I thundered up the three flights of stairs, stopping on each of the three landings to gather strength and collect my thoughts. Finally, with even more keys, I entered my three room pad and went directly to the bedroom - tossing clothes and shoes on the closet floor.

I was tired, sleepy and cranky. My canopied bed with its crisp sheets and downy comforter looked achingly inviting. Hair brush in hand, I traipsed naked to the bathroom to brush and wash my kinky mop under the bathtub faucet. I then I lit a few candles and sprinkled rose-scented oil beads in the fresh hot water that filled the tub. Finally, with my wet hair conditioned and wrapped in a towel-turban, I leaned back in a long-awaited soak.

Time to plan my attack on the mortgage company. How in the world would I ever pull this one off?

I've got to be convincing. Who do I know that'll vouch for me? No one's going to buy into any lies. Unless....

Dragging myself out of the warm, soothing water, I was just able to reach around the bathroom door to the hall phone without dripping, too much, on the carpet. I snatched the telephone off its nook and sat on the commode lid to dial an old number.

Up until a scant three months ago I had worked as an office manager in an up-and-coming law firm. I'd quit because the stress was too hard to leave behind when I went home at night.

Ha. Don't I wish....
The receptionist answered on the second ring. "Brady, Blankenship and Morehead Offices of Law. May I help you?"

"Hello, Samantha. This is Kathleen. Remember me?"

She remembered me all right. A few years ago, she'd been dating a guy by the name of Casey for some time and invited him to our office Christmas party. By midnight, the married couples and those who had someone to go home to had gone, leaving the serious drinkers and the singles to sort things out and sop up the last of the booze. She'd been blathering on for an hour, drunk as a skunk, with one of the other secretaries about the newest gossip making the office rounds and ignoring her date completely. He and I had struck up a conversation which developed into a friendship. Later on, we had started to date - ultimately, ending their relationship. She'd blamed it all on me, of course. And, I supposed, with some veracity.

On hearing my voice, her coolly polite tone dropped a couple decibels. She frostily admitted she did indeed, remember me and asked what could she do for me?

You mean besides dropping dead? Out loud I said, "I'd like to speak to Darrian."

She stated, in her snippy little way, that Darrian wasn't there. A fact which I had been counting on.

Darrian was a devout Roman Catholic and had been planning an extended trip to Seville and Barcelona, Spain for the World Expo and Summer Olympics. For the last year, he'd been giving long lectures about Spain and Catholicism to anyone not smart enough to have preplanned an escape route.

Pretending to be disappointed, I said, "Oh, darn it. He's got a book on Real Estate Law he said I could borrow." In my mind's eye, I could see Samantha's simpering gloat. "Oh well," I said, "I'll just come by and pick it up." I hung up the midst of her babble about not loaning things out.

Silly girl. She'll never learn.

CHAPTER TWENTY ONE

Dressed in my finest suit, a lightweight navy-blue wool set off by a seagoing-print scarf, I marched into the old office like I'd never left. Sam's pencil-thin eyebrows arched in an inverted V over her nose when I breezed in, all set to tell me all the things I couldn't do, since of course, I didn't work there anymore. Those same brows soon plummeted to a full-blown gape when I whisked past her desk, my chin jutted forward, my scarf fluttering daintily to the back.

The little twit actually thought I would ask her permission.

Over my shoulder I said, "Hi, Sam," as I continued my fast trek down the hall.

Leaping up from her desk, she came after me in a short, high-heeled trot, "You can't go in there," she yapped. "Stop. You can't go in there."

Luckily, Darrian's office door wasn't locked. Slamming the door wide, I marched to the shelves lining the wall to my right. I actually had used the book some months before as research on a difficult court case our firm was representing. The book was still where I had left it, next to an encyclopedia of contract law - Darrian's specialty. I took it down and thumbed through it, ignoring Sam's repeated squawk at my elbow.

"What's that?" she cried. "You can't take that out of here!" The papers she referred to were of that research, a rough draft sketched in pencil and folded as a marker to keep tract of that particular chapter.

The gods were with me that day. Just then, the phones began to ring. First line one's annoying bray and then line two. Assuming my old role as office manager and her immediate superior, I gazed down my nose as if I were three feet taller and said, "Aren't you going to answer that?"

Right on cue, she emitted an exasperated cry and spun on one dainty little toe to flee back to the front desk. I could hear her down the hall, her condescending twitter to an obviously irate customer. She'd probably forgotten to send him something.

Quickly, I grabbed a handful of office stationery and envelopes from the bottom cupboard. A rubber stamp toppled to the floor. My old notary seal. I stuffed it and the paper into my purse. Sam met me on the way out, yelping at my heels like a crazed terrier. Tightening my grip on the big book and on my purse, I bit back a snotty remark about a muzzle and forged by her to the outside door.

The law firm was on the same floor and just down the hall from Northwest Properties Title Company. I'd shared many an elevator ride and a lunch or two with the clerk who worked there. Knowing Sam could well have called the security guard, I ducked in the title company's double glass doors and leaned over their counter. "Hey, Bertha. Are you back there?"

Bertha's round, black face poked from behind a wall of dingy yellow files and smiled sweetly when she saw me. "Kathleen. Well. What on earth are you doing here?" She waddled out, every ounce of her extra 90 pounds jovial and jiggling, and asked, "How you gettin' along on that new job of yours?"

Circling the counter, I hugged her, comforted by her warmth. "I need your help, Bertha." Holding me at arms length, her big black eyes peered solemnly into mine. Waiting. I said, "I don't have time to explain, other than to say there's at least two lives at risk, not to mention my own. Two teenage girls are in trouble and they're counting on me to get them out of it." I took a deep breath, debating if I should tell her all of it. I then said, "Their dad was killed over a development project on the Suquamish reservation. He was the chairman and the only dissenting voice of the Tribal Council. With him gone, all that's left is his two twin girls. And I'm afraid they're next."

Bertha asked, "What do the police say?"

From the corner of my eye, I could see the elevator through the front windowed door. As I watched, the elevator doors slid open and a pair of uniformed guards emerged. Good ole Sam. They strode, as if with purpose and intent, past us and out of my field of vision towards the law firm.

With one arm still around Bertha, I calmly led her to the back of the room, saying as we walked, "Not much. Every time I've called, since making the original statement, the sheriff hasn't been there. And if he's returned my phone calls, I haven't been at the paper to receive them and he hasn't left any messages." Spying her old Remington typewriter, I pulled up a scarred wooden chair and began to roll a page of my former law firm stationery into it.

"What do you need, girl?"

"I need time, Bertha. Between you and this book," I said, holding it so she could read the cover, "...I've got to come up with some documents to hold the wolves at bay."

Fear flashed across her face, a fear that I could well understand. If caught being involved in this, she could loose her license and therefore kiss her job goodbye and the ability to care for and feed her four little kids at home. "Hey," I said. "I've got my old notary seal with me." I dug it out of my bag and held it up for her to see. "And some of my old letterheads. There's no way anyone could trace any illegal acts back to you or to this company. I'll do it myself. Just show me what I need and how to write it up."

She squared her rounding shoulders and said, "I didn't say I wouldn't help. Let me see what we've got here. There's an old plat map of North Kitsap County in the back." She went to the back of the room and came back carrying a tattered roll about four feet long. "You say it's out on Hood Canal?"

"It's called Hideaway Island, and part of the Suquamish reservation."

"Yes, here it is. The old treaty and covenants will be on microfilm, but I don't have them here. It's not our county. Hold on, let me call North Kitsap." She dialed a number from memory. "Carol? This is Bertha at the Seattle office. I need a covenants and restrictions on the reservation. See if you can find the original treaty and anything pertaining to Hideaway Island." Pause. "No. I need it faxed, ASAP. My client is here now." Hanging up the phone, Bertha looked at me, a mischievous glint in her eye. "She's not happy with your methods but she will send it."

"Thanks, Bertha. Now. Here's the fun part. I know for certain, that I saw some marshy ground on that island and a small pond. We're talking wetlands. Plus, the hill overlooking the pond is supposed to be some old burial grounds for the tribe. Couldn't I write up some kind of a stay to shut them down for a while?"

Line 3 on the phone lit up. Bertha answered it and took a quick message. When she was finished, she turned to me and said, "You could, but it wouldn't mean much without a court order." She rolled her eyes at my seal and stationery. "You'd have to find a judge to sign it and hope to God he wouldn't call for Darrian at the office and confirm." When I didn't answer that, she said, "Let's try it this way instead." In the back of the room, a machine moaned and advanced a sheet of paper to its holding tray. "Ok, here's the fax. Bingo. You've got it. When this Abrahamson character signed his lease, he would have had to promise not to disturb or touch or alter the hill, in anyway. It would have to be left undisturbed, in spiritual communion for the tribe. The pond and the marsh is another story. He would have had to apply to the Department of the Army Corp of Engineers for a permit. From there, a hundred different environmentalist agencies are made aware of his intentions. And if what you say about the existence of wetlands is true, there's no way his application would ever be approved and a permit issued."

"Well, I don't know about any permits, but they're bulldozing up there, right now. As we speak. Using the dirt from the hill to fill in the marsh. I saw them myself out of the bedroom window." To her questioning blink, I added, "David was out there with them. They work for him."

I peered over her shoulder, remembering the day that Camille had pointed out the hill above the pond to her sister as their tribe's old burial grounds. And that brought back some other, more painful memories. The day I'd first seen the island - David's formidable stance at the prow of a sailboat as it sliced through the choppy bay, the clean bite of a salty wind in my hair.... Drawing a jagged breath, I turned and stepped back so that my friend wouldn't hear me.

Bertha was pawing through the other papers, and frowning. "This is strange," she said. "If there's that much marsh there, why is there no environmental statement? It should be here, in fact the restrictions refer to an attachment D. But there is no attachment D. Hmmm."

"Bertha, don't tell me, you're suspecting foul play."

"Hold on. Let me call Carol back." Into the phone, Bertha said, "Carol? Would you look and see if there's not more to this file? Say, an environmental study for wetlands? And there should be something there from the BIA about the burial grounds." Pause, Bertha frowning at the receiver. When she hung up, she looked at me, doubtfully, and said, "I don't understand it, but she swears that's it." Chewing her bottom lip, Bertha stared at the faxed copy.

"Bertha," I asked. "What's wrong? What did Carol say?"

"OH, nothing. Just that...she agreed. There is reference to a restriction, but it's...just...missing." Still chewing, Bertha went over and over her papers. "There was something else she said." Bertha carefully spread her pudgy hand over the faxed papers, choosing her words to me very carefully. "She said the reason she was able to get these papers back to me so fast was that the microfilm was lying right there on the counter. Right on top of her 'in box.'" Bertha stared at me. "That property's getting awfully popular. Someone had been looking at it while she was out to lunch."

"Ask her if one of the other gals had looked it up and possibly mislaid it. Bertha.....It's got to be there, somewhere."

"That's just it, Kathleen. She's the only one there. Her clerk just quit a couple weeks ago. I remember her telling me about it. One day she just never came in to work. About five days later, Carol got a postcard. The girl said she was sorry about leaving that way but didn't give any reason for it. Just gave her an address for her last paycheck."

"An address? Bertha, this is important. Did she say where that address was?"

"Sure. How could you forget it. It was the same place I saw on T.V. the other night. You know, that big hotel - the Imperial Palace. That new one in Las Vegas."

"Oh, God. And it could take forever to push a new statement out of the federal office. Especially if they get it tied up in the courts. They and their high-priced attorneys. Damn, they're cagey. Well, that's it, Bertha. I'm too late. If I approach these Capital Mortgage people now, they'll know that we know that it should be there and it's not. It would give them that much more time to get ready." I jerked the stationary out of the old typewriter, crumpled it, and chucked it in the wastebasket.

"If they have the unmitigated gall," I said, snatching the notary seal off the desk and shaking it at Bertha like a misshapen finger, "....to buy off that clerk and swipe some of that microfilm, they won't mind at all any new investigations to see if they did, indeed, apply to the Army Corp of Engineers for a wetlands permit." I made ready to fling it in the same direction as the stationary then changed my mind and stuffed it into my purse. "And then they'll have one court hearing after another to see if this particular Indian nation will have to follow those guidelines. You see what they're doing? It puts everything off long enough for them to finance it. They can wipe out that marsh with a bulldozer and no one will be the wiser. Just scrape some gravel off that hill, fill up the pond, and we'll play hell trying to prove it."

Reaching into my pocketbook, I retrieved a business card. I then snatched the phone off the desk and dialed the number on it. Mike

Hampton answered on the third ring. I said, "This is Kathleen. Will you be around for awhile? I've got to talk to you."

He agreed and said, "Do you remember the park down by the bay? I'll be in my car, in the graveled area lot of that park in half an hour."

I had Bertha check the outside hallway for the security guards while I watched from behind her counter and through the large windows. She also thumbed the up-arrow for the elevator. As I stepped inside it and just before the doors closed, she said, "Be careful, Kathleen. These guys are slick. There's something...almost mafioso about them."

CHAPTER TWENTY TWO

It took all of that half hour to get there. At the entrance, I down-shifted the old red bomb into second gear, enjoying its rumble and grumble as we lagged down the side of the steep park hill. The tires slid sideways in the gravel as I parked alongside Hampton's car, a late model Chrysler. He was alone.

Small waves swished around the pilings of the old dock and slapped at the rocks of the shoreline. Looking out over the bay, the wet sky seemed to sag, depressed and heavy, over the water. As I walked around to the Chrysler's passenger side, I breathed deeply. I wasn't sure if it was the air or the activity, but I was starting to feel better. Inside, I still hurt. But I'd get over it.

I would survive.

I climbed into Hampton's front seat and slammed the door. There wasn't time for small talk. "Mike - I can't stall anymore. The paper is breathing down the back of my neck and I've got to get them a story. Now, you have all the legal means at your disposal and I don't. And I understand your tribe's need for the income from the casinos. But, I also believe you're as concerned about what is going on, and the lives of these kids, as I am. Probably more. So, before I run this, I'll need to know where you stand. Let me warn you. Don't say anything you don't want to see in print."

Leaning back, Hampton rested his arms on the steering wheel. "You know, Kathleen, I can remember something my grandmother used to say. Probably heard it a hundred times. 'Let every step upon this earth be as a prayer.' Do you understand?"

I nodded.

He watched a hawk circle lazily overhead until it was chased and run off by a pair of crows. Then he turned to me and said, "This land is our essence, Kathleen. Of course it can't be owned. By anyone. We belong to it. We're attached to it by our own history - our traditions. And up until the Boldt decision, we'd been through five generations of humiliating disempowerment. Our culture has been assaulted time and time again and we still must fight for the right to govern ourselves as a free nation." Great clouds of soft fog settled around the car as we huddled in our coats. Overhead, the mist clustered in the cedar branches and huge drops of water drummed on the roof of the car. "You know, when we gave the government our land they made some promises, too. For one, they promised they wouldn't take away our heritage - which includes the way we eat. And what happened? The state absolved our

115

hunting and fishing rights, in direct opposition to our treaty. They continued to turn a blind eye upon this violation for eighty years. Then what did they do? They promised this little piece of land, commonly called a reservation, was ours. Forever. To do with as we pleased and within those borders we could govern ourselves as we've always done. The treaty is in the Library of Congress. Send for a copy sometime, and read it."

"What's that got to do with the Cloud kids?"

"I'm getting to that." Hampton loosened his tie and unbuttoned his shirt collar. "So. Finally, we won a few cases and were able to set up a few government services but not nearly enough to staunch the flow from the wounds we'd received."

A few large rain drops plopped on the dusty windshield like small toads. Hampton paused as if trying to decide just how much to tell me. "Let me start from the beginning," he said, taking out a cotton handkerchief and wiping the condensation off the inside of the glass. "When my grandparents were small, the government decided, in all its wisdom, that our children would go to their schools. Learn to be REAL Americans. Work. Be productive."

"So, how did they do it? They came out to the reservations, telling us that we're not fit to raise our own children. They put them in trucks and buses and took them to a boarding school. There they kept them, a thousand miles from home. The children were forced to learn the white man's language and beaten every time they spoke Indian. They were taught to be ashamed of their parents and grandparents."

I gaped, unabashedly. "They could do that? Just take their babies? How?"

He seemed tired. Resigned. Touching his forehead, Hampton said, "Yes. The white people decided they had the right to take our children away from us."

"Is that what happened to the Cloud twins?"

"Something like that. In the 1960s, more laws were passed. We gained a few rights, but the situation was still deplorable. Then, in order for a child born of an Indian mother to be taken by the child protective services, due cause had to be shown as to why the child could not be cared for in their own home. But, once that was determined by the state, the child became a ward of the state. Right there in the hospital, as soon as they were old enough, say two or three days old, the Welfare could send in a social worker to simply take them. With no prior knowledge of the mother, or habits - other than maybe some hearsay. Whether or not she had a home or even drank, she was many times labeled an alcoholic and her babies were removed. To be raised in foster homes, not even of a Native American culture."

I gasped. "Why didn't the parents sue? Take the state to court and make them prove it? For crying out loud, they should have first rights to their own children."

"The parents had no recourse. No rights to a hearing or to an appeal. And since the records they kept were sadly inadequate, and what court files they had were sealed, we couldn't even find out where the child went. We never had a chance."

"So that's...", I ventured....

Hampton nodded. "When Mrs. Cloud went into labor, the attending women, your term would be a midwife, thought there was something wrong. The first baby was sideways in the womb. Breech. Wouldn't come out. She insisted that the father take her to the county hospital. Well, as it turned out, by the time he got her there she'd been in labor too long and had lost too much blood. She went into shock and from there, into a coma. She never came out of it."

By now, the mist had thickened to a light pattering rain. The larger drops streaked down the car windows and hood, making teary paths in the dust. Hampton was visibly shaken. "The doctor performed an emergency caesarean section to save the babies but one of them was small and had been severely stressed. She was placed in an incubator. The other one, the one they call Cerese, was taken by the state the next day and placed in a foster home. We've never been able to find any kind of a paper trail, so evidently, she stayed in that first home and grew up there."

Hampton wiped again, the inside of the windshield, as if he was still searching for her. "When Joe Cloud came back two days later as he'd been told to do, an over-zealous social worker had found out that they weren't legally married. They were according to tribal tradition, but the courts didn't recognize our customs. It was then that they told him his Indian wife had died and that one of the babies was gone. Without him even being notified. The smaller one, the breech, was still in an incubator. Joe went in and took the child out of the incubator to take her home. There was a scuffle - he had to push one nurse out of the way and break the lock on the door. Later on, they tried to stop him from keeping the child. And even tried to bring action to terminate his parental rights - what little he had. That nurse claimed assault and battery."

"But once Joe had his baby home, here on the reservation, the state couldn't find him. He hid out in a shack up on the meadow. I guess his father had built it as a honeymoon cottage and Joe was born there. Since then, it's always been a kind of special place for the family. Before the mother died, she grew a few vegetables there...something about some wild onions."

He rubbed the back of his neck and cracked the side window. "I was struggling to get through law school at the time and hadn't passed my state boards yet. But our professor was a just man and helped me prepare and file the documents. When I talked to the social worker, she had the audacity to preach to me about getting the children off the reservation. 'So they can have a decent, Christian life,' she said. She claimed she knew some GOOD people."

Hampton's controlled exterior seemed to be wearing a little thin. He fidgeted with the dials on the dashboard, then rolled down the window and looked out. "The courts finally gave up. Through the years, we've tried to find out something about Cerese through the schools and doctor records. But, they'd also changed her last name and we had no idea in which county to look or even which state. We found some little Indian girls but we had no idea which one was his, and he had to prove parental rights before he'd be allowed to see her. I believe this particular foster parent did move her out of the state and it made matters almost impossible. At least, they were for us."

"I see. So, Joe Cloud did know about his other daughter.

"He knew. He also did everything he could to find her. Wouldn't you know it, they finally grew up enough to find each other."

DEADLY DECEPTIONS

CHAPTER TWENTY THREE

I drove the short distance back into town and over to the service station, just above Frank's motel room. It looked like Jack was just leaving. The lights were off, the *CLOSED* sign propped up in the window. He was leaned up against his pick-up, smoking a cigarette.

I pulled into his parking lot and rolled down my window. "Hey, Jack. How's it going?"

"Kathy. Good to see ya."

"Closing up a little late, aren't you?"

He blew out a cloud of smoke from a corner of his mouth, and said, "Been a long day."

Jack didn't look as dirty as he usually did. His nails had been cut and he wore a cowboy shirt and a pair of jeans - both old, but they were clean. I assumed he'd already washed up and left his coveralls in the station. He jerked a thumb at the cabin door. "Remember them folks you asked me about? Don't look like they'll be partying anymore for awhile."

"What makes you say that?"

"Reservation cops come and took that loud, foul-mouthed guy away. He shore don't mind what he says to anybody." Jack dropped his cigarette stub on the dust and ground with his shoe. "Did you ever see the pile of junk he drives? That old Buick? Oughtta be a law against having crates like that on the road." Wrinkling his nose, he said, "Just the smell of 'em would gag a maggot. He's gonna kill 'at kid one of these days. Bad business, them exhaust fumes."

Something in the back of my mind clicked and began to roll, like a cog sliding loose from its groove in a wheel. "What did you say?"

Jack blinked, pulling his chin in and eyeing me.

"No, really," I said. "You mentioned something about a kid and that old car?"

"Yeah," he said, and propped a foot up on his fender. "Hell of a way to treat a kid. You get a bad muffler like that, the fumes'll get sucked up inta the car. Carbon dioxide. You get too much of it, you're gone, Dude."

"I understand that. But the kid. What was it you said about a kid?"

"The way he treats him. Dragging him around by the hair like that. Making him ride in the trunk. There's a better way to discipline a kid than that."

My heart began to thump so loud I was sure Jack could hear it. "This guy has a kid in the trunk? What's the guy look like? Kinda swarthy, fat, stands about five foot six?"

119

Jack shrugged and nodded. "I guess you could say that."

It had to be Frank. And he's got Cerese. "When was this? How long ago did you see him with this kid?"

"Number of times. He hauled him outta the cabin again this morning and throws him in there. Kid was just a-kickin' and a-bawlin'."

The gears in my head were turning, the cog getting closer to the slot. *It could be Cerese.* "Him? You mean 'her', don't you? How old would you say the kid was? Would say she was a teenager? Did she look Indian?"

"Naw, that's not the one I was telling you about. This'n here's a boy. I've seen that girl too, with her Mamma. She pretty well comes and goes as she pleases. The kid he's so mean to, is a boy. Can't be more'n seven, maybe eight years old. Blond. Oughtta be a law against treating a kid like that."

The mechanism in my mind connected, locking onto an image I'd had that first day I'd seen Frank and his brood at the ferry. While Cerese had jumped out, running away from the car, Margaret had been holding onto a boy. He'd wiggled and tried to run away, and Frank slapped him.

Jack was shaking his head and repeating himself. "I'm telling you, it don't make sense that they haul the guy away, then leave the kid in that cabin. Mystery to me."

I geared the Porsche into reverse. Shouting over the sound of the engine, I said, "One more thing I wanted to ask. Last time we talked, you said there'd been a tall blond guy, also here with a kid. In a BMW. Was it this same teenage girl with him or was it this boy you just told me about?"

"Neither one. That other one was a kid all right, but more like a young man. Looked different from the others. Kinda like he was foreign 'er something'. Naw, that boy, that seven-year-old, that's the one he was mistreating. There outta be a law against treating a kid like that."

Migod. We keep this up, I'll have an orphanage. Out loud, I said, "There is a law against it, Jack. But we'll have to catch him at it, first." I then pulled out of the parking lot and into the street.

First things first. Driving past the entrance to the motel, I looked for the old Buick and didn't see it. There didn't seem to be anyone home. Although it was dark enough for lights to have been turned on, nothing showed in the windows. I parked my car about two blocks down in an alleyway behind a closed hardware store and followed the alley as far as the back door to the Blue Goose Tavern. I was in luck. The band was blasting out a loud, if not well-done version of *Rocky-Top* and covering any noises I could have made.

There was just enough light from the tavern's neon sign and side windows to make out Frank's Buick. Since Frank was in jail, Margaret must be having a night out on the town. The car was parked on a side street, facing the sizable yard of an old house. The house appeared to be vacant, with what looked like old sheets tacked up on the windows. The yard was overgrown with uncut grass and weeds. A hump in the middle of the yard, its weeds taller than the others, I took to be a long-neglected rock garden.

The Buick's doors were locked. Just to be sure, I thumped three times on the lid of the trunk, and called out, "Hello? Anyone in there?" No answer. The boy must have been taken to another location. I picked up a fist-sized rock from out of the garden and broke the side wing window, being careful to bash the glass all the way to the rubber molding. I then popped the lock and opened the car door to began a search of its rubbish-piled floors and glove compartment.

Within a few minutes, I found all I needed. A large manila envelope, hidden under a folded wool blanket on the back seat, held a wealth of letters, all addressed to the same mailbox in Suquamish. One of Frank's duties, evidently, was to pick up the mail. Quickly, I thumbed through them. Holding my breath, knowing my actions could well land me in jail too, I opened the envelope from the Federal building in Seattle. Bingo. David must have been waiting for this - his newly-issued passport, with a picture that included a young boy - a blond boy, said to be his son, about eight years old. Another letter, I saved to open later when I could study its contents thoroughly, was also addressed to David. It sported a return address of Capitol Mortgage, also from Seattle. The same mortgage company I'd tried to hold at bay with Bertha's help and my old notary seal.

I tucked the letters under my arm, then loped across the yard and back down the alley. Locking them in the trunk of the Porsche, I walked to the empty lot behind Frank and Margaret's cabin, to the same spot where I'd gone over the stone wall the first time.

The soggy sacks of grass clippings were still there. Holding my breath to keep from smelling the decaying crud, I took a little running jump up and over the sacks and flopped on the top of the wall. The blouse of my suit skirt had come up. Little pebbles, inlaid into the cement, ground into my belly. I adjusted it to keep from getting scraped and rolled off - landing on the inside of the yard with a thud.

I retraced my steps to the back door. Still no lights. I tiptoed to the window, listening intently. Nothing. The door handle rattled loosely within the old wood of its round hole - the lock had been turned but didn't catch. When Margaret left, she hadn't closed it hard enough. I nudged it, and the door creaked open.

Inside, the room reeked of stale cigarette smoke and beer. A jacket drooped off the back of a kitchen chair and a blanket was crumpled on the end of the couch. They'd be back. I searched most of the rooms, hating the feeling of invading someone else's privacy. I'd turned and was making ready to leave, when a thump came from the smaller bedroom.

I froze.

Not wanting to see, up close, their crumpled sheets, I had only peered around the corner of the doorway, without going in the room. Could someone be asleep? Cerese was long gone, Frank was in jail, and Margaret was partying in Franks absence at the Blue Goose. Only one left to be accounted for.

I listened, standing stock still and quiet. Another sound - not quite a sigh, but a simple discharging of air. Keeping myself ready to leap back and run, I peered into the room, creeping ever closer to the bed.

There he was.

Propped up on a cot alongside the bed, his pants caked with urine, his cheeks streaked with old tears, sat a little blond boy. I recognized his picture to be the same one as in David's new passport. At first, he cringed away from me, frightened. I put my finger to my lips, a sign to stay quiet, and winked.

He seemed to realize I wasn't there to hurt him. Still on guard, my head pivoted to the left and right, making sure the boy was alone. When I took the gag out of his mouth and untied the stringy scarf from his hands, he started crying. "Can I go home now? Please. Can't I go home?"

"Yes. Of course you can go home." I hugged him and felt his little body shake against me. "But first we have to get out of here. Can you walk all right?"

The boy and I snuck out the back door, his little hand firmly gripping mine, his blue eyes filled with fear. I didn't want to try for the back wall. With nothing to climb up on, I might never get us over the top and we could be cornered if Margaret came back early. We'd have to go out the front entrance. The boy and I followed the fence around to the driveway.

Once out on the street side, we started to run parallel with the rock wall towards the alley where I'd parked the Porsche. It was also in the direction of the Blue Goose Tavern. Up ahead, I could hear an old car turn the corner and chug down the street towards us.

The Buick.

With no place to hide, the car lights raked across the boy and I. I started running, pulling the little boy behind me. Panting hard and terrified beyond belief, he lost his footing fell. The kid must have been in shock - or possibly hyperventilating. He couldn't get up. I stopped, patted his round cheeks, and set him right on his feet. "Run. As fast as you can. Hurry!"

Margaret had seen us. She did a lumbering U-turn in the entrance to the motel cabins and pulled up behind us. "Where are you going with him," she screamed. "Get back here."

We started running again, the Buick coasting alongside. Another block and a half to my car. Suddenly, she screeched to a halt, the Buick's engine sputtered and died.

Margaret got out and started running after us. The boy was sobbing, couldn't keep his legs under him.

We'd never make it. I turned to face her, the boy behind me, stumbling and scrambling down the sidewalk. "Leave the kid alone, Margaret. He doesn't belong to you."

She outweighed me by a good sixty pounds. "Why don't you mind your own damn business and go home. You ain't wanted here."

Behind her, the steady barrage of noise from a well-tuned engine and some hyped-up carburetors pulled out of the service station and throttled down the hill. To keep her attention on me instead of the oncoming pick-up, I lowered my head like a fighting cock going in for the kill and screamed, "You can't just steal other people's kids, Margaret. He's not yours."

She screamed back, "Who said he's not mine? What's it to you?" She then elbowed me out of her way and made a lunge for the boy, hollering at him, "Billy! Come here. Get over here, with me."

The force of her heavy body slamming into my side, bowled me over. I landed on my left hip, the palm of my hand sliding in the dirt by the wall. Seeing her descend on him, the boy finally found his feet. As she started after him, he sprinted for all he was worth, down the sidewalk.

The souped-up truck rolled past me and stopped just ahead of Margaret. It was Jack from the gas station next door. I scrambled to my feet and came up behind her. Swinging my purse on its strap around my head, I bashed it into the side of her skull - dead center. She was dazed but she didn't go down. From his elevated seat, Jack reached over to the passenger side, rolled the window down, and stuck his head out. "What's goin' on?" The boy was still running and almost out of sight. Margaret blinked at Jack as if she had just recognized him, then started after the boy.

I swung my arm in their general direction and hollered at the mechanic, "Go after the kid." As he geared into low and accelerated down the hill, I beat feet in Margarets direction. Too far ahead. I'd never catch her. As a last ditch measure, I again swung my purse around my head, building up steam until I could hear its whistle. I then threw it as hard as I could. Bingo. It caught her right behind the ear.

She dropped like a stone in a pond. Jack's pick-up had disappeared around the corner. Keeping a watchful eye out for him and the boy, I wound my purse straps around Margaret's hands in place of a pair of handcuffs. There was no way to tie them off. With nothing to do but wait, I tugged my purse each time she moved, to keep a tension on the straps and prayed that Jack would get back before she woke up.

Margaret wasn't out for long. Within minutes, she was moaning and trying to get up. After scraping her face on the sidewalk several times, she seemed to better understand that her hands were tied. She rolled to her knees, and stared to the back and up at me. Feeling as if I had shackled myself to King Kong, I kept tugging on the purse straps and listening anxiously for the grind and shift of Jack's pick-up.

Finally, he roared up the street. The boy was in the front seat, next to Jack, his little face lost and forlorn but hopeful. His face changed to sheer terror when he saw Margaret. To him, she must have looked like death incarnate - her hair disheveled, her face bleeding from the scrape on the sidewalk, and screaming obscenities.

The pick-up stopped in front of us. Jack opened the door and got out - giving Margaret a full view across the front seat and over to the boy. He'd flattened himself against the far window.

She bellowed like a wild cow and lunged to her feet. I couldn't hold her. The purse straps jerked out of my hands. In a split second, she was in the pick-up and had her hand wrapped in the boy's shirt. He screamed and kicked at her.

Jack lunged for her, and missed. My heart was racing. The fury mounted in me, pumping adrenalin like water through a hose. I leapt on her back inside the pick-up cab, and yanked her hair - pulling her head back and causing her eyes to bulge. But she wouldn't let go of the child.

Jack was behind me, shouting encouragement to me, accusations at Margaret. With two struggling women and a boy in the front seat, there wasn't much else he could do.

Some tools had been stored behind the front seat. The overhead light glinted off the edge of a large wrench. I dove after it, brought it up, and swung - catching Margaret on her right shoulder.

It slowed her down but didn't stop her. With that arm dangling helplessly, she grasped the boy with her left hand and started backing them both out of the pick-up. I swung again at the back of her head, missing her entirely. The wrench bounced off the inside of the pick-up door.

Finally, Jack ran around to the other door of the cab and tore it open. He dove for the boy - when Margaret wouldn't let go, he popped her full-face and bloodied her nose. She still clung to him, crying, "Billy! Come to me, baby." Wedging my right leg up, I found enough clearance on my side for a good kick and the corner of my two-inch heel ground into a knuckle - forcing her to let go of the boy. The boy leapt into Jack's arms. Ignoring her own pain and blood, she in turn socked Jack in the jaw and grabbed the kid back. Holding Billy tightly to her bosom, she began a stumbling run toward the Buick.

By now, they were a good five feet away. I took careful aim, lost it when Jack moved across my vision running after her. As she turned with an elbow into Jack's belly, I aimed again, throwing the wrench sideways like a boomerang. This time, it hit her broadside on the temple. She moaned and crumpled to the ground.

CHAPTER TWENTY FOUR

Jack helped me tie and toss her into his truck bed and drove to the reservation police station. The officer behind the counter was Highbear - the same one who'd come to Camille's house after I'd been beaten. This time, I told him everything I knew, leaving nothing out including my theories on David and where the boy fit into the scheme of things.

With Margaret trundled away and out of sight, the boy stopped shaking long enough to tell us where he lived. He'd been picked up, coming home from the playground, in Sacramento. Deputy Highbear immediately called the California State police. Sure enough, a boy by his description had been missing for more than a month. Arrangements were made for the parents to fly up and identify him.

Margaret cried openly as she strained for her last glimpse of Billie's blond head, ducking into the Tribal Police van. Betty Hampton had offered to take the boy in for the night, feed him, clean him up, and let him talk to his mother on the phone.

Highbear agreed to let me sit in on Margaret's first session of questioning. There was no other woman present and she'd refused her rights to an attorney. Margaret was sullen, distrusting, and distraught. "I kinda got attached to the boy, see," she said, blowing her nose on a kleenex. "Never had any of my own. But I did not steal that boy. I ain't even been to California. I was living in Montana. On the southside of Bozeman, to be exact. Friend of mine told he'd been abandoned and they were looking for someone to keep him. That's all. I'm a babysitter. A professional babysitter."

"And the name of that friend?" Highbear glanced up from his note-taking to study her face while she rambled on with her declaration of innocence. When she finally sputtered to an end, he asked her again. "Ma'am, I have to have the name of your friend."

"Friend? Why do you need her name? She was just my neighbor there, in the apartments. Everyone called her Sheila. I'm not sure of the last name. Said she'd seen an ad in the paper, somebody needed a babysitter. I answered it, and here I am. With all this work going on, you know, construction and everything, I thought I'd open a day care center."

"And your friend Sheila's last name?"

"Uh, I'm not sure. She claimed to be married to this fella she was living with, but I didn't believe it. He was milking cows at one of the dairy farms, let's see, I think his name was Hastings."

Too pat. I was sure Margaret was lying. It would have meant that Cerese's appearance in Suquamish was purely accidental and was also totally contrary to what I knew about Frank. Highbear's expression - bright yet unreadable, gave no sign of whether he believed her or not.

My skepticism must have shown. With a sniff, Margaret glared at me and folded her muscular arms at her bosum. "Frank and me had been dating for some time. When he found out Cerese was born in this area, he did some checking and found out she had blood ties to the tribe. A sister and her natural-born father was still alive. It was that, mostly, what got me the job. Frank was working on and off as a security guard and put in a good word for me. I kinda helped with the security checks, but the babysitting has always been my best business."

I was determined to blow the lid off her lies. "And your little scheme to have Cerese sit in on Camille's seat at the council? What about that? And the conk on the head in that tunnel. I suppose that was also a coincidence? You just happened to be hefting a big wrench and it unfortunately fell on my head, maybe?"

"You was trespassing! Frank got picked up, and I asked for some of his security-guard hours. We needed the money. As for Cerese's little part, Abrahamson said they wouldn't hurt her any. Said she was just supposed to sit there and pretend she was her sister. Not too nice, maybe, but no law against it. Just take an hour or so of talking and there'd be a bonus in it for us. A big bonus. Enough to get us into a nice place and start the paperwork for proving Cerese was a member of this tribe. Get her started in a decent school."

"You contributed to my abduction that night in your cabin."

"I did not. You'll remember, that I argued with Frank. Told him I wanted no part of it and that he should let you go. Besides, you were trespassing again."

Exasperated now, to the hilt, I handed her back to Highbear. He continued his line of questions. "Do you remember the name of the person or persons who asked you to babysit? And do you know if that person would be the same one who abducted this child from the playground in Sacremento?"

"Well of course I remember. I've just been telling ya how it was. Could I do all that if I didn't remember?"

"The name, Ma'am. Can you tell us this person's name?"

"Of course I can. His name is David Abrahamson. Do you want me to spell it for you?"

Bingo. We've got him. Highbear seemed to agree. In the only change of expression I ever saw him have, his black eyes twinkled and he gave me a wink and half of a nod.

Later on, I asked about Frank and was told he'd been transferred to the Sheriff's office in Poulsbo. They would hold him there until the hearing. Margaret was around the corner of the other room when I inquired about why they had moved him. But she heard me and answered. "'Cause he ain't Indian," she said. "The agency turned him down when he applied for his papers. Course, in the beginning, he lied to me and said he was. Lied to us all. But he ain't. I'd been wondering about him for some time. Just didn't act right. He was dark alright.

Looked the part. But he had a bad attitude. More like a white man than one of our people."

I accepted that slur as one I probably earned and asked to use their phone. I again called Sheriff Belltower. He still wasn't there. "Still not in?" I asked, letting my voice go shrill and hard with the officer on the phone. "What is the deal with this guy? Is Old Bucket Belly on vacation or just a permanent lunch break?"

"That information is not available at this time," he said, and slammed the phone receiver down. I also called Mamma, letting the phone ring and listening to her taped message, all the way through.

Her and Belltower were both gone. Humph. She did say something about Hawaii. Could they have gone and not told anyone? No. Mamma might have snuck out of town for a few days if she hadn't heard from me in a month and wasn't expecting to. But, to tell me she'd be home that night, then take a taxi to Sea-Tac on the tail-end of a long shopping trip was too farfetched. No way. That was not Mamma's style.

Jack gave me a lift back to my car and waved goodbye. I had a hunch he was glad to see the boy safe - and to rid himself of me. I couldn't much blame him. I would have loved to wash my hands of the whole affair. But there was one more item to take care of.

I felt restless. That same nagging worry had settled in my chest, all balled up and fermenting. Plus, I hadn't put a face to it or defined it.

Time for a good confab with my Mamma. Surely, she'd be back by tonight. *Just wait until she hears that Belltower was so worried about her kid that he didn't even show up to investigate my case. It's been a week now, since their big date. Could the big romance have flared and gone out already?* I had to admit, I wouldn't be sorry to see it end.

I turned right at the Big Valley turnoff and 15 minutes later, pulled up into the driveway. No sign of anyone home. The Sheriff's patrol car was gone, but so was Mamma's new Nissan.

I tried the outside door. It was locked. Thank goodness, there was an extra key on the GMC's key ring. As I jiggled the lock trying to open it, I could hear Timmy's quick yaps slide into a long, mournful whine.

That's odd behavior for him. Usually, he's incensed over the idea that someone's coming in the door.

I opened the door slowly and called out, "Mamma? Are you home?" Timmy gained in enthusiasm when he saw me, yammering and yapping at my feet for a few minutes. But then he ran off a ways with his tail tucked under his belly, whining, and rolling over on his back.

Something wasn't right.

I stepped into the porch, assaulted by the strong odor of doggie-doo. Timmy had messed directly in front of the outside door. He saw me step over it and began a diversionary tactic which was to race back and forth just out of reach. He barked and howled as if to convince me that some terrible monster had come to his porch in my absence, forced him to do this terrible deed, and would soon return. I called to him to let him know I wasn't mad and let him think I believed his outrageous story. "Timmy. It's OK boy. Quiet down, now." I was a little surprised, though.

Timmy hadn't had an accident since he was a tiny puppy and he'd never made this much of a mess. As I stepped to the kitchen, around more puddles and piles, I noticed his bowl had been licked clean and rolled under the table. "Are you hungry, boy? Huh?" His one bark I took to be an enthusiastic, 'yes.'

As I unlocked the cupboard door where his food was kept and ground the lid off a can of Alpo with the electric can opener, Timmy went nuts. He jumped, wiggled, barked, and sniffed all at once and as joyously as he knew how. Spooning half of the can into his bowl, I sat it on the floor.

Timmy immediately began wolfing it down with all the ferocity of a wild animal. He emptied the bowl in about four chomps, licking it and whining for more. I hoped he wouldn't get sick, decided to wait awhile before I gave him anymore.

Eyeing his loins underneath all the hair, I was again surprised - amazed - at how skinny he was. I filled his water dish and looked again in the cupboard. I had fed Timmy myself on that morning Mamma left with the Sheriff. I'd broke open a new six-pack of canned dog food at the time. That left five cans. This can I just opened, would leave four. And if Timmy hadn't been fed since I was last here...

I counted the cans still in the cupboard. Four. I looked under the sink for an open sack of dry dog food. Nothing. I counted again the cans in the cupboard. No matter how I moved them, they continued to add up to four.

Migod. Has he not been fed since I left? That means...

Mamma. The last time I'd seen her, she was with old Bucket Belly. *What has the Sheriff done with my mother?*

I hurriedly picked up as much of Timmy's mess on the porch floor as I could with paper towels while he paced the kitchen, whining as his toenails tapped a quick rythmn from his now-empty water and feed bowls to the door. A quick slosh of warm soapy water on the porch and a swipe of the mop, was about all I had time for.

I checked Mamma's phone messages - most of them were from me, a few from Sears haranguing her about the insurance on her refrigerator. Everything else was just like I'd left it, almost a week ago.

I rummaged through the kitchen junk drawer until I found a pen. Using the back of an old envelope, I scribbled a message; *Mamma - just in case you get home before I get back, Timmy's with me. Call me at* (here I copied down Camille's phone number) *or at the office as soon as you get in.*

I then collected the little dog, threw the four cans of dog food in a paper sack along with an opener, and headed out to the Porsche. Just in case he threw up, I spread a copy of last weeks *Gazette* on the front seat and down on the floor. That done, I climbed into the driver's seat and amid Timmy's face-licking and excited yelps, I cracked the window on his side, and took off.

As I drove, I mentally went through this last week's events in an effort to find the similarity, if any, between the Cloud disappearance and my mother's. Cloud's daughter, an obvious witness to the crime, was left unharmed. In my mother's case....

Oh shit. So also, am I a witness. Almost. If not to an actual crime, they know that I know who's company she was keeping when she left. I had to find her. Cloud had met his maker soon after he was abducted. Somehow, I would have to prevent the same fate from happening to Mamma.

I glanced over at Timmy. He seemed to have survived his ordeal well enough. His nose was thrust into the wind that poured in through the half-open window. His ears were once again alert, catching every sound and nuance that chanced to drift his way. As we drove by some kids playing baseball on the far side of a cow pasture, he barked and waved his tail. By the time I reached the police station, he had settled down on his side of the seat and except for the occasional roll and blink of his huge black eyes, he seemed content and happy. He was definitely a lot happier than I was.

I rolled into town, past David's condo-church and the old GMC, and into the parking lot of the Poulsbo Police Station. I breezed in the front door and up to the counter. "Where's the Sheriff," I demanded of the officer on duty. She was a new one, I hadn't seen before.

"He's not here..." she started to say.

"Marconi, then. Where's he?"

"I'm sorry. This is not his shift..." Her eyes widened, probably in reaction to my expression.

I took a deep breath, and said, "How about the Mayor? Has His Honor deemed the citizens worthy of his presence today?"

"He has an office in a law firm. The building behind the drug store, facing the water." As she pointed down main street with one hand, I saw her reach with the other into the knee-space of her desk drawer. Probably to summon the guard from the jail cells in back. As I slammed open the front door and turned to follow the sidewalk to my car, a large burly-type cop stomped up to the front counter and watched my retreat through the glass. He had a knobby face and a bulbous nose, and his uniform cap was perched on a wide, fleshy head with a sweep of hair up the sides the color and consistency of yellow sandpaper.

I rumbled the car to the Mayor's office, taking care to stay within the speed limit and watching to see if I was followed. No one in sight. I then breezed into the law firm's door, giving the receptionist a little better treatment than the cop, but not much. Without comment or argument, I was shown to the Mayor's office.

I could hear voices as I swung down the carpeted hall and a thump that could have been a fist hitting hard wood. A man shouted, "That's bullshit, Ted. You try to take that kind of story to the stand and the jury will hang you up by the nuts. No. You've gone too far." The placque on the outside door, read Mayor Mullins.

I waltzed in without knocking, cutting short his visitor's nasal plea. "Damn it. If you'd just see me through, this one time..."

The Mayor, a tall, balding man I guessed to be in his late fifties, stood at the window, looking out. The man who'd come begging favors was slumped on the Mayor's brown couch. When he saw me, Sheriff Belltower straightened to an upright sitting position like a kid in grade school who'd been caught shooting spit wads at the girls.

"Young lady," the Mayor said. "... how dare you barge in here. If you want to see me, you'll have to make an appointment at the desk. Now please leave. I'm in conference at the moment."

I paused, hoping to keep the temper in check. Of course, that meant I wouldn't bash his desk over his pointed head. *A good tongue-lashing just kind of gets things out in the open.* I turned to the Mayor and said, "Your conference can wait. Last week, a man disappeared and later drowned. The state says it was accidental - I say they're wrong."

The Mayor sucked in a big breath, and knowing he was ready to expound on the intricacies of a death by drowning, I interrupted, saying, "My mother has now disappeared, under very suspicious circumstances. And I'm not leaving until I find out what your fair-haired boy here...," I leveled a finger at the Sheriff, who had by now taken on a 'don't-look-at-me' attitude by catching the Mayor's eye with a palms-up, head-shaking shrug, "....has done with her."

The Sheriff said, "You know Kathleen, it's strange that you chose this morning to come in here. I was just telling Roy," he gestured towards the Mayor, "how concerned I was about your mother."

"That's odd. You haven't called my mother's house once, or returned a single one of my calls. You also haven't made the first move to investigate any of these crimes I've been reporting."

This time, it was the Mayor's turn to butt in. "Young lady, I'll have you know that there has been an ongoing investigation since day one for this case. I take it, you're also the same complainant who filed the assault and battery charge?"

I nodded.

"That too, is being worked on. You have to understand, Miss....?"

"O'Shaunessy. Kathleen."

"You see, Miss O'Shaunessy, even though you haven't actually observed our law enforcement in the field, doesn't mean that they're not working. Quite the contrary. It means that BECAUSE you can't see them, they're doing their job correctly. Now, I suggest that you go on home and let the police handle this."

I hate being patronized, hate even more being made a patsy. I ignored the Mayor's suggestion. To the Sheriff, I said, "At least tell me where she was when you last saw her. Surely, you've gotten that much of your story together by now."

The Mayor didn't give Belltower a chance to answer. Probably knew he'd screw it up. He strode to his desk and, in a futile attempt to frighten me, he mashed the intercom button on the phone and picked up the receiver, saying, "Young lady, I'll have to insist that you leave before I send for a squad car. And I'll advise you, one more time, to go home. I'd hate to see you get hurt again, unnecessarily."

"And let me suggest something to you, Mayor. While you're doing your investigating, you'd better look into the shenanigans of your Sheriff. I am not in a forgiving mood and if I don't get my mother back, REAL SOON, neither one of you will be electible for the position of garbage collector." With that, I started for the hall, then turned to add another thought. "And, by the way, I'm keeping a complete log on everything that's happened, including my suspicions, with the *Gazette*. You better make damn sure nothing does happen to me or my Mamma and, for that matter, those kids out there on that reservation. My editor has been directed to hand it all over to the feds, the first time he has to go for more than an hour without hearing from me. Have a good day, gentlemen."

CHAPTER TWENTY FIVE

I drove back to Camille's house, put Timmy on his leash, and let him out. No one was home. I walked with the dog down the trail to the hall where they'd had the pow-wow. Bobby was sitting outside, under a tree. "Hi, Bobby. What are you doing out here? Where's Camille?"

"They're having a meeting," he said, thumbing in the direction of the closed door. "They call it a 'talking circle.' Kinda private. Just the tribal members and the family...I wouldn't go in there."

He'd piqued my curiosity. "Why? What's happening?"

"Camille. She says it's her time. She's found her song. It's like, she's discovered her guardian spirit."

Just then, an old Indian woman waddled down the path towards the hall. Huge clouds of smoke billowed from the doorway when she went in and I got a brief glimpse of a bonfire in the center of the room.

The old woman stepped inside, then turned to wag a finger 'no'...I was not to attempt to come inside. I shrugged a shoulder and started back to my car.

If they'd rather handle it themselves, then good luck. I was tired of arguing.

Suddenly, I heard someone call my name. "Kate? Kathleen. Wait." It was Camille. She was calling from the doorway. "Can you come in? I'd really like for you to be here."

"But, I'm not supposed to..."

"I want you to. You saved my life and brought me together with my sister." She moved aside, making room for me in the doorway. "Please. I'd really like for you to come."

I couldn't resist. I handed Timmy's leash to Bobby, and said, "Can you try to find him some water? Here's a sack of his dog food. Let him have the rest of that open can, but watch him, that he doesn't drink or eat too fast and get sick."

With the hairs on the back of my neck at full mast, I tiptoed in. The old woman nodded in a way to show me she'd meant no harm and ushered me inside, gesturing for me to stay quiet. From her seat, Camille announced to the small crowd, "Kathleen is our guest. She has shown great bravery in the face of our enemies. She has earned the right to sit in our circle." Behind us, drums began to beat and Camille began to chant.

From a cloth on the floor, the old woman picked up a beaded leather purse and drew out what looked like an eagle's wing. Using an oyster shell as a bowl, she filled it with some weeds and lit it. Then she went around the circle, sweeping the smoke into each of our faces, using the eagle feathers as a fan. When the old woman had finished her ritual, she stepped behind Camille and sat down.

Camille stopped chanting and began to speak. "Kathleen. A great spirit has come and wishes to speak to you." Then she became placid, breathing with great, heaving sighs. She looked the same but her voice rumbled several octaves lower than usual and seemed to boom as if keeping beat with the tom-toms of an ancient time. The personality emanating from that voice was old and it was male.

She/he said, "Welcome, the one who is known as Kathleen. You are a friend to my children and their children. It is good that you have come. Your brave heart sings out for the needs of my people. Is there anything, my child, you would like to ask? I must tell you, that I may not have the answers you seek. But I shall try."

I started to ask, "What should I do..." But in the asking, I felt terribly stupid. Besides, I already knew.

There's only one man who can stop this nonsense. And only one place to find him.

He seemed to understand what I was thinking. "Your loved one has been detained by unfriendly forces, although she is safe and awaiting your arrival. You will know what to do and I believe you will have the courage, when it is time." The stately old presence paused, and when I didn't answer, *what in the world would I answer to something like that,* he said, "Do you have another question I may help you with?"

I swallowed, hard, and nodded. "Oh, well...uhm...maybe just one. It's silly, really..."

He waited.

"...it's just that...when I first talked to Camille, the very first time, she said that someone whom I had written about recommended that she call me. And I couldn't imagine...who..."

"In your writings, you told of an unfortunate soul, I believe your term is 'homeless', who was one of our people. You words were kind and sincere. You were distraught, in that, the man had had no home. And with his demise, he had no name."

"Oh. You mean, that article I did on the homeless? But, that guy, when they found him...he was already dead."

"Exactly."

"Oh. I see." *Great. Now I really feel stupid. Of course he was dead. And so will I be, if I don't get this case solved, find my mother, get my story written, and scoot on out of here.*

"Are there any more questions, my child?"

Noticing my mouth gaped large enough to be in danger of catching flies, I snapped it shut, checked the bottom lip for drool, and rose clumsily to my feet. "No...uhm, I have to go now."

I came out of that hall faster than I went in. *Well. If they're nuts, I guess I am too. I swear, Camille was NOT making that up.*

Timmy barked an animated greeting as I came out, running over to lick my hand and gouge my leg with his claws. Bobby threw a stick for him which he raced after with all of his old, enthusiastic energy. "I see you two are getting along."

"He's a neat little dog. He's yours?"

With a brief shake of my head, I said, "He belongs to my Mom. Name's Timmy." I wiped my eyes with my hands, hoping that Bobby wouldn't notice the tears that had suddenly welled up. When I saw him watching me, I gestured toward the hall I had just left and said, "How can they breathe in there, with all that smoke?"

My tears were only the tip of the iceberg, as compared to the emotions that churned at my insides. The more I investigated David and Frank, the more worried I became about my mother's disappearance.

There was one more place to look. "I need to run a little errand, Bobby. Can you watch Timmy and the twins for me?"

"Yea, I could do that. But I'd just as soon go with you. Where ever it is that you're off to Kate, I don't think you'd oughtta be alone."

"Thanks, Bobby. But it's better this way." I didn't take the time to explain. Maybe I should have. Bobby would have remembered Mamma. Probably thought highly of her, like everyone else. But first, I'd have to understand her myself and in my thirty-one years of life, that hadn't been accomplished yet. At the dock, I untied Camille's small outboard boat, steadied it, and jumped in. Yanking the Evenrude's rope with a clamped-jawed determination, I listened to it settle into a constant, deafening roar, and set out.

Skimming across the waves, the small boat sliced neatly through the foamy spray like a hot knife through whipped cream. I thought of the deep, reverent words coming from Camille's mouth when I first entered the hall. Whoever was speaking had no interest in Indian economics or monetary achievement. He'd cared about the people and about the land.

Across the way, a stand of evergreen and rhododendron bushes looked like it had jumped right off of a picture postcard. And the damp fog gave it a breathtaking, almost ethereal quality. *If the scenery is this moving for me, what does it mean to this tribe?*

OK. So, their spirituality, their heritage, it's all attached to this place. And maybe they're even more involved with the development than I thought. But - there's still nothing being done about it.

Maybe I can, though. Through the paper, at work. This naked, ugly racism that I had witnessed this last week, each side as guilty as the other, perpetuating with each generation - year after year, has got to stop. Needless hatred, taught to the babies at their mother's breast, continues to snuff out any hope that these kids, be they black, brown, red or white, might learn to trust and to let each other be.

That would be the focus of my article. And if the paper won't print it, I'll find another one that will. Or a magazine...or even a book.

The cold wind whipped around my head, the salty air refreshed and healing to my jelled brain and battered heart and body. I shook my head like an old, grizzled hound, blinked a few times, and faced into the blustering bay.

Hideaway Island, coming up.

CHAPTER TWENTY SIX

The little boat nosed into the inlet several yards from shore. After switching the noisy motor off, the engulfing silence was nice and I let the boat rock in the water for awhile, listening to the slosh of each incoming wave and its hiss as it drew back to the sea. The boat's easy sway soon crunched to a halt as the prow plowed into the gravel on the beach. After lassoing a large rock with the rope and tying it off, I headed for the path leading to David's house.

Opening the tunnel door, I fanned it in hopes of replacing the dank, foul air with the wonderful breeze off the bay. The sour draft coming out of the hole smelled a lot like a refrigerator's bottom storage bin stuffed with a plastic sackful of last summer's lettuce.

This time I'd play it smart. Running my fingers along the edge, I found a piece of the same loose wire I'd tripped on before and followed it to a spot just inside. I could hear a light bulb clink against the sway of a short chain.

A sharp pull of the chain brought a string of flickering lights that were hung off the sides of the weeping rock wall. I held my breath against the stench of dead bugs and rotting timbers, wondering if I'd ever again, breathe fresh air. And careful not to touch anything that was wet or wiggly, I climbed in.

I walked as quickly as I could. Every ten feet another light bulb rocked in the draft of the open trap door, illuminating large round spaces that shimmered and gleamed with the same crazy, rocking motion. My own bent and shivering shadow crept alongside me on the wet walls.

Overhead, a 4 X 4 stud creaked. A loosened pebble rattled, dusting my hair. Breathing in quick, short gasps, I hurried on - refusing to think any farther than my next move. I had to reach that computer room.

Finally my foot bumped the bottom of the last wooden step. The hatch loomed just ahead. As quietly as I could, I climbed the five steps and grasped the hatch door handle with both hands. Leaning on the steel bar, I felt it wiggle and nudge down a notch but it wouldn't open. I bashed it until my hand hurt. It still wouldn't open.

Maybe it's locked from the inside. Desperate now, I threw my full weight on it, straining with everything I had. Something clicked. I felt a tiny movement. An airy whir sounded from inside. Then slowly the ponderous cold steel moved and the hatch door slid, silently, to the inside.

I perched on the edge of the office chair and switched the IMAX computer on. The moment it was ready I brought up the Scout program. Cruising through the menu, I found the file for accessing his portable

PC on the boat and highlighted it. It loaded with crunching little noises while I waited.

Let him be there for me...just this once.

As I typed, the tap, tap, tap, of the keyboard resonated in the dead air. *'Brown Bomber to Grey Ghost. Where are you?'*

Come on, David. I know you've seen it. COME ON.

I tried it again. Tappity-tap. *'Grey Ghost. Acknowledge, please.'*

The blank screen stared back at me, unblinking, noncommunicative. A square green eye, bloodless and vacant.

The hell with secrets.

Tap, tap, tap. *'Damn it, David. I trusted you. I loved you. ANSWER ME!!!'*

Then - a letter - a word - a sentence. *'Hello, Beautiful. Where have you been?'*

For a moment I touched a kinky curl, drawing it across my lips, remembering.... Inhaling jaggedly, fingers poised above the keys, I began.... *'Oh, hanging around. You know, spent some quality time with the twins. Saved a tribe from extinction. That sort of thing. How about you?'*

He replied, *'About the same. Made another couple of million. Played God for awhile. Typical day at the Old Lazy D.'*

'Well, Pilgrim. How about you and I mount our ponies and ride off into the sunset?'

'Anything to please a lady. Mind telling me where we're going?'

Lifting the hair off the back of my neck, I jutted my chin at the ceiling and breathed deeply before returning to the keys. Tap, tap, tap. *'To see the Head Honcho. Mr. Moneybags. The Big Boss.'*

His hasty answer. *'I AM the boss.'*

'No. No, you're not. You wouldn't do this to me if you had a choice.'

I waited a long, dragged out, tortuous minute. *'David, my mother's still missing. Either tell me right now that you've already killed her, or help me find out where she is.'*

Then...*'Meet me at the mouth of the inlet.'*

I tappity-tapped. *'You got a date, cowboy.'*

I closed down the triple X. An old hand now with the hatch, I moved through the menu, looking for the T-DR command that would open the tunnel door and let me out.

Suddenly, a red light flashed over the hatch door. From somewhere in the depths of the wall, a siren emitted a doleful bleat. Then, on the same glass sign, a message moved from left to right, letter-by-letter, word-by-word. DANGER. INTRUDER IN TUNNEL. DANGER.

I quickly brought back the Triple X. *'David. If you're there, and Frank's in jail, who's in the tunnel?'*

He answered. *'Frank's out on bail.'*

Tappity-tap. *'He's also on the other side of this steel door. How do I keep him out of here?'*

'See a little bar at the top of the screen?'

'Yes.'

'Use the mouse to open another file. Look for a small window at the bottom of the screen to open up. Click twice, then each time it questions if you want the tunnel door to open, click on NO.'

I did as he said. Next question. *'Do I click at close and seal?'*

'Yes. Then again at red blinking emergency signal.'

The siren screamed. The over-hatch light blared, a single word spelled out, repeatedly. DANGER...DANGER...

'David. He's forcing it!'

'You'll have to leave. On the other side of the room, on the left, there's a panel. Do you see it?'

'Yes.'

'About waist high, there's a piece of loose molding. Push it in. Hurry.'

The end of what was probably a crow-bar, poked through a newly forced crack between hatch and wall. I could hear Frank's grunt and strain. "Lemme in," he pleaded. "I gotta talk to you."

I clicked the command to tell the computer 'NO', do not open the hatch door. I then pivoted my chair on the plastic, and ran across the room.

"Wait, Lady," Frank wheezed. "I'm sorry. I didn't mean to hurt you, back there. It's just....well, you shouldn't have said what you did. You're so darn pretty and all...I kinda got carried away. Will you let me come in, so we can talk?"

I bashed at the molding with the heel of my hand. Nothing. No doors opened. No way out.

Behind me, at the hatch door, Frank's knee and part of his hip was wedged in the opening. Angry now, he snarled, "I know you're in there, you bitch. It was you who put me in jail, and by God, you're gonna pay for it." Again, I whacked at the panel.

Damn thing's not going to open.

I streaked back to the desk. Tappity-tap. *'David. The panel won't open. Frank prying hatch. HELP.'*

His answer. *'Go to menu. Find RAID. Hit enter.'*

A segment of Frank's face and one bulging eye appeared in the crack between hatch and doorjamb. Four hairy fingers, white-knuckled from strain, curled along the edge.

The command switched the warning in the overhead sign, a taped, monotone voice gave the same instructions.

WARNING. EXPLOSIVE ASSAULT IN 10 SECONDS. SIT ON FLOOR - FACING WALL. DETONATION IN 8 SECONDS. BEND HEAD TOWARD THE KNEES AND CLASP TIGHTLY. DETONATION IN 6 SECONDS.

Then the countdown began. 5 SECONDS, 4 SECONDS...

On the computer screen, a message blipped. AUXILIARY ENGAGED. CLOSE AND SEAL? CLOSE AND SEAL? I took a chance that it meant the hatch door and clicked the Y for yes. Then, somewhere inside the walls, some kind of gear came alive with an odd groan. It snapped the hatch door shut, the tip of Frank's finger protruding like a bright red bulb. I heard him gasp and scream as the warning sign blinked;

ONE SECOND. DETONATION READY.

Then, a terrible blast. The room rocked, dislodging several pieces of ceiling tile. Still holding my head as I'd been instructed, I waited for the floor to stop shaking.

CHAPTER TWENTY SEVEN

The panel door slid sideways quite easily - once I deciphered David's directions. His 'waist-high' was more like my shoulder. Coming into the pantry from the back, I stepped into the small space behind the shelves and peeked past a large jar of spaghetti sauce. The house must have been built like a fort. Other than a sack of loose tea leaves crunching under my feet and an opened box of cornflakes, I could hardly tell the room below had just suffered a blast.

Straight ahead, the light of a quarter moon caught the beige glint of an electric range. Catty-corner to that a double-doored refrigerator hummed for a moment and then shut off.

I felt for a latch and found it. The wall of shelves, with groceries teetering precariously, sprawled open like a cafe door. The sheen of that same moon was my only light. Slicing through the venetian blinds, it lay in glowing strips on the kitchen's hardwood floor and bounced off a delft blue-on-white vase sitting to one side of the window sill. I tiptoed past the range and down the length of the countertops to look outside.

The blast had done something to my hearing. Rotating my little finger in my right ear, I tried to stop its deafening roar. It didn't help. The click my shoes should have been making on the floor could have been two cotton balls patted together for all I knew. That dizzying sound was the only thing I could hear.

Peering between the beveled slats at the window, I studied as much of the outside porch and yard as I could see. It was mostly dark, except for the dull glow off the white bark of a birch tree. The quick flutter of its shiny leaves was the only perceptible movement.

Doing a quick check of most of the rooms and their closets just in case Mamma might have been hidden there, I mentally hardened the jell in my knees and reached for the place where the knob on the outside door should have been. But, this was, after all, David's house. I found the knob four inches higher and a dead bolt four inches above that. I opened them both and stepped out on the deck.

In a flash of brilliance I remembered he'd kept a flashlight on the wood box. Scrounging it from the back of the shelf and turning it on, I started down the path to the beach. Picking my way past the rhododendron bushes and the cedar trees, a creepy feeling started about middle-back, slithered up my neck and raised the hair on my skin like little antennae.

I shrugged and jiggled my shoulders as I hurried down the path. The flashlight cast its beam on the eerie, threatening shapes of the dark and turned them into sensible objects - the hulk of a burnt stump, the spiny tips of a pine tree swaying in the breeze, and the large, blinking eyes of an owl.

Behind me, a menacing rustle of leaves and brush gripped me with anxiety. I stumbled and went down - scraping my hands in the dirt and gravel. "Uhnn." The flashlight rolled crazily down the hill, making large, bright arcs across the trail.

My wrist hurt....

Damn. I must have sprained it.

....but my hearing was coming back.

I squatted on my knees and rubbed the sore places on my hands. The flashlight had rolled against a small bush. I retrieved it and once again, pierced the darkness with its glow. Carefully, I got up and crept down the path with measured steps - touching each spot of ground first with my toe.

Finally I felt the crunch of clam shells and beach gravel beneath my feet and the cold rush of wet, salty wind on my face. I climbed over the driftwood and found the shoreline with its hard surface of wet sand, heard the splash and gurgle of a low tide. As I stretched out for a fast-paced walk to the inlet, small waves took great, sudsy licks at the sand less than a yard away. I couldn't shake the feeling of being watched.

After a long twenty minute walk, I thought I could see David's boat anchored just off shore. Hopefully, he also saw the bob and glare of my flashlight. I walked on, hurrying now, eager for the company of another person, anxious for the end to this nightmare.

With a quick intake of breath, I felt and then saw him as he stepped from the shadow of an overhang on the cliff wall. "Well," he said, dryly and somewhat distant. "If it's not the Rebel of the Irish Republic. You were born too late, Kathleen. God, could they have used you in the Irish Uprising of 1914. The British wouldn't have stood a chance." He came closer, peering down at me. "Mixed up in this mess, you just seem to be in the way."

"So, why not get me out of the way? Level with me and let me go home."

"I have leveled with you, Kathleen. All along."

"Yeah, sure. What about the tricks your buddy Frank pulled? Are you going to tell me now, it was all his idea?"

"Kathleen, I swear. I never, in a million years, told him to hurt you or the kid. Please, Katie. You've got to believe me."

I hadn't seen this side of David before. Remorseful, wretched.... I watched him with interest.

David reached out to stroke my arm. I moved just slightly out of his reach. He pleaded, "Frank was supposed to put you in the cellar to cool off for awhile, ONLY. I thought we could scare you into going home and get the kid to cooperate in the bargain."

"Well, it's too late, anyway. He won't be hurting anyone else."

"You mean....the blast? He didn't get out? Uh...before the tunnel blew?" I shook my head.

"I saw it from the boat. Got a little rocky out there for awhile. Which reminds me, we better get outta here. If I could see and hear it from my position, it stands to reason that someone else could have heard it from the mainland."

We walked toward the waiting row boat. I didn't get in. "Say, uh, David....," I said, folding my arms to the front. This habit of his, of moving people around like pawns in a game of chess, was beginning to tick me off. "I know you want to talk, Kate. So do I. But we better do it on the boat, where I've got some protection and maneuverability."

"That's just it, David. Where's my protection and maneuverability?"

"I guess you'll have to trust me." When I didn't answer, he said, "I see. You don't trust me."

"You're damn right, I don't. My Mamma didn't raise any fools." I thought about what I'd said for a moment, and the ache of missing her and wanting to see her safe came flooding back. Covering my mouth so David wouldn't hear or sense my moment of terror, I flashed my light on him - up close. His chin and cheekbones stuck out from the deeper hollows like a skeletal mask. His eyes were indented and dark.

"Kate," he was saying, "you've got to trust me. I am your protection. The only one you've got. Since you won't mind your own business and you refuse to go home, you'd have been dead long ago if I hadn't have stepped in. What can I do to convince you of that?"

"I don't know, David. But, before I get in that boat, that and what you've done with my Mom, are just a few of the things that will have to be explained."

"I'm not sure about your mother. But I'll do what I can and get back to you on it. What else?"

"We found the kid. The boy from Sacramento. I want to know what Margaret was doing with him. And what was your role in the little scheme? White slavery, perhaps? Sell him as a male bond to some kinky oil-rich bastards overseas?"

"Kate, I swear to you. I didn't have anything to do with the abduction. She said he was another Welfare custody case."

"He was kidnapped off a playground in California."

"I'm sorry. But I had nothing to do with it. She raised that girl from a baby and I had no reason to believe anything else."

"Damn it, David. Stop lying to me. I saw the passport. I suppose Frank did that too?"

"You're snooping in my mail, now? Opening a letter from the Federal government? Don't play with me, Kath. I told you I'd help, now let it go."

"And that makes it OK to you? The fact that I opened your damn mail makes us even?" Even though I was spooked, exhausted, and highly pissed off, and my nerves strained to the breaking point, I forced my mind to dump the myriad of reactionary curses it continued to supply. Tampering with federal mail was the one indiscretion I'd made and, with David's connections, the only one they'd need to have me conveniently jerked off the case and thrown in jail. And I wouldn't be able to solve anything or help anyone in there. Not even myself. I'd have to let it go - for now. And think logically. *Everything I say, from here on, will be crucial to our survival. All of us.*

"OK," I said, hoping I wouldn't hate myself in the morning for caving in. "You may have something there. And I realize that I never would have gotten away from Frank without your help. But there's more." I rubbed my arms as a buffer against a cold blast of wind, and said, "Something I have got to know."

"Shoot," he said. "But hurry up. It's cold out here and getting late."

"Frank was evil and a dull-witted dope. But - he was also very confident. If he was going against your orders, and that's a big IF, then why didn't he show a little remorse when he was found out? If you were his boss, why could you not have called him on the carpet? Read him the riot act? I mean, at least cut back on his fringe benefits?" I was beginning to shout and I didn't care. "For crying out loud, couldn't you dock him a day's pay? I want to know what's going on, David. And no more lies. Why did he come back, even more beastly, more smug, than when he left?"

"He was following Charlie's orders. Not mine."

"Charlie? And who, pray tell, is Charlie?"

"Charlie Wong. It's...just a nickname."

"I don't believe you. Why haven't I heard of him before?" The crawly feeling on my back was getting worse. Behind me, something splashed in the surf. It could have been anything - a fish, an energetic wave, or the Loch Ness monster for all I knew. But in David's new-found moment of truth, I didn't dare take my eyes away from him long enough to check it out. And he didn't seem to notice.

"You have met him...once. He was the driver, that night when I picked you up on the road."

"Your chauffeur? You mean that first night? You're kidding."

"No. That...was him."

"You son-of-a-bitch. You dirty son-of-a-bitch! It was a set up, wasn't it? The whole thing!" I could have scratched his eyes out. Gladly. But someone else beat me to it.

David's face screwed with panic as feet slapped on wet sand behind us. As I spun on one heel, someone streaked past me to pounce on David, teeth and nails extended - screaming insults. "Murderer! You stinking scum bag. You killed my father!"

They struggled. A knife flashed, a wild shriek split the night air. I backed up, out of the fight. Only half David's size, she tore at him with the fury of a hellcat - thrusting her knife for his throat then whistling it past the soft part of his lower belly.

She was everywhere - a feign, a dash, then suddenly she would leap, cut, and jump back. And David was left bleeding.

I suddenly knew why she had run away and where she had been hiding. *She wanted to kill him.*

"Cerese! Stop it! Please. He's not worth it, Cerese. He's just not worth it."

She backed up, crouched and wheezing, her knife level and square against his gut. "I've been waiting ever since I can remember to find my parents. My real parents. And now, he...."

I interrupted, "I know you have, honey. I know. But, it's not up to you to get even with him. That's for the courts to decide. He's not worth going to jail for."

The knife, still pointed at David, had started to shake. "Daddy," she sobbed, "...my father...was here, waiting all these years. We could have been a family...a real family..." Hate crackled in her voice. She spit on the ground and said, "He deserves to die, Kathy. And I'm going to see that he does."

Calmly, I said, "Yes, you're right. David deserves everything you can hand out and more. And he will get his due. I promise you, someday, all his crimes will come back to haunt him. But we can't do that right now. Besides, you've got the wrong guy. David here is just an agent. He doesn't have any power to speak of, and I'm beginning to think, not all that much money. Someone else was giving the orders. And David's going to help us find him." Turning to him, I said, "Isn't that right David? Do you know where Charlie is?"

He nodded, his face a phantom white. "Yes. I know where he is. He's got a yacht anchored in Liberty Bay."

"Then let's go."

"Go?" David stumbled back, his face etched in fear. "Good God, Kate. I can't take you there. And a kid too? Forget it."

"Oh, you want to take the heat yourself? Fine. We'll just go on back and I'll call the Tribal police and the Kitsap county sheriff from home. Maybe you could share with them, your reasons for wanting to forget it."

"All right, all right. I'll show you where Charlie's boat it. Then, will you lay off?"

"Lay off? You still don't get it, do you David? This is not some kind of personal vendetta."

"Then what is it, Kate? There's got to be some reason you won't go home and let the authorities take care of things."

He had me there. But - I could no longer be sure of which of our 'authority' to trust. *This could be the most incredibly stupid thing I've ever done. But, if I didn't do it, I'd be looking over my shoulder the rest of my life, running away from God-knows-who, and I might never get my Mamma back.*

"Yes," I said, eyeing David carefully. "There is a reason. In fact, there are a number of reasons." I drew a deep breath and holding up a finger for each one, I started counting them off. "If I'd have gone home, would you have responded to the authorities like you did to me? Would you have told them the password and how to get access to your personal files? Would you have told them about Charlie? Or would you rather have run off, spread some money around in some high places, and kept it all hushy hush. You think I don't know that the only way I'm getting any respect around here, and even that's not much, is that you're all scared my paper will set off a scandal and a federal investigation? And bring your little house of cards tumbling down around your ears?"

"All right. Then, we'll go talk to Charlie. But it won't do any good. And I cannot, for the life of me, see why you would even want to. It's...pointless."

"You want to tell Cerese it's pointless?" I stopped. *There's no use arguing with him.* A cold wind had come up. It felt as if it was blowing directly on my bones and whistling through the crack in my broken heart. "Let's go. Cerese? You can't stay here. God only knows who else is creeping around. Come and get in the rowboat. We're going to pay a little visit on Charlie."

CHAPTER TWENTY EIGHT

Cerese and I huddled in the lower cabin while David cranked up the anchor. The small engine moved us out into deeper water where he readied the boat to whisk us off towards Poulsbo. Through the cabin walls we could hear the sharp snap of the white canvas as the buffeting wind grabbed the sails and started shoving us along. The sea was rough. Not yet a storm, but the winds were high.

I rummaged around in the galley and found a tiny closet packed with David's extra coats. Handing a hooded rain jacket with a warm liner to Cerese, I put on another jacket - a polyester-padded, navy-blue number that hit me at knee-level and made me feel like the Pillsbury dough boy. But they were warm and the cabin was dry and after a little while we stopped shaking.

The boat veered sharply to the left in a tight turn. The sudden cant of the floor threw me into the dinette seat and Cerese against the closet door. We grabbed tables, walls, anything within reach, and hung on. There was no way to tell if David was actually taking us to Charlie or if he was headed out to the high seas where we'd be thrown over the side and drowned.

"Uck," Cerese said. "I'm getting sick to my stomach."

"So am I," I grumbled. Motion sickness, or seasickness in this case, can be a killer. "Let's go up on top. The fresh air will do us good." We zipped our jackets snug to our chins and I tied the string on Cerese's hood close around her face. She looked like a little brown rose bud. At the cabin door I grabbed the handle and said to Cerese, "Ready?" She nodded and I pulled the door open.

A strong, cold gust of wind smacked our faces with salty spray. We steeled ourselves against its force and clambered up the four steps to the deck. David was at the helm, facing the boat into some fairly high waves. "Be careful," he shouted. "Sit down, up close to the cabin wall and hang on." On the aft-deck, a small, dugout space had been lined with benches - formed out of the fiberglass. Plastic covered cushions were set up along the seats with straps on each side. He gestured at them with his chin, "Those are floatable. They go on like a backpack. There's some life vests under the seat. I'll have to insist you put them on. Right away. Hand me one, too." Although I didn't like his tone, I knew he was right. With much cold-fingered fumbling, we each strapped a life vest on over our coats.

Snuggled up close to the cabin wall, Cerese and I managed to stay out of the worst of the wind. David's white-blond hair flapped in a sudden gust as he peered anxiously around the cabin wall. I could only guess what he was watching for. In the wind-whipped moment, I said a silent prayer....

Out in deeper water now, the boat skimmed the length of the bay, streaming the waves from its hull. Cerese and I gazed dully across the whitecaps to the wink and glitter of the occasional beach house window and the moving lights of the cars on the highway. After awhile, the lights seemed to be more frequent.

Then David dropped the largest sail with a hydraulic winch, winding it down to wrap neatly around the beam. The boat's movement slowed considerably. Next came the smaller sail and the boat began to heave and groan, tossed about by the current. Finally, he started the engine and thrust it into reverse. The boat came to a full stop. He then geared it into low-forward and maneuvered it into position.

Having set the sailboat at just the right angle, David shut the engine down. No longer in command of its own bulk, the boat floundered helplessly in the high, night winds. The three of us rode the deck, staring at the luxurious yacht some thirty feet away.

I had seen the lookout and all of the top level of the yacht even before we jockeyed around. Now, the three-tiered deck and the wide span of its hull made a cursory roll in the surf even though the wind had whipped the waves to a considerable size. It was a huge thing, over eighty feet long and mostly white. A deckhand flipped on the outside lights as he watched us approach.

I couldn't see Charlie.

David lowered the anchor and cleared the deck of loose ropes. He then swung into the cabin and muttered something I couldn't hear into the sea-to-shore radio.

While he was busy, I pulled on the rowboat's rope and brought it up to the side ladder. From pure habit I slung the strap of the camera over my shoulder, and made ready to board the tiny craft that we would row over to the cabin cruiser. Cerese sniffled and crowded close behind me. Patting her arm, I said, "There's no need for you to go. You'd be better off staying here, out of their reach."

"But I want to," she argued. "This involves me too, and I'd like to hear what he says."

Thinking fast, I nodded vigorously in agreement. "Oh, I didn't mean that. You're not being left out, kiddo. I really need you here where you can call the coast guard if I need any help. In fact, it'd be better if you stayed down in the cabin with the radio on."

David was back on deck by then and had heard us. "I don't want some kid messing with my radio," he griped. "What do you mean, telling her to call the Coast Guard?"

"Well, that's tough," I snapped. "I said, only in case of an emergency. If you're going to eavesdrop, at least get the whole conversation." Fuming, I honked my nose into a handkerchief and said, "We don't know what's going to happen over there. If you don't care about our lives,

DEADLY DECEPTIONS

what if they blow YOU to bits? Would you like knowing help was on the way, then?"

His lip lifted in a sneer. "You just can't resist putting me down, can you Kate?"

I stared at him, but didn't answer. "All right." Motioning to Cerese, he said, "Come on. I'll have to show you how to use it."

Cerese cast a quizzical glance at me which I answered with a nod. She then followed David into the cabin and watched carefully while he explained how to give and receive messages and how to send an SOS.

After David returned to the deck and made ready to climb aboard the rowboat, I stuck my head in the cabin door to tell Cerese we were going. The wall clock read 11:25 p.m. Pointing to it, I said, "If you don't hear from me by 12:30, and I mean me, not David, send out an SOS." Quickly, while David was busy and out of earshot, I dropped to the galley floor to give her a quick hug and whisper in her ear. "If everything's OK, I'll start my conversation by saying 'hey kiddo.' If you don't hear that, no matter what else I tell you, call the Coast Guard the minute I hang up."

Her eyes glittered like shiny black marbles in her round face. "Be careful, Kate. I couldn't stand it if anything happened to you." Then showing me the rounded edge of some cold steel, she said, "Here. Take my switchblade with you."

"Oh, I don't know...."

"You might need it," she urged. "Hold still and I'll slip it into the hem of your jacket." I turned, and felt her fumble while I pretended to examine the radio's microphone. "With any luck, they won't find it if you're searched," she whispered to my back.

David couldn't stand being ignored. He growled from the doorway, "Are you coming, or not?"

Bounding up the steps, I flashed a bright-eyed and hopefully guileless smile and said, "Let's go."

To Cerese he said, "Don't go playing around with that," and pointed at the radio. "Wait until you hear from me. If there's an emergency, I can probably handle it myself from over there or come back here and do it." He scowled and fingered his bandaged forearm where she'd cut him. "Got it?" She nodded woodenly. That and a quick gleam, was her only expression.

David paused, obviously waiting for a better reaction. When he didn't get it, he said, "Just don't be going off half-cocked and start broadcasting a lot of false alarms. You could get us in a lot of trouble."

Again, no answer. She could have been carved from mahogany.

My heart swelled with pride as I waggled a tiny hip-high wave to her and turned to leave. Behind me, I could hear David's angry snort and his grumble, "I don't know why you had to show her my radio. I wish you'd learn to ask me first." We then clambered over the side to step into the rowboat. Perched high on the back seat, I watched David pull the oars through the water as he rowed us towards the big yacht - favoring his sore arm. It probably hurt. Vaguely, I wondered if it was still bleeding.

147

All the while, the knife in my jacket hem had been bumping comfortingly against my bottom as I moved from one boat to the other. I felt its smooth bulge now as I sat.

CHAPTER TWENTY NINE

Charlie waited for us on the main deck. He wore a smocked, black satin kimono, beautifully embroidered in an oriental pattern of peacocks, mums and bamboo leaves. His eyes were inscrutable slits and hard to read, but I felt his stance suggested arrogance. Overhead, a scattering of stars twinkled and blinked like a panel of control lights in a vast and high-tech universe. We reached the side of the yacht. A crew hand unrolled a rope ladder and motioned for us to climb aboard.

It could be a trap.

Was it a mistake to come here? Had I passed the point of stubbornness and become foolish?

From the bridge of the yacht a beacon of light flooded the area, casting long, dark shadows to the choppy water below. David steadied the tiny rowboat against the yacht's ladder and tied it.

Stubborn or not, it's too late to turn back now.

I glanced back at the sailboat. Cerese's shadow wavered past the cabin window then dropped out of sight. I stepped onto the bottom rung of the yacht and started climbing.

That same crew member pulled me up the last few feet and ushered us into a surprisingly large and lush stateroom. A padded couch lined one wall, upholstered in a nubby, Chinese red and turquoise-blue silk. On the other side exquisitely carved teakwood went from floor to ceiling with tiny recesses built in to hold a pair of Ming dynasty vases.

At the end of the room, three small, carpeted steps led up to a raised platform. Staged on top, as if he were part of the furnishings, stood Charlie. Shaking off the feeling that I had somehow entered the era of an old Charlie Chan movie, I entered the room a little behind David.

David bowed to him from the waist, prodding me with a hooked thumb to do the same. Then in a studied, theatrical gesture Charlie returned the bow with a slight nod and flicked a jeweled hand to two high back chairs strategically placed below and facing the bottom step. To David he said, "Welcome, comrade. Allow me to apologize for the humble accommodations."

He didn't speak to me.

"I apologize for any interruptions we might have caused," David said.

Charlie sniffed, his arms folded, his hands hidden in the kimono sleeves. "It is nothing. Please. Due to the late hour I fear it necessary to dispense with my normal formalities and the serving of tea. I will hear your requests now."

A cool rage began to fester as I sat in the chair. It was as if I, a mere woman, was subject to a lower class. And even though I knew his whole purpose was in gaining a psychological advantage I couldn't help but feel somehow subservient. And David definitely appeared shorter.

This little shrimp's beginning to tick me off.

With a mental grip on my composure I folded my hands primly in my lap and cleared my throat. It didn't help. Staring at the slitted cat-eyes I interrupted David's homage and said, "Excuse me. I have a request."

David thumped me in the side as if to remind me of my lowly position. Head bent, he seemed to be speaking to the steps. "There were a few matters that deserved your immediate consideration. If I may be so kind, I shall bring them to your attention."

David's cow-towing was making me sick. I inched away from him on the seat and stared again directly at Charlie and said, "I asked David to bring me here for a reason. Two men have died and there are others whose lives are in danger. I'll have to have your assurance that my mother and those twin girls will not be harmed before I leave here. If not, I can't guarantee the consequences."

Acting as if he'd heard or smelled something irritating to his senses, Charlie whipped out a handkerchief and dabbed the end of his nose. David took it as a sign. I shook his hand away from my arm and kept staring at Charlie.

That wizened little bastard is going to pay for this.

I cocked an eyebrow and sneered. "What happened, Charlie? You lose your job?" David gasped and dug at me again with his thumb. Slapping his hand away, I kept my attention on the little Asian. "Too bad. There for awhile, you looked like a real guy, driving around in that big limo. Of course they had to prop you up on cushions so you could see out the window. But that wasn't so bad, was it? David. Next time, remind me to get him a car seat."

Even from four yards away I could see Charlie tremble, his eyes scuttle wildly around the room. They settled on David. With a sniff, Charlie puffed up and said, "You will instruct your wench to be silent."

David was going nuts, trying to look humble and command me to shut up at the same time. I ignored him. Hands propped on my thighs I leaned back and looked Charlie straight in the eye. "Wench? Get real, you sawed-off little runt."

Charlie was staring at a point somewhere above my head. With a wry sneer, he jerked his head once and fluttered that same jeweled hand. Suddenly, two goons rushed me from behind. I managed one quick squawk and a kick to David's shin before they trundled me off down the hall to a back room. There I was tied, gagged, and shoved onto a small cot.

When they left, I heard their gibberish as they closed the door and fussed with the lock. It didn't work from that side. I could hear them jabbering all the way down the hall and finally slam the hallway door. Then it was quiet.

OK, Kate. You proved you had a big mouth. Now it was time to find my Mamma. I inched my way along the cot until I could lean my back to the corner. On the other side of the left wall would be the hallway. To the right - another room of some kind. With my left ear pressed tight against the paneling, I took a deep breath, held it, and listened intently to the murmurs and the occasional bleat from Charlie. He was scolding David.

Where'd that knife go? With the life vest still on, the goons hadn't bothered to check the back of my jacket. Inching the fabric up with my fingers, I pulled the part of the hem that held the switchblade into the palm of my hand. Grasping it firmly, I fumbled for the button that would eject its sharp blade. Once open, the smooth steel poked easily through the polyester padding of the hem and was in a perfect position to slice through the tape on my wrists. The one-hour time limit I'd given Cerese should be just about up. I automatically looked to my left wrist to check the hour before I realized my watch was gone. The goons had taken it along with my camera.

I almost left the life vest in the room but thought better of it. It'd be harder for them to drown me. Tiptoeing down the hall, I peered into the two extra rooms - if Mamma was on the boat, this is where they would most likely hide her.

The first room was empty, except for two more cots and a cloth bag with dirty clothes. The goons' bedroom. The other was a galley with a tiny bathroom off to one side. Opposite that was a circular staircase - leading to the upper deck. Charlie's quarters. I doubted they'd keep Mamma there, but I had to check for clues.

Charlie's futon bed was neatly made up, his clothing stored in a handsome cedar closet - including the chauffeur's uniform. A cordless phone, tucked inside a small nightstand, produced a score of buttons, all marked in Japanese. I tried a few and on the third tap, I discovered a bonanza. An intercom. Evidently, Charlie had the boat wired for sound, or at least the room they were in, and this phone was a receiver.

David's voice came through, loud and clear. Now that HIS life was on the line, he wasn't quite so humble. "You want me to take the shipment to Germany? Hey. Forget it. You know I can't make another trip in there!"

"Yes. You must. But - do not fear. Since the unification of East and West, the communists have lost power. Besides, I've arranged for everything. You have new identity - Norwegian passport and drivers license. I have seen to everything."

"No, Charlie. I'm not dealing with the Bundesbank. Not even a unified one. No way. What happens when they find out I don't even speak Norwegian? I'll just take it to the clothing factory. Taiwan's banks aren't nearly so damn particular and I can channel it from there to Hong Kong, as usual. In fact I'll leave tonight."

This answered a lot of questions for me. The women's clothes in David's condo, the imported liquor and cheeses without the normal U.S. stamp and labeling, not to mention their need for secrecy. David must be running some kind of international underground operation from the hidden room under his cabin.

"You will obey me! My Hong Kong sources are being watched. The Bank of England has sent auditors to examine our system of foreign exchange. It has become dangerous to deal with American-owned companies, everywhere. Your stupid government has allowed too many bank failures in your own country. Your world banks are scandalized. Now, even the Chinese have become distrustful of anyone coming from the West with money."

"But what happens when they find out I don't even speak Norwegian! This hotel/casino deal is contingent on getting that money in a form that I can use within the next couple of weeks. I'm already late. The first disbursements were due last month and Hampton's starting to ask questions."

"That is why you're going to Deusendorf. Your American tongue will be acceptable. My advisors tell me that you are expected and sufficient lodging has been reserved. Now, quickly. There is little time. The shipment will be ready, this time, in Bremerton. There will be an old Ford pick-up parked across the street from the main gate, in front of an old service station. A sign will be placed on the side that says 'Landscape Design.' The shipment will be under the tarp in the back. You will be there at 2:40 tonight. The plane leaves from Sea-Tac at 3:55. You will go through customs in Frankfort, then take train to Deusendorf. The customs agents have been well imbursed. You will have no problems and your bags will not be searched. Herr Grossenburger will meet you at the bank on Friday and handle all the transactions from there. Enjoy your trip."

I knew it. The creep is laundering drug money. Hauling it overseas, then funneling it back here and using it to fund his development schemes. No wonder they're so filthy rich.

"But Charlie," David whined. "For God's sakes. Let me at least sift it through some kind of business. What about that jewelry company? I could pretend to buy some jewels, pay for them with American travelers checks, then say I changed my mind. At least, that would give me a draft in yen. There's no way I can just walk up to some European bank and flop a suitcase full of unaccountable American dollars on the counter. Even if I manage to sneak it through customs, the bank will have to report it. You know that, Charlie."

"There is no time. Kobayashi want it now. He is not a man who is told to wait.

"Who? Kobayashi? You mean that big car manufacturer? What's he doing in a German bank? You know, I remember hearing something about him. Something about the Tokyo Stockmarket. Isn't he the guy that started this whole bashing business of the American labor unions? Yea. I saw it in *Man of Means Magazine*. That's what he wants with the dough, isn't it? To cover his ass. His stock took a nosedive and the dividends hit the skids. Probably played hell with their profit margins. And with the economy the way it is, I wouldn't doubt that Kobayashi's out more than a couple of bonuses. If he don't watch it, he'll be out of a job."

Charlie sounded like he was in the grips of an apoplexy. "You will excuse your vulgar tongue before I have it cut from your vile mouth. The name of Kobayashi will not be tarnished by the speech of a contemptible American dog."

"Hey, I'm sorry. Charlie, I, uh, don't get so upset. I didn't mean anything disrespectful. But there's no way I can get into Germany and back out. You know that."

I'd heard enough. Charlie, somehow, was in full control and had David eating out of his hand. I chanced a peek down the staircase, and up the hall. It was empty. Hurrying now, I moved back down to the area outside the main room and chanced a peek around the doorway.

David's back was to me, standing on the raised platform next to Charlie. There was something about the way the two of them looked....

That's it. Jack had said there'd been a tall guy and a kid at Frank's door. A funny, foreign-looking young man. Charlie was half his size. From the back and some distance away, he could have looked like a small boy.

That was the tie-in. In addition to the drug money, David's also helping to sell other people's children. If they could sneak boxes of cash out of the country, a few kids here and there wouldn't hurt. Some nice pocket change. Margaret took most of the risk, and was probably paid well for it. All the while, scooping up a nice check from the state for keeping welfare kids. They were still arguing. "Go," Charlie demanded. "And do as you're told. This discussion has made me weary."

I better get outta here. Where's the Coast Guard? Cerese should have called them by now. Trembling, I gauged the distance between the spot where I now stood and the door leading to the outside deck. About ten feet. But I'd have to cross in front of the open doorway.

"I don't mean to be arguing, Charlie....." David's voice sounded closer.

Oh, God. He's coming.

"....but it's much safer for both of us if I take the private jet."

"The answer is no! And next time you will remember not to bring your foolish women on board. Get out of here. Before I lose my temper and have you all fed to the sharks!"

"The women are all taken care of. I've already called the switchboard and warned them that there's a girl on my boat messing with my radio. They promised to ignore anything she tells them."

That bastard! So much for the Coast Guard. Palming the switchblade, I took a deep breath and crouched - ready to lunge for the outside door.

That was my biggest mistake. I should have been paying more attention to the hallway behind me. One minute, I was alone. The next minute, a cold gun muzzle poked in the soft part of my side. I jumped a foot high when an unfamiliar, unaccented voice muttered, "Don't move." He searched me for weapons, missing the most obvious place for the knife - still in my hand, hidden under the long sleeves of David's jacket. The sights on the gun barrel gouged painfully when he pushed me inside the room, saying, "Get in there."

Charlie squealed when he saw me. "What's this!"

The stranger shoved me into a chair. "I caught her eavesdropping." Hands on his middle-aged hips, he said to David. "This the broad I've been hearing about? I thought you were told to get rid of her."

Who is this guy? I watched the stranger warily, trying to determine how he fit in. When no one was looking, I tucked the switchblade under my thigh.

David blanched. "Christ, Joe. We can't keep killing these people off. She works for a newspaper. If she don't show up for work, every paper and T.V. station in the country will be on us like stink on shit."

Joe? I've seen that name somewhere....Yes. On the files I had sent to the Gazette, a memo had been signed, Joseph Platt.

I purposely leveled a stare at David and asked him, "Who do you mean, 'these people?' Mr. Cloud? Is that who you've been killing off?" But before he answered, I swung around to face the stranger - operating on pure intuition and raw nerves. "Or maybe it was you, who killed him. The big Indian was too much for Charlie's little bozos, and you had to step in to finish him off. Is that it?"

A purple rage rose up from Joe's neck like mercury on a hot day. *Good God, I was right.* He stepped forward, his hand groping for my neck. He didn't reach it.

Sliding to the floor on one knee, I slashed upwards with my knife - laying his palm bare to the bone. He gasped and stumbled backwards. I then sprang to my feet and leapt to the center of the room. Joe screamed and fell back, moaning. David stood stock still, watching...calculating...

Charlie flapped his arms like a red and blue robin about to take flight. "The woman! Go after her, you fool."

"Don't try it, David," I warned. "If I go down, you're going with me." Edging into the hallway, I slammed the door on them and shoved a chair under the doorknob.

Scrambling up the steps, I paused on the outside deck. I had to get off the yacht. A cold wind flung a spray of cold salt water in my face and stung my eyes. In the distance a small boat motor roared, its solitary light bobbing as the fast-moving craft smacked into the waves. The sailboat was still a good thirty feet off the stern.

I heard the splinter of wood. Probably David - bashing through the door. Quickly I climbed over the rail just as he barged up the steps. "Kate. Take it easy, now. You won't live ten minutes in that water. It's too cold."

"Back off, David. I've had about enough of you."

"Kate. Listen to me. You'll never make it. Don't jump!"

Squatting on the edge of the deck, outside of the rail, I took careful aim....and slid off.

CHAPTER THIRTY

I landed with a thud in the little rowboat. It dipped dangerously, taking in water. I dropped to my knees and hung on to the seat with one arm while slashing at the rope with the other - to free it from the ladder of the yacht. David peered at me from the deck of the yacht, then turned and disappeared from my view. I had to suppose he went back inside. Suddenly, Charlie's men ran up to the side rail, jabbering. Their tone seemed to change as they pointed at the speedboat - closing the gap, headed directly for them.

Maybe Cerese did reach someone.

Within minutes, the deckhands started up the yacht's engines and activated a small winch on the side of the cabin.

David. Lowering himself a lifeboat.

Positioning the ends of the oars over the water, I dipped and pulled as hard as I could - rowing out into the wild and choppy darkness of the bay. With any luck at all, David would take it for granted I'd be heading back to the sailboat and would be more worried about his own escape than coming after me.

Fat chance.

David stepped aboard his small craft and yanked the rope on its outboard motor.

Suddenly, the yacht's huge propeller also began to churn, whipping up a wake of sea water behind it. Just then, the speedboat appeared, streaking between the yacht and the anchored sailboat, throwing up a four-foot high wall of water as it circled around them. Doubling my efforts on the oars and using every ounce of energy I had left, I managed to stay on the outside of the wake of both boats.

The yacht's engine squalled as the large craft picked up speed, ignoring the efforts of the smaller boat to stop them. Soon they were running neck and neck, going north on Liberty Bay.

The speedboat's appearance must have frightened David off. Caught in the worst of the wake, his little boat threatened to capsize in the mountainous waves. Struggling to stay afloat, he turned the boat, heading into them straight on.

I had no idea who was in the speedboat, but I was grateful. David and Charlie were sent scurrying for cover, trying to save their own necks. As my tiny rowboat pulled away from them both, rocking precariously in the agitated waves, I was consumed by the black gusty night. The only boat left, besides my tiny craft - bobbing clumsily in the surging swell of whitecaps, was the sailboat. And by the looks of the activity on board, that wouldn't be there for long, either.

The steel chain clinked and groaned, as David pulled up the anchor. Framed in the window of the lighted cabin, a small brown face peered out from behind the curtain.

Cerese! What will David do with her now?

The sailboat's engine sputtered, then burst into gear, even before the anchor was fully up. The main sail jerked up the mast, burgeoning in a sudden gust of wind. For one moment, David was silhouetted against the white canvas. Then he was gone. And with the force of the wind combined with the engine, the sailboat whisked up the Puget Sound and in what seemed like only minutes, had disappeared from sight.

I'd been clutching both sides of the rowboat. My fingers were curled, white and numb, around its edge. Painfully, one by one, I loosened them. The wide expanse of the choppy water reached out for miles on every side of me. I could only guess at its depths. The little boat swayed with each play of the waves, turning and whipping, until I was no longer sure of any direction.

As the tiny boat topped a large wave, I could see the wink of a light from the shore. I wasn't sure which shore or even if it was the closest. But it was better than the nightmarish dark all around me. Wearily, I picked up the oars and began to row.

The crunch of gravel under the rowboat's prow and the sudden stop of its sway, startled me out of a deep sleep. I must have dozed off, and during the night, the boat drifted to shore. Shivering, I rubbed the back of my sore neck and looked up.

The first light of dawn lit up a forest of evergreens, crowding the edge of a rocky beach. Nothing looked fámiliar and there was no sign of humanity in sight. I stretched my stiff legs and tried standing up. They wobbled and my knees ached but I thought I could walk to get help.

Where in the world am I?

I jumped out onto the hard sand of the shoreline. A cold wind brought the scent of pine to my nose and blew down the gap between coat and neck. I hunched it up around my ears, shoved my hands in the pockets, and started down the beach.

About thirty feet away, I found a path. It wound around a small marsh reeking with skunk cabbage, then meandered up a slight incline. The trees would be a welcome shelter from the cutting wind. On the top of the hill, huffing and blowing from the climb, I flopped down on an old log and rested. I was on the edge of a meadow. There was something about this place.... A tingle scampered across the back of my shoulders and nibbled the nape of my neck. Facing into the meadow, I noticed a movement in the lower branches of a cedar tree.

Please... let it be a deer.

But, of course, it wasn't. As the morning sun broke over the tree tops, an old man stepped from behind the large tree. "Hello," he said, raising his old, gnarled hand above his head and nodding good-naturedly.

Am I seeing what I think....

I blinked and rubbed my eyes. He was still there.

"Welcome," he called, and walked into a swath of light spread like melted butter across the meadow. "Come this way."

Too tired to care if it was coincidence or fate, I stretched and lolled my head to the side and back. I felt spacey but ready to go on. Half numb, I stood up and started to walk towards him - feeling the swish of the tall grass against my legs and the hard earth of a somehow familiar trail beneath my feet.

I'd been here before.

Even before I looked up, I sensed the old man would be gone. But the path was there, firm under my feet, and I knew where I was and how to get home.

There to my left and a little behind the spot where the old man had stood, was an old shack. And splayed out on that side of the meadow wafted the scent of wild onions. A honeymoon cabin and the mother's old garden patch.

Camille's house would be just down the hill.

CHAPTER THIRTY ONE

When I walked into Camille's house, Hampton was waiting for me. "We were hoping you'd come back here," he said. He was alone.

"Where's Camille? Did Cerese make it back? She was on the boat with David." I blinked, trying to clear my mind. On wooden legs, I clumped to the phone. "We've got to stop him before he absconds with her....." The Tribal Police number had been scratched into the paint. I began to dial.

Hampton walked up and depressed the receiver button. I glared at him. "The girls are fine," he said. "I've sent them out of the county, to stay with some friends. They'll be safe there, until this all blows over. Something I should have done a long time ago."

"Cerese, too? Did David let her go?"

Hampton nodded. "She called last night from Poulsbo. Evidently, he saw no advantage to holding her hostage. He let her off at the dock, and I went in myself to pick her up."

"Oh. Well...as long as they're safe..." I was relieved, and I should have been more grateful to Hampton...

"I realize you consider us a band of inept savages. But if you'll bear with me for a moment, I..."

"Now that's where you're wrong. I've never said that. Actually, I see this whole tribe as being at the mercy of an uncaring government, oblivious to their needs. Stuck out here in the boonies without any of the human rights and privileges any other American takes for granted. Not even decent access to our Judicial System. Don't you see? That's what I've been trying to do, since I've been here. I do have access to them, and in a way that demands immediate attention. The media."

He nodded, softening a little. "Your enterprize and concern for the lives of those girls have been greatly appreciated. You've shown great vigilance and bravery. And many times, we have feared, without prudent regard for your own safety."

"So, if we agree on that, what's the problem?"

In answer, Hampton turned to the back bedroom door and gestured with one hand. Sims walked out, pulling a small wallet from the inside pocket of his vest.

I stifled a frightened gasp. "What's the meaning of this? What were you doing, hiding back there?" As his vest flapped open, I could see the edges of a gun - held fast to his shoulder by a holster. "Now wait just a minute," I said, beginning to back up. "I still have places to go. My mother's missing, and I've got to find her."

"And that's what we been trying to tell you." said Sims. His wallet now open, he stuck it up in front of my face, so close that I had to lean back a bit in order to see it. It was a badge. "FBI agent Sims at your service, Ma'am. I hear you've been busy, trying to solve our case for us. And doing a pretty fair job of it, too. If you don't mind, I'd like to be in on a little of your 'detecting.' Let my boss think I'm earning my keep."

To Hampton, I said, "Why didn't you tell me the FBI was here? What's the big damn secret?"

Sims replied for him. "Wasn't up to Hampton to tell you," he said. "For one thing, you don't have a security clearance. And for another, I believe we been suffering from what's commonly called a breakdown in communications." He paused for a moment, then said, "You wouldn't listen."

I absorbed that for a moment, not wanting to admit he was right.

"Now," he continued. "If you don't mind, I'd like to tag along while you go to fetch your Mamma. Who knows? Might even pick up a stray crook or two."

"Of course, I don't mind." To Hampton, I said, "You sent for the FBI?"

"That I did. Even before Cloud was found missing. Sims is an old, personal friend of mine. He's been conducting an ongoing, top-secret investigation for weeks now."

"Well. I'd been wondering why there wasn't more being done."

With a weary blink, Hampton said, "We just this morning got the clearance we needed, before we could reveal Sims identity."

I felt a nudge at the elbow. It was Sims. "Shall we go, then? Ma'am? The longer we wait, the harder it'll be to catch up." For the second time, his strong brown eyes riveted my attention and I was reminded again of a hawk. A golden hawk, not native to this area. "I'm ready. I just wish I knew where to find her."

Another look exchanged between the two men, then Hampton reached into a side jacket pocket and produced a crumpled piece of paper. "Will this help?" he asked. "Camille asked me to give you this, before she left."

Using the back of an old envelope, Camille had drawn the shape of a building, built out of what looked like brick, with porticoed windows and sashes on each side. The front entrance had wide steps leading up to double wooden doors. To one side, she had written a note. *'Kathy. I saw this in a dream last night. I don't know where this place is, but the people there care only for money and power. Your mother is locked inside.'*

Giving Hampton a quick nod of thanks, I said to Sims, "Now I'm ready to go."

"Will that help?" Hampton asked.

"I think so. It looks kind of familiar...." I turned to Sims and said, "C'mon. We can take my car."

"Yes, Ma'am." As Sims held the door open for me then followed me out, he said, "Riding in a red Porsche with a pretty Irish lass to drive it.... Huh. And they call this work. Wake me when it's over, would you?"

"Fine. Just quit calling me Ma'am."

The drive into Poulsbo was spent with Sims filling me in on some of the details. David indeed had a background of shady money deals. Very little was known about Charlie. "I've been on David's trail since before he left Vegas. Then when I heard that Hampton was doing a preliminary check on his credentials, we went to the Tribal Council to ask their support in exposing this whole drug-running, kidnapping scheme. At that time, it was scheduled as a simple fact-finding mission. Then when Cloud came up missing and later was found dead, we had to update it to a fullfledged, tactical operation. Now, don't get mad at me for telling you this, but that's why we wanted you to go home. Besides fearing for your safety, you were getting in the way." He watched me a minute while I drove through the tight turns of the little country highway. "There's one other thing you need to know. Just in case - say I get wiped out or you can't reach me."

I gasped at that, and turned to stare at him. "Wiped out?"

He crooked an eyebrow at me, his finely carved cheekbones and thin beak-like nose standing in stark relief against his dark skin. "It could happen. You know, some of our old warriors had a saying, 'It's a good day to die.' But, don't worry. That doesn't mean I'm going to die. Just hear me out. You remember the guy with the big gold ring? The one you were arguing with that day in the parking lot, right after they found Clouds body? He's my number two man. Came all the way from Washington D.C. to be my back-up. We died his skin and hair so he'd pass for Indian. He's in the area on a stake-out. So if you see him on the case, try not to blow his cover. See this?" Sims asked, waggling a set of car keys with an odd looking rectangular piece of plastic, emblazoned with the letter 'S.' "If you get in trouble and I can't help, twist the bottom section to the right, like this." He demonstrated. "My buddy has the receiver, and will be able to find you with it." He leaned closer to my arm and I realized he was looking at my bruises. "Are you healing up alright? You took some pretty bad hits. We should have been watching David closer. But we were trying to solve the problem from this end." He let me digest all of that for another few minutes, then said, "Now it's your turn. What's the scoop on your Mamma and how in the world did she get involved in this?"

I told him what little I knew, and this time, I included what I suspected. "Sims, the guy's got a lot of connections - political and financial - in this country and overseas. We're talking money laundering and kidnapping." He nodded and asked me what else I knew. I told him as much as I could, to the point of 'motor-mouthing' - rattling on a little too much and probably repeating myself a little too often - but I didn't really care. It felt good. Sims was an extremely easy person to talk to, never scoffing at me for having less than perfect control over my anger and acknowledging the areas in which I didn't have complete faith in our local fuzz. The only time he interrupted was to ask me to repeat - verbatim - what I'd seen, heard, and my impressions of the dispute that day in the Mayor's office with Belltower.

By the time I'd finished, we were cruising past David's church-condo. The sleek grey fender of the limousine bulged from the garage door and David's BMW had been sloppily parked behind it. It was canted off to the side of the driveway, the right front wheel sunk into the grassy yard and the driver's door was partially open.

Dad's old GMC was still across the street, right where I'd left it. At least no one had tampered with it.

"Pull in here, a minute," Sims said, thumbing at the empty lot. "I want to watch these guys for awhile." I did as he asked, parking on the other side of the old pick-up behind the same group of trees. They'd be hard-pressed to spot us - there weren't any windows on that side of the building and the GMC hid the little red car from their view. I was just getting ready to tell Sims the history of the old pick-up truck when he interrupted to say, "Looks like they're all there, for now. Probably getting their stories straight and destroying evidence while they plan their exit. I'm going to try to take them as they come down. You stay here in the car and don't let them see you. Lock your doors and if there's any gun fire, get down on the floor." He then got out, pulled his gun from its holster, and ran to the edge of the lot behind a tree. From there, he dashed across the road to the opposite side of the glassed-in entry way. I could just see his outline through both walls of the murky glass brick. He was around the corner, crouching in the flower beds.

I couldn't stand the suspense. Although Sims had practically ordered me not to, I had to watch. Removing the keys so that the buzzer wouldn't sound, I got out of the Porsche. Creeping low to the ground, I peered around the pick-up's front fender.

Within minutes, David, followed by Joseph Platt and several other men whom I took to be bodyguards, burst through the entry way door and propped it open. They each carried an armload of large boxes. Making their exit single file, the boxes piled up under their chins, they were forced to feel for the steps with their feet. Except for Platt - I was pleased to see that he had his left hand bandaged, obviously due to our little scuffle in Charlie's boat, and in a sling. He carried only a briefcase in his right hand.

Halfway to their cars, Sims hollered, "Take one more step and I'll blow your fuckin' heads off."

They stopped. The bodyguards bristled, casting dark, expectant glances at David.

Sims moved up behind them. "Now, set your boxes on the ground," he said. "Easy. And don't turn around." One of the hired guns tried looking over his shoulder. Sims immediately placed the barrel of his revolver against the guy's temple. "Go ahead. Look. While you're about it, why not try reaching for your revolver?" The guy's head swung back, staring straight ahead. Sims kicked their legs wide so that they stood in a spraddle, then ordered them once again to put the boxes down. Carefully. "Now drop your hardware - all of it." He jabbed his gun into the neck of the same body-guard. "You first, tough guy."

I'd about decided to crawl back, elated that things had gone so well, when a stout figure leapt from the still-open entryway door. *Sheriff Belltower.* One large, hairy arm locked under Sims chin. They struggled, knocking Sims off balance. The bodyguard snatched his gun off the ground and whacked it over Sims head. He went down.

Instantly, the men turned and hurled their boxes and briefcases - as many as would fit - into the trunk of the limousine. Slamming that shut, they piled in - the two bodyguards in the front seat, the rest of them in the back.

All but David. He ran toward the BMW.

The instant I saw Sims drop, I was on my feet. Crawling into the old GMC, I started it and roared across the street. The side door of the BMW loomed just ahead...

David saw me coming. He gunned the engine, jolting across the yard and over the top of the rhodie bushes. Barely missing my target - a broadside hit - I managed to clip his back fender. The pick-up hardly felt the jolt but David's car spun crazily to the street.

The hit jounced me slightly to the left and in direct line to the limo. I rammed it - head on - as they were backing out of the parking garage. The length of the limo saved their lives. Although the back of the car had squashed like an accordion and the right rear axle twisted in the shape of a pretzel, the men's seats were forward far enough to escape a direct hit.

The bodyguards tumbled out of the car and hit the ground rolling. They fired, shattering my windshield. I tried backing up - the engine had died. Tried starting it. Nothing. The truck wouldn't budge. They fired again, the bullets zinging within inches of my ears. Throwing my arms up, I hit the seat - crawled to the other side - and cranked down on the door handle. It wouldn't open. The impact had sprung the lock.

More shots. The side-window burst into a hail of flying glass. The bullets peppered the door on the driver's side, some of them piercing the truck body and ricocheting around in the cab. I threw my arms up to protect my face and rolled onto the floor.

I laid there, waiting.... What had Sims said?

This would be a good to die.

But, I'd always wanted...thought there'd be more. A husband. A baby. A home.

NO! God help me. I'm not ready to die! Not yet.

A volley of gun-fire erupted. Crawling into the area under the dash - a surprising amount of space - I inched my way over the top of the gas and brake pedals and burrowed up against the engine wall on the passenger side.

Suddenly, the firing stopped.

Silence, except for the ringing in my ears. The shots had all but deafened me.

They're coming. A few tiny sounds - *that was a man's voice.* I didn't know who...but I could guess. He entered the cab.

Hold my breath. Don't let them hear me.

Too late. He pulled on my ankle. I kicked, sobbing - "Get away. Leave me alone."

"Hey. Kathy. Take it easy. It's me, Sims. Your friendly FBI agent. Remember me? Come on out, honey. Everything's okay."

CHAPTER THIRTY TWO

Sims held me while I shook - sobbing uncontrollably. The eery smell of death lingered in the air like dust. I blew my nose, again and again. It didn't help.

The bodyguard lay spread-eagled on the ground. On his chest, a shiny, dark maroon spot dirtied his grey suit. He was dead. Across from him, Joseph Platt sank on rubbery knees to the ground. White-faced and bleeding from a shot to his upper left shoulder, he watched helplessly as siren-screaming squad cars and unmarked sedans filled the parking lot. His left arm dangled uselessly, his right had been handcuffed to the crushed body of the limousine. The other bodyguard, whom I now recognized as Sims back-up with the gold ring, had just finished tying the last knot on Sheriff Belltower's feet.

Whipping out a white handkerchief, Sims dabbed at the cuts on my face. The blast of gunfire had showered me with pieces of the shattered windshield. Blood flowed, warm and pasty, from several of the larger wounds and I could feel him plucking shards of razor-sharp glass from their depths.

"Well, Doc," I said, making a mental effort to pull myself together. "Am I going to live?"

"It actually looks worse than it is," he said. "A couple cuts could stand a few stitches, but other than that, you'll be alright." By now, his hand-kerchief was red and soggy from sopping up my wounds. Trying to keep me from seeing the sight of my own blood, he stuffed it in his back pocket and said, "Some nice big bandages would come in real handy about now."

I jerked a thumb at the GMC cab, bullet riddled and bashed beyond recognition. "There used to be an old army-issue Red Cross kit under the seat." As Sims searched for it, I added, "Look for a narrow metal box with one of those funny, hinged lids on it."

"Got it," he said, flipping the latch and forcing it up. "Gauze, tape, and here's some bandages still sealed in plastic."

Sims had just finished dressing the larger cuts when an ambulance arrived and three medics jumped out. Two of them paused to check the dead bodyguard and began the procedure to resuscitate him. The other one quickly examined me - my facial wounds and any evidence of my going into deep shock. "I'm OK," I said, waving them on. "Check out the guy over there with the bullet holes." From the corner of my eye, I'd seen Sims drag the Sheriff into the back seat of a squad car.

By now, twenty or more cops and medics hustled in what space was left in the graveled parking lot, examining, grilling, and reporting into their shortwave radios. Approaching Sims from the back, I got there just in time to hear him interrogate Belltower. "You got one chance," he said, "...to tell me where Kathy's Mamma is being held." He drew his gun and pointed it at the Sheriff's leg. "Lie to me, and you lose a knee-cap."

"I tried to talk him out of it," the Sheriff whined.

"Who?" Sims demanded.

"Platt. He said I had to get rid of her. Said she knew too much."

Mamma. I stumbled as if I'd been hit in the stomach. I was afraid I'd be sick.

"You son-of-a-bitch." Sims set his jaw and aimed. "Say goodbye to walkin'..."

"No! Don't shoot. No, wait! I didn't...do it. I couldn't. I swear to God, she's fine. I got her hid away. Been bringing her meals and everything. Even let her get up and walk around when I can."

"Where?"

"Can't tell you that. You let me go though, and I'll see to it that she's turned loose and gets a ride home."

Sims shook his head. "No deals, Belltower."

"Fine. But you won't prove a damn thing in court. And Kathy's Mom will starve without me there to feed her."

Sims looked at me. "You heard him?"

I nodded. A cool, bubbling rage had begun to replace the nausea.... "Never mind, Sims. I just realized where I've seen Camille's drawing. The Capitol Mortgage building in Seattle."

"I'm going after her," he said. "Mind if I borrow your car?"

"Won't need to. I'm going with you."

"Kathy, you're in no shape to be...."

"I said I was going. She's my mother. I'll either go with you or I'll go alone."

Sims grabbed my hand, stomping towards the street. "Women," he growled. "What ever happened to the days when they did what they were told." "Look, Chief," I said, swinging into a running walk to the car. "I want my Mamma home. Safe. You help me do that, and you can order me around all you want."

"Will you listen?" He got into the drivers side of the Porsche.

I ran around and jumped into the passenger side. "Sure. I'll listen to you. Anytime." I handed him the keys.

"Will you do what I say?"

"Simply because you told me to? Probably not."

He grinned, winked, and spun onto the road. "I didn't think so."

On the way back to Seattle, I asked Sims to fill me in on some details.

"It looks like Belltower has been David's front man, all along. At least, here in Washington State. Gave Abrahamson the credibility he had to have, in order to pull off this whole development scheme. Covering up for him, shredding a little paperwork here and there, strong-arming a few permits through the city planning department, and giving credence to David's lies to the passport office with his own sworn testimony. We can nail his nuts to the wall on that one."

"But why did he go after my mother? What did she ever do. Or was it simply a way to get to me?"

"I don't think so. From what you've said, the Sheriff and your Mamma were romantically inclined way before you ever showed up. Belltower probably liked her. Maybe even thought he was in love with her. He was up for retirement next year." Sims shrugged, thoughtfully. "Who knows why these guys cross over the line from cop to crook. Sometimes there's not a hell of a lot of difference. Still, most of them walk the straight and narrow right up to the end. Saw a chance to make a big bunch of money - enough to take his new bride on one humdinger of a honeymoon. Evidently, he couldn't pass it up. But as far as your Mamma's concerned, I think he really wanted someone to enjoy his golden years with."

He parked in the alley, next to the Capitol Mortgage building. It looked strangely vacant until I realized that today was Sunday.

We ran to the back side of the building. The door there was a sheet of metal overlaying solid wood - set into a fortress of brick with no windows. Sims flattened himself against the wall, next to the right hand side of the door and pulled me in behind him. His gun was out and at eye level. We waited, listening intently.

No one came, no sounds were heard. Nothing.

Sims pulled a wad of keys and little silver prongs from his pocket. The lock was easy - it gave way to one of his master keys on the fourth try. The dead bolt took longer. With his ear resting on the metal of the door and to the left of the bolt, he delicately tried each tined prong in the key hole - using only the slightest pressure. Suddenly, a quick twist and the bolt slammed home.

We were in the building.

To the left, a short hall with offices on each side dead-ended with the sign *Conference Room* over the door. Ahead of us, another hall gave rise to more offices and a staircase with polished wooden banisters next to the front door.

To the right - a small elevator.

Sims pushed the down button but didn't seem surprised when the red window lit up, saying *Restricted Area. Use Code Card.* "That little weasel," he mumbled. I supposed he meant the Sheriff. "Come on. There has to be some stairs going down." We thumped along the wall and under the staircase. He pointed to the first office. It was unmarked.

"Gotta be in there," he said. "Only place it can be."

A jingle of keys, another quick turn, and we entered a large, plush office. Behind the receptionist's desk a plaque over another door read, *President, Joseph Platt.*

"Bingo."

The door had been propped open with a small paperweight. He motioned with a finger to his lips to keep quiet. Assuming the same position as we had outside, the revolver clutched in both hands, Sims entered the room. Except for the office furniture and a root-bound tree sprouting from a hammered-brass urn, the room was empty.

But it hadn't been empty very long. Behind the polished cherry-wood desk, a portion of the wall containing an exquisite mural of wild, galloping horses had been scooted to one side on hidden runners in the carpet. It exposed the front of another elevator. The person who had used it last had either left it open in their haste or was still down there.

"We'll have to take it," Sims whispered. "It's the only way down." He pushed the button and waited - gun aimed and cocked.

A moment later, the elevator opened. It was also empty.

Sims stepped in first. He thudded each of the interior walls with the heel of his hand, then motioned me inside. At the last moment, he blocked the accordion doors from closing. Going to one knee, he indicated that I should step onto his shoulders. As I did, he stood up - positioning me just under the ceiling tile. "You'll be safer up there," he said.

I shoved. It wouldn't move. Shoved again, then shook my head. Whatever disaster may be down there, we'd be facing it head-on. No one was escaping through the ceiling. Not even us.

"Shit," Sims muttered under his breath. "A solid, metal box. Kathy, I think you ought to stay up here. You can be look-out in case they get past us."

"Forget it, Sims. She's my mother, and I'm going."

"Alright." He then removed his foot and the door slid shut. And in less than a breath and a heartbeat later, we were on the basement floor. Mamma couldn't be far. *Please God, let her be alone.*

I was wedged behind Sims in the corner when the door slithered open. He motioned for me to stay back, then burst into the room - gun blazing at the ceiling lights.

Then...silence. No return fire. No screaming.

It was dark and I had no idea where'd he'd gone. The suspense was too much. I peered around the edge of the doorway, hoping I could see Mamma - praying I would hear her cry out in relief... No such luck. I couldn't see her or Sims, either one.

It was a large, full basement with several rooms portioned off so recently that the glued tape on the drywall still looked wet. With an angry gesture, Sims signaled from behind a short stack of lumber that I should stay inside.

I waited - edgy from the hollow sound of my hammering heart and faint from a growing dread.

Mamma.

The minutes ticked by, I checked my watch continually.

Suddenly, the sound of shuffling feet...a muffled gasp...a shout, "Drop it. Drop it, I said, or I'll kill her." *That voice. I know that voice.*

It belonged to David.

"Don't push me Sims," he growled. "I'm not in to shooting women, but you better know I'll do it if I have to." *He's coming this way.*

In my agitation, I'd been fiddling with the key doo-dad Sims gave me. The transmitter that sent an SOS to his sidekick. I twisted the yellow 'S' on, watching for it to respond. It did not blink or emit bleeps. I had not idea if the signal worked or if it was received. Or if it would reach all the way to Poulsbo.

"Then I'd advise you not to use that elevator," Sims warned him. "There's a slew of cops on the top floor, both in the office and the hallway. Just waiting for you to appear and mow your ass down like a wooden duck in a shooting gallery."

"I have no intention of using that elevator."

There WAS another way out.

I then heard sounds like someone kicking. "Jerks," David said. "They put the damn drywall up with one measly door and forgot to leave me a key."

Taking advantage of the confusion, I peeked around the corner. Sims was across the room, his hands up. With an almost imperceptible shake of the head, he tried communicating the idea that I shouldn't take any chances.

Too late. His way didn't work. Now we'll try mine.

David's back was to me, bashing at the lock with his foot. Mamma stood next to him - David's gun leveled at her chest while he kicked.

Her hands were tied, her mouth taped, but her eyes were wide open. She looked over and saw me. Quickly, I shook my head and winked. The proud shine in her gaze told me all I needed to know. We were on the same wave-length. She looked back at David and resumed the same expression of fear, but I sensed in her a new vigor and assurance. I then dropped down on all fours, crawled out of the elevator, and behind a stack of boxes.

Their attention was now on Mamma as she began to gyrate and work her jaw. Her muffled yells, smothered by the gag over her mouth, demanded David's attention. He pulled enough of the tape aside to hear her speak.

She said, "If I'm expected to go with you, I'll have to use the restroom first."

"There isn't time. You'll have to wait."

"Then make time," she insisted.

"Look, Lady. You'll just have to wait." There was little left of the doorknob but a splintered hole. He shoved the door wide and jerked a thumb at a vehicle which had been parked in the make-shift garage. A new, four-wheeled jeep. Motioning to Mamma with his gun, he said, "You're coming with me. Get in, and let's go."

Drawing herself up to her full, five-foot-two height, and with a huffy sniff, she said, "Mr. Abrahamson. I am a grown woman and old enough to be your mother. Please believe that I am quite capable of knowing when I can wait and when I cannot. Now before I embarrass us both any further, I intend to use the sorry excuse of a lady's room before we leave." And with head held high, she proceeded to disengage her arm from his grasp and turned on her heel. On her path to the bathroom, she walked right past me. As she pretended to smooth her skirt over her hips, she glanced and returned my wink without once breaking in her stride. Once there, she made a point of locking herself inside.

That-a-way Mom.

But it wasn't over yet. David had merely swung his pistol toward Sims. And this time, he used both hands, at arms length, and aimed. "Looks like as good a time as any to get rid of you. Dead men don't tell any tales."

Sims glared back, tall and unafraid.

I had to do something. Next to me on the floor was a stack of boxed nails, the one on top already opened. The large ones, I'd seen used for framing. I grabbed as many as one hand could hold - stood up - and threw them at David as hard as I could. Then ducked back down behind the boxes.

It worked. Caught off guard, he jerked his head in my direction. A volley of deafening gun-fire followed. Hands over my ears, I crouched down behind the boxes, staying there even after the shooting stopped. At least one of them had to be dead. Maybe both. Again, I waited, wondering...

I looked up, to see David hovering over me.

"Are you ever going to learn," he growled. "C'mon. You and your mother, both. I'll have to decide what to do with you on the way."

"No, David. Take me with you but leave Mamma alone. Otherwise, I swear to God, I'll make your life so miserable you'll wish you'd never been born."

"You probably will. But don't forget. That can work both ways. And I'm the one with the gun."

I had to do something. Standing up, making it a point to have full eye contact, I said, "That's what I've been trying to tell you." Hopefully, I sounded sultry enough to be convincing. I then walked towards him, swinging my hips with exaggerated bump-and-grinds. "Remember that day on your sailboat and later on at the beach? I do. I can't stop thinking about it." Sidling up to his side, I leaned into him, my pelvis brushing his thigh. "It seems to me, we've got some unfinished business to attend to." Deliberately, I arched my body and pursed my lips as if poised for a kiss while mashing my hard belly against his manhood. "Oh, yea," I purred. "Something has got to be done about this."

He responded, his left hand kneading the hard muscle of my butt. His other hand still held the gun. "You little vixen," he said. "Don't think I don't know what you're up to."

"Of course you do. You're a business man. Trade me for my Mamma. Let her go, and I'll come with you. As long as she's safe, I'll work for you, be your lover, anything you want. Just let her be." As my fingers played inside his lapel, I kept the eye contact going. "We could have a lot of fun, you and I."

Behind me, I could hear Mamma fumble with the bathroom doorknob and come out. "No, Kathleen," she said. "I can't let you do it."

169

"Shut up, Mamma. It's the only way." With a blatant thrust against David, trading him stare for stare, I said to her, "David says he's agreed to let you go. Go ahead and take the elevator up, call a cab, and go home, Mamma. I'll get in touch with you when I can."

"No, Baby. No. I can't let you do this...."

"Go, Mamma. There's no other way." To David, I said, "She's not going to make a statement to the police, or testify, or cooperate in any way. Are you Mamma?" I paused. When she didn't answer, I said, "She's going to go home and keep her mouth shut. She'll do that in order to keep me safe. I'm going to go with you and everyone's going to mind their own business."

Ignoring my efforts completely, Mamma walked up to the side of us and said, "I take it, your name is David?" He nodded, his gaze finally leaving mine to watch her.

"David, you're obviously an intelligent man. And you've got to know, that this is no way to begin a relationship. If you really cared one whit about my daughter, you'd see the fallacy of this whole escapade. Love is not a thing to delivered on demand, like a pizza. You must earn it. Be deserving of it. And that is done by showing respect and a high regard for the other person's well-being. Now, you can swing that gun of yours around all day. But it won't help. Eventually, she will end up hating you for it. And you'd feel forced to shoot her and me, both. Is that what you want? Go on your way, David. And leave us to pick up the pieces of our lives as best we can. Do that, and you'll have our respect and our promise to 'keep our mouths shut' as Kathy so aptly put it. I doubt there's anything we could tell the courts that they don't already know, anyway."

For one breathless moment, Mamma and I waited - watching his eyes change colors like a chameleon. Just then, the elevator door slid shut and whispered its way up to the main floor. It had to be Sims back-up man, responding to the transmitter. But David didn't know about that. "Looks like the troops upstairs are tired of waiting," I said, backing up. "You better make up your mind, David. Time's a-wasting."

He grabbed me, giving me a long, tonguey smooch - his gun still wavering in mother's direction. "I'll talk to you, later," he said. Then he was gone.

The four-wheeled drive started up, and a garage door lifted. And as he drove away, I said, "Holy shit! I can't believe we got away with it. You talked him out of it, Mamma. You really did."

"My brave, brave little girl," she said, hugging me. "Did you really think I was going to let him take you away from me? She then got up and walked over to Sims. His buddy had arrived on our floor and gone straight to his side. "This poor man. Is he a friend of yours, dear?"

"Mamma, don't. He's....dead. It's best you don't go over there."

"Don't be silly. Kathy, get to a phone and call an ambulance. This man's been hurt, and appears to be unconscious. But he's not dead. Not yet, anyway."

"You mean he's alive?" Running over, I grabbed Sims wrist and tried for a pulse. The back-up man nodded and loosened Sims belt.

"Of course he's alive," Mamma said. "But he's been hit and he'll need a doctor's care. Hurry, now. There's a phone on that desk in the corner."

CHAPTER THIRTY THREE

A few weeks later, the tribe held a feast - serving some of the most delicious barbecued salmon I'd ever eaten. The twins shared the spotlight as the guests of honor and I'd been invited. Hampton sat across from me.

"So," I said. "How's your casino deal going?"

Digging into his shirt pocket, Hampton produced a letter and gave it to me to read. It was from a group who worked for the Department Corp of Engineers. They'd put a permanent stop to any more building on the island. "We'd still like to have a casino. But it would be more feasible to simply add it onto the bingo hall, here on the mainland. It won't be so exclusive and a lot easier to get to. We're looking for another mortgage broker, now."

"I'm sorry I was such a pain in the neck," I said. "I don't mean to be that way."

"It's not uncommon for misunderstandings to arise between the white man and the Indian. It's a problem that's been going on for generations." With a show of affection normally reserved for private, he grasped Camille's hand, then fumbled for Cerese's, drawing it away from her lap. His adams apple bobbed - the veneer on his intensely guarded emotions beginning to wear thin. As I pretended to be intrigued by a fuzzball on my sweater, he cleared his throat and said, "We all knew you had the best interests of the girls in mind."

Touched to the quick, I asked Cerese as gently as I could, how she managed to call for help out there on the bay. Camille laughingly answered. "That wasn't Cerese. It was me, all along. Things were happening so fast, I just never bothered to correct you." She looked downcast for a moment for having lied, and then said, "It was like, I finally knew what it meant to be a twin. There for awhile, I sort of felt I was Cerese."

Surprised, I mumbled something bane and questioned Camille as to who she'd called with no phone on board and the Coast Guard having been told by David to ignore her calls for help. "Well, when the SOS didn't work," she said, "I called the ham radio station and asked them to hook me up to Hampton. I found the phone number on a pamphlet in the drawer. Hampton said that Mr. Sims would be coming right away."

Cerese then piped up and said, "I'm sorry about Frank."

Thinking I'd be big-hearted on this one, I replied, "There's nothing for you to apologize for. You didn't do anything."

"No, I mean, I'm sorry about setting him loose like that. I should have known he'd come after you. Just didn't think."

This was a bit much. I was flabbergasted. "You what? What does that mean - set him loose?"

"I just had to go to the jail for awhile and see my Mom. Or anyways, you know, Margaret. I always called her 'Mom.' We talked for awhile and I promised her I'd finish school and stuff. And I also paid Frank's bail. I hope you're not mad, Kate."

"But why? What did he ever do for you besides bat you around a lot?"

"Well, that's it. Don't you see? I hated him so much! And I knew they'd get him off, somehow. The cops had to have proof. These guys break the law all the time, Kathleen. And just run off in their big jet with their wads of money, like they're better than everybody else. I'm sick of it."

"So you..."

"I took your extra camera and followed him. I was going to catch him in the act. And I knew where Mamma had some money stashed. It was under the back porch there at the cabin. There's this opening on the end and she shoved a bag of it under there." I nodded, remembering the cat fight under my feet and my sudden fright. "There was just enough to get him outta jail. Then I hid in the trunk of the Buick. I'd fixed it last week, so that the next time he shoved little Billy in there, he'd be able to get out by pushing on the wall and crawling out around the back seat. Man, does that trunk ever stink of fumes." I nodded again, prodding her to finish explaining. "So anyways, Frank drove right to the dock. Camille's boat wasn't there, so he stole Hamptons. Right after he left, I saw Camille come out of the meeting hall. When I told her where I was going, she insisted on coming with me. She knows this guy in Lomolo that rents out boats and we got one of his. We were in David's house when we heard this really big blast from the basement. Like dynamite blowing up. Then when you sort of appeared in the kitchen, we hid in the shadows of the dining room. Camille's the one that followed you outside. She's got this idea that she's safe - no matter what. Says she's got spirits guiding her. I stayed back trying to find some money." She paused, giving me an impudent glance. "We're orphans, Kathleen. We're gonna hafta live somehow."

A discussion followed about the old man in the onion field. Camille insisted it was her grandfather - or rather a vision of her grandfather. He'd died some six years ago. When I told her I didn't think that I was up to having visions, she babbled on about how my bravery had brought me power and wisdom. She felt certain that some divine being had appointed me a guardian spirit.

Me? Who am I to say? I wasn't sure what to believe. Their answers to the age-old questions of the meaning of life seemed to be as credible as anyone else's. And if some their gods wanted to take me under their wing, I could use all the help I could get.

They had set up long tables in the park for the feast. Most of us were groggy from eating too much, the others had begun to bat a baseball back and forth and run a few bases. Sims sat a few seats down from me, still eating. I nursed a cold beer, and Mamma went in search of a rest room.

After Sims and I found Mamma in the basement of the Capitol Mortgage building, scared and roughed up a little, she insisted on speaking to the FBI immediately. I told her she already was speaking to the FBI and explained about Sims and his gold-ringed back-up. She made their case. More than willing to testify against Sheriff Belltower in the Superior Court hearing next week, Mamma gave the statement and signed it as to how Joseph Platt - the mortgage broker from Las Vegas, happened to be on the same ferry as Belltower and her. Saying she'd swear it on a stack of Bibles, she told how he'd approached the Sheriff at the counter as he paid for his coffee, and said, "Be sure to burn Cloud's autopsy report the minute it comes in. And get me some blank forms, including some of those death certificates, so I can write up something we can use." He hadn't realized that her and the Sheriff were together until it was too late.

Mamma had evidently overheard and seen just enough to make her dangerous. Belltower then testified that Joseph Platt was the one who insisted that she be 'put away.' The Sheriff had indeed defied the orders to kill her and hid her away in that basement as much for her protection as his own, until after the election and Platt went back to Vegas. The Mayor seemed to be clean but was still under investigation.

Mamma came back from the ladies room, straightening her blouse and swinging her pocketbook with some of her old, jovial manner. Timmy bounced at her heels, sniffing every leaf and bush, and hiked his leg at a rock.

The girls had started a baseball game. Timmy spied a baseball flying through the air and before it had time to hit the ground, he stormed after it - barking excitedly. Mamma went after him, and was soon drug into the game by Camille and handed a bat.

There were a few things that didn't make sense and I still felt uneasy. "Sims," I said. "If that was you in Hampton's speedboat, what did you hope to accomplish by tailing that big yacht? You must have known you didn't stand a chance of getting on board."

"I'd called the Coast Guard before I left. Remember, that was before we learned that David had already squelched any possibility of their help, and I had no reason to doubt they'd come."

"So, where's Charlie now? I wonder if we've really accomplished anything with him and David still loose. Of course, the Indians are better off without them around. But won't David start up his little game, somewhere else?"

"The last time I saw Wong, he was headed north up Puget Sound and I figure he'd be going out to sea. That boat of his could take some pretty high swells if the deckhands were any good at all. And I have a suspicion they were. David? I have no idea. He's one of those guys you just can't predict. That's what's made him so hard to catch."

I'd already given Sims a copy of my notes, all of David's mail from Frank's car, (Sims never asked who opened it) and the sheet of paper I'd taken from David's computer room. They'd deciphered it as a warning from Vegas that Charlie was about to double cross David. It had said,

If you're going to make your move, you better do it now. I now told him about their arguing on the yacht and Charlie's insistence that David go to Germany.

Sims nodded and said, "There was bad blood between those two, all along. David must have known for some time, where Charlie was getting the drug money from. And when David found out about the double cross, he had to start making plans to eliminate Charlie and take his place in the very lucrative money-laundering business. Evidently, he had to stove up the ties with Hong Kong or find an even better outlet for the boxes and boxes of cash he took over there. But - and keep this under your hat." Pinning me with a piercing stare, until he was sure I could be trusted to with top security secrets, he said, "We can't prove it yet, but we think he might be forging new ground with Saudi Arabia. Sources have it that he's approached a world bank in England, about taking American cash - no questions asked. It's owned by one of those oil-rich Sheiks. I believe, that was the purpose for the kid. The little blond boy. As payment to this Sheik for a little arm-twisting with the banking regulators. You know, Hong Kong is going back under the thumb of the United Kingdom, pretty soon. There's bound to be a lot of audits going on." The computer print-out also had the dates and pick-up places for the next two weeks' worth of drug money. Of course, the event in Liberty Bay had put a kibosh to that.

"So," I said, "Has your tail on Charlie turned up anything? I hate the thought of them getting away, scott free."

"Ah, don't worry your pretty little head about it. There was anony-mous phone call - definitely from some Chinese guy. Could hardly speak English. He fingered Charlie, docked in a San Francisco port and hidin' out in Chinatown. We got a warrant and a searched the yacht. Found a big bunch of cash in one of the rooms on the yacht. You know, them big old garbage sacks? The kind these little home-owners put grass clip-pings in? The money was in them sacks. Just layin' loose in there, tied up with one of those little twisty things. The heavier baggies, like the ones my wife...well, exwife I should say - the ones she uses to cook a big ole' pot roast in, these baggies were full of heroin. His goons been peddling it up and down the coast. We promised them immunity though, if they'd testify. Usually, the agency follows the 'bird inna hand is better than two inna bush' rule. But they're going for the cheese on this case. Big time. Going to hold Ole' Charlie's feet to the fire. Looks like we've got the evidence and eye-witnesses this time, to make it stick."

Just then, I heard the crack of a bat hitting a ball. The game had attracted a small cheering section, and everyone of them were shouting encouragements. "Come on. Run, Mamma, run. Go, go, go."

Sims and I watched for a moment, my heart wanting to burst with pride. "Would you just look at her? Can you believe, that's my 52-year-old mother? Migod, she's going to make a home run."

Sims smiled and winked broadly. "Your Mom? Yep. I wouldn't expect anything less."

I wasn't surprised at his flirting. Just undecided what I thought of it. *I am NOT going to rush into this.* Lowering my eyes to the table, I shrugged and said, "Well, what can I say?" We watched them playing a little longer, saw Camille and Cerese hug my Mom and clap each other's back. "Looks like they won the game. Now, if we just knew what really happened to Joe Cloud... Damn it, Sims. One of these apes had to kill those girls' Dad. I refuse to buy this crap about drowning...."

"Hold on there, Irish. We got Cloud's killer, long time ago. Didn't you know? That Vegas dude - Joseph Platt. Him and Frank killed him. We got him dead to rights. You remember those memo's you sent over from that computer in the tunnel? There ain't no way he can weasel out of that one. He's in there as we speak, spouting pages of facts, names, and dates on these other birds as a trade-off for a lighter sentence."

"Oh. Wow. No, I uh, didn't know about that." I thought for a moment, humbled by all that had happened. "I don't know how to thank you. I did the best I could, but...."

"Hells bells, girl. You don't know your own strength. Without your contributions, we'd still be muddling around in this mire up to our necks. You were the one to expose these bozos. Alls we did, was the clean up."

"Well, thank you for saying that. And for going with me to get my Mom, and....just everything."

"Aw, c'mon, Katie. You know, it seems to me, that any man that can be trusted with a girl's Mom should ought to be safe enough to escort her to a movie. What do you say? Next week sometime?"

"I will, if you'll tell me one more thing. What happened to David?"

"David got away. Can you believe it? The biggest catch of all. And we lost him."

"I thought Charlie was the big...."

"Yea, Charlie's the cheese alright. But this guy's the rat. He's been on the 10 most wanted list for years. We been close, time and again, but right at the last minute, he gives us the old slipperoo. Ever damn time. It's all that equipment he's got. There was stuff in that tunnel I didn't know was invented."

The dismay and extreme agitation I felt must have been written all over me. Sims patted my hand and said, "Hey. Don't worry about it. We'll get him. OK? You know, this guy's history goes all the way back to the second World War. We've heard that his Pappa was an SS Troop in Germany. Carried out Hitler's little schemes. War criminals. His Mom and Dad, both. What threw us for so long, was that they actually took on the name of a Jewish family. The Abrahamsons, was a real family. A family they disposed of. When they were faced with having to flee Europe, they used this family's papers and adopted their name. Now, that's cold. Anyway you look at it."

"He's got stuff imported from Germany, all over that house of his."

"Buys it on the black market. Hong Kong, Taiwan, just about anywhere. The thing is, he don't dare to set foot on German soil. The German prosecutors are right serious about hunting these holocaust criminals down. We're getting closer all the time, though. With Charlie and his hoods under lock and key, we just might have a case. We'll get him, Kath. I swear to God, we will."

CHAPTER THIRTY FOUR

Back in my cubicle at the Seattle Gazette, I sat wondering how I could, or even if should try to tell the whole story. Only the facts were pertinent. But, how much of it was... factual? At my last trip to the reservation, the council had decided to move Camille and Cerese into David's house on the island. There'd been enough money stashed in the bureau to get them through their last years of High School and, with the help of a grant, put Camille through nursing school and Cerese through her first four years towards a degree in Engineering. At the office I'd been promoted to full-fledged reporter, which meant that never again would I suffer through another lady's tea or an obituary. Gunner had in fact, given me the run down on the immoral Tacoma Mayor with the armful of cocaine. His Honor had turned down his bid for re-election and ran off with his girlfriend Ruby. I was asked if I wanted to do a piece on his wife who had ratted on him in the first place and then had mysteriously disappeared.

Blowing a loose-lipped sigh, I stared back at the gaping green square of my computer screen. Then did some finger stretches and poised them over the keys. I still felt drained, and mildly depressed. I typed in my byline and made an attempt at a title. Tappity-tap.

Suddenly, a message over-rode my own writing.

Hello, Kate. Still mad? I miss you. My pony is corralled at the San Antonio Steakhouse in Kent. Buy you lunch? The Duke.

I knew the restaurant well. They had the best steaks around and individual dining rooms in the back. I made a quick phone call to Sims. "I smell a rat," I said. "You interested?" I told him about David in the steakhouse in a strangely hoarse whisper.

"You're damn right, I'm interested."

"I assume you can take care of the details without me?"

He agreed.

I hung up.

Snatching a kleenex from the box in my drawer, I blew my nose and wiped a watery eye. I then tapped the delete key to erase the message and began to write my story.

The whole story.

It no longer belonged just to me.

THE END

This speech was made by Chief Seattle on the shores of Elliott Bay, in 1854 and in his native tongue, at a spot that is now in the heart of the City of Seattle.

"The son of the White Chief says his father sends us greetings of friendship and good will. This is kind of him, for we know he has little need of our friendship in return because his people are many. They are like the grass that covers the vast prairies, while my people are few; they resemble the scattering trees of a storm-swept plain.

The Great-and I presume-good White Chief, sends us word that he wants to buy our lands but is willing to allow us to reserve enough to live on comfortably. This indeed appears generous, for the Red Man no longer has rights that he need respect, and the offer may be wise, also, for we are no longer in need of a great country.

There was a time when our people covered the whole land as the waves of a wind-ruffled sea covers its shell-paved floor, but that time has long since passed away with the greatness of tribes now almost forgotten. I will not dwell on nor mourn over our untimely decay, nor reproach my paleface brothers with hastening it, for we, too, may have been somewhat to blame.

Youth is impulsive. When our young men grow angry at some real or imaginary wrong, and disfigure their faces with black paint, their hearts also are disfigured and turn black, and then they are often cruel and relentless and know no bounds, and our old men are unable to restrain them.

Thus it has ever been. Thus it was when the white man first began to push our forefathers westward. But let us hope that the hostilities between the Red Man and his pale-face brother may never return. We would have everything to lose and nothing to gain.

It is true that revenge by young braves is considered gain, even at the cost of their own lives, but old men who stay at home in times of war, and mothers who have sons to lose, know better.

Our good father at Washington - for I presume he is now our father as well as yours, since King George has moved his boundaries farther north - our great and good father, I say, sends word that if we do as he desires he will protect us.

His brave warriors will be to us a bristling wall of strength, and his great ships of war will fill our harbors so that our ancient enemies far to the northward - the Sinsiams, Hydas and Tsimpsians - will no longer frighten our women and old men. Then will he be our father and we his children.

But can that ever be? Your God is not our God! Your God loves your people and hates mine! He folds His strong arms lovingly around the white man and leads him as a father leads his infant son - but He has forsaken His red children, if they are really His. Our God, the Great Spirit, seems, also, to have forsaken us. Your God makes your people wax strong every day - soon they will fill all the land.

My people are ebbing away like a fast-receding tide that will never flow again. The white man's God cannot love His red children or He would protect them. We seem to be orphans who can look nowhere for help.

How, then, can we become brothers? How can your God become our God and renew our prosperity and awaken in us dreams of returning greatness?

Your God seems to us to be partial. He came to the white man. We never saw Him, never heard his voice. He gave the white man laws, but had no word for His red children whose teeming millions once filled this vast continent as the stars fill the firmament.

No. We are two distinct races, and must ever remain so, with separate origins and separate destinies. There is little in common between us.

To us the ashes of our ancestors are sacred and their final resting place is hallowed ground, while you wander far from the graves of your ancestors and, seemingly, without regret.

Your religion was written on tablets of stone by the iron finger of an angry God, lest you might forget it. The Red Man could never comprehend nor remember it.

Our religion is the traditions of our ancestors - the dreams of our old men, given to them in the solemn hours of night by the Great Spirit, and the visions of our Sachems, and is written in the hearts of our people.

Your dead cease to love you and the land of their nativity as soon as they pass the portals of the tomb - they wander far away beyond the stars, are soon forgotten and never return.

Our dead never forget this beautiful world that gave them being. They still love its winding rivers, its great mountains and its sequestered vales, and they ever yearn in tenderest affection over the lonely-hearted living, and often return to visit, guide and comfort them.

Day and night cannot dwell together. The Red Man has ever fled the approach of the white man, as the changing mist on the mountain side flees before the blazing sun.

However, your proposition seems a just one, and I think that my people will accept it and will retire to the reservation you offer them. Then we will dwell apart in peace, for the words of the Great White Chief seem to be the voice of Nature speaking to my people out of the thick darkness, that is fast gathering around them like a dense fog floating inward from a midnight sea.

It matters little where we pass the remnant of our days. They are not many. The Indian's night promises to be dark. No bright star hovers above his horizon. Sad-voiced winds moan in the distance. Some grim Fate of our race is on the Red Man's trail, and wherever he goes he will still hear the sure approaching footsteps of his fell destroyer and prepare to stolidly meet his doom, as does the wounded doe that hears the approaching footsteps of the hunter.

A few more moons, a few more winters - and not one of all the mighty hosts that once filled this broad land and that now roam in fragmentary bands through these vast solitudes or lived in happy homes, protected by the Great Spirit, will remain to weep over the graves of a people once as powerful and as hopeful as your own!

But why should I repine? Why should I murmur at the fate of my people? Tribes are made up of individuals and are no better than they. Men come and go like the waves of the sea. A tear, a tamanamus, a dirge and they are gone from our longing eyes forever. It is the order of Nature. Even the white man, whose God walked and talked with him as friend to friend, is not exempt from the common destiny. We may be brothers, after all. We will see.

We will ponder your proposition, and when we decide we will tell you. But should we accept it, I here and now make this the first condition - that we will not be denied the privilege, without molestation, of visiting at will the graves of our ancestors, friends, and children.

Every part of this country is sacred to my people. Every hillside, every valley, every plain and grove has been hallowed by some fond memory or some sad experience of my tribe. Even the rocks, which seem to lie dumb as they swelter in the sun along the silent sea shore in solemn grandeur thrill with memories of past events connected with the lives of my people.

The very dust under your feet responds more lovingly to our footsteps than to yours, because it is the ashes of our ancestors, and our bare feet are conscious of the sympathetic touch, for the soil is rich with the life of our kindred.

The noble braves, fond mothers, glad, happy-hearted maidens, and even the little children, who lived and rejoiced here for a brief season, and whose very names are now forgotten, still love these sombre solitudes and their deep fastnesses which, at eventide, grow shadowy with the presence of dusky spirits.

And when the last Red Man shall have perished from the earth and his memory among the white men shall have become a myth, these shores will swarm with the invisible dead of my tribe; and when your children's children shall think themselves alone in the fields, the store, the shop, upon the highway, or in the silence of the pathless woods, they will not be alone. In all the earth there is no place dedicated to solitude.

At night, when the streets of your cities and villages will be silent and you think them deserted, they will throng with the returning hosts that once filled and still love this beautiful land.

The white man will never be alone. Let him be just and deal kindly with my people. for the dead are not powerless.

DEAD - DID I SAY? THERE IS NO DEATH. ONLY A CHANGE OF WORLDS.

DEADLY DECEPTIONS

Taken from the book: Chief Seattle's Unanswered Challenge; Spoken on the Wild Forest Threshold of the City That Bears His Name.
By John M. Rich.
Publishers; Ye Galleon Press, Fairfield Washington, 1970

FLYING SWAN PUBLICATIONS
ORDER FORM

Did you borrow this book? Find it in the library? Like to give one as a gift? Would you like to have it autographed? If so, send name you'd like to have mentioned along with payment and order form. Special discounts for quantity purchases.

Personally autographed copies of *HAYSEEDS IN MY HAIR; A Memoir,* are also available, directly from the author.

Send order to:

Flying Swan Publications
P.O. Box 46
Sedro-Woolley, WA 98284

Make checks payable in U.S. funds to Ruth Raby Moen.

For 4 books or less, include 1.50 shipping and handling. For more than 4 books, freight pre-paid.

Qty.	Name of book	Price each	Tax	Total Per Book	Total Amount
___	*Deadly Deceptions*	$ 7.95	.60	8.55	_____
___	*Hayseeds In My Hair*	$12.95	.97	13.92	_____
				Shipping	1.50
				Total	_____

Please print your complete mailing address below:

Name: _____

Organization or Company: _____

Address: _____

City, ST, Zip: _____

Phone number: (_____) _____